IT WAS ALWAYS YOU

SARAH K. STEPHENS

BLOODHOUND
— BOOKS —

For Joshua, with love

1

It's early afternoon and exactly two days too late when Justin and I set off for our romantic weekend.

When he recommends we take the scenic route, I nod in agreement.

The snow-sleet default of northeastern Ohio winters stops as we're ready to pull out of my apartment's parking lot and onto I-680, heading north. Wilting December sun cuts across the sky at a low angle, casting the library tower of the university and the dilapidated buildings surrounding it in a fraudulent glow.

Justin asks to drive, and even though I'd prefer to be behind the wheel—self-confessed nervous driver that he is—I let him. After our fight, I'm the most agreeable girlfriend in the world.

Annie would hate me right about now.

I move to pull out my phone from my purse to use for directions, but Justin tips his head towards the middle console of the car. He's tucked his phone in one of the cup holders and the screen shines back at the two of us. "I already have the address entered in," he says, and the kindness in his voice multiplies my doubts like a cancer.

Sure enough, the map shows a red flag labeled "Wolf Mountain Lodge" next to a lake and a winding road. I put his phone into the hands-free holder next to the steering wheel, so we can both see it during our drive. Justin's phone case is bright red, with a sticker declaring "I Voted" stuck on the back. When I first saw his phone, the randomness of it struck me as charming.

It still does.

Justin puts the car in gear, but before we start to move I grab his hand and offer an apologetic squeeze, although I don't quite know what I'm apologizing for.

Annie wouldn't like that either. If she were with us in the car, she'd side-eye me into oblivion. Maybe chuck her well-worn copy of *The Awakening* onto my lap from the back seat. "I thought you might need some leisure reading for your trip," she'd deadpan, trying to make me laugh and cringe at the same time.

But, then again, she doesn't know what I've done.

At least that's something she and Justin have in common.

Justin and I stay like this for a few quiet breaths, hands entwined like the lovers that we are, until he edges my Chevy Corsica into the light traffic of Youngstown city proper. After trading in and out of a few highway exits we move off the interstate, and the scenery turns picturesque: red barns and white houses with laundry still hanging from the line despite the cold.

The sun is starting to set as we transition from farmland into forest, and cleared fields give way to foothills. The landscape becomes denser with trees, and the berm on the side of the road is littered with remnants of past snows. Looking out the window, I catch a glimpse of myself in the rearview mirror. My brown hair is longer than it's been in a while, and the tips poke out from underneath my knitted cap. I've always looked young for my age, and my students at the university often mistake me for a fellow undergraduate. I try out a smile for myself in the mirror, and in my reflection I look happy.

I turn from the window towards Justin, and the smile strips away from my face.

Something is wrong.

His hands grip so hard at the wheel that his knuckles are white and bloodless. My first assumption is that his anxiety about driving has been triggered by something—the enclosing woods, the hill we seem to be descending—and I reach out to touch him again, but as I do he jerks the wheel violently to the left and my hand glances his skin and instead lands firmly on the steering wheel.

I grab the soft leather and hold on, trying to calm the rising panic in my gut.

"Why don't you pull over? I can drive for a little while."

He ignores me and gives another jerk to the wheel, this time to the right. I lose my grip, my hand falling with a dull thud onto the side of my seat. I hear our tires gnashing into the debris on the side of the road.

"Take a deep breath," I say, my voice calmer than I feel by a million times over. Because I'm certain now, watching Justin twist the wheel as he pushes on the accelerator, that this isn't just a panic attack. This is something more. Something else.

The headlights of an oncoming car appear around a curve. In the dusk I can't see the car fully, but something inside tells me that Justin is going to jerk the wheel towards this other car, and so I reach out to grab the steering wheel with both of my hands. My chest is held back by my seat belt, which seems to be so enamored with its job that it's locked itself into a shorter length, and I can only get my hands around the right side of the wheel. Still, it's enough to counter Justin's swerve to the left that comes a second later, and I manage to shift our car back into our lane.

Sweat pricks at my temples and under my arms. My mind is full of the sound of crunching metal and the feel of shattered glass sprinkling my cheeks. Memories I haven't retrieved for years. Memories I didn't even know I had.

Déjà vu floods my senses, followed by the spiky thrusts of dread.

"What are you doing?" I ask Justin, desperation turning my voice into Valley Girl upspeak. Like I'm asking him why he came home with farm-raised beets instead of wild-caught. I'm still trying to free myself from the seat belt, which is clinging to my body and won't release me, no matter how much I rail against it. I want to shift forward to look him in the eye, to have him look at my face and stop this, whatever it is he's trying to do.

I love you, I want to say, but the words get swallowed by the thrashing of the wheels as they skid along the road.

And then his phone rings, and a name pops up on the screen.

"*Mom*" is calling, it says.

Justin and I look at the phone together in an odd duet. My mouth opens and closes, a bilge pump of fear. When he turns to me, our eyes lock, mine wild and erratic and his two steadfast pools of blue. I think I see something shift in his face, a flicker of a feeling I can't identify. He looks back at the road, unbuckles his seat belt, and pushes his foot hard down on the accelerator. We are coming up to a hairpin turn, and the inertia of our bodies and the car encasing them wills us off the road, so I fling my hand out to the steering wheel one more time. Justin's skin is hard as a stone. The pads of my fingers prickle.

I hear the squeal of tires, the crunch as we move from the road to the berm, and the sickening crack of the car's front end making contact with the trunk of an ancient tree. Justin's hand goes limp underneath mine.

There again is that familiar shower of shattering glass, followed by a cry of pain. The voice I hear could be Justin's, or mine, or both of ours mixed together in a polyphony of terror.

Until the cry is replaced with another voice—*her* voice.

My mother's.

"Morgan." The sound of my name hums like a buzz saw. "Morgan."

Her voice creeps out from behind lead-lined doors.

My mind is playing tricks on me. Again.

And just like all the other times, hearing her say my name is not a wish my mind is making.

It's a nightmare.

The podiums at the front of classrooms are really all the same. By this point in the semester, just a few weeks away from final exams, they are chock-full of jettisoned belongings, left and never claimed by their owners. In my classroom there's an earring with two musical notes dangling from the post, an umbrella, a pathogen-experience of a coffee cup with the remnants of coffee from several weeks ago, three Five Star notebooks, and a miscellaneous gathering of pens and pencils. I push all of this aside to make room for my lecture notes, my water bottle, and my phone.

After I set it on the faux-wood desk, I check my phone is on silent. Only a month or so in, Justin and I are already settling into familiar patterns. For instance, Justin likes to text me in the middle of the day. For no reason really, just to tell me he's thinking about me, and as much as I find it kind of mid-century adorable, I also don't need my students hearing those little pings and getting distracted. It's hard enough keeping their attention without my social life on full display.

When I look up I notice a young woman sitting in the front row, smiling at me.

I don't know her in particular—my classes are large and full of students in both my department and from other majors—and her nondescript features make her blend into other young women sitting beside her. All are pretty, brunette or blond with matching ponytails, wearing sweatshirts emblazoned with Youngstown State's name and insignia.

I make eye contact until she looks away. Maybe it's a display of dominance by me; maybe it's just me seeking out some odd version of camaraderie because today's topic always leaves me feeling like I have no skin by the end of it. Anticipating how I'm going to spend the next seventy-five minutes, that part of my brain—the part that I've sectioned off through sheer force of will, and with more than a little help from Dr. Koftura—buzzes inside my head. I've gotten used to it over the years, like the murmur of static playing at a low volume in the background of my life. Just sometimes—not too often—the volume gets turned up.

I check my phone to see if Justin got back to me. I called him on my way to class, but he is in a meeting with his advisor and can't really talk.

Yes, we're one of those couples that still talk to each other on the phone. Justin actually asked me out on a date in person, after sitting in on a lecture I gave about language development. And the other night I found a handwritten note waiting on my pillow when I woke up. Dare to dream, but I think I've found an old-school romantic.

Ever still, my blank home screen stares back at me, except for the clock on my phone as it ticks down to the deadline to begin the lecture. I look up at the girl who smiled at me before, but she's now engrossed in her laptop screen.

I take a breath to focus, but as I'm exhaling, a green bubble pops up on my screen. My podium vibrates and my heart does a little involuntary flip, which makes me smile and cringe simultaneously.

I have a new text.

Are you okay?

I pause, caught off guard. It's a weird thing to ask just because I called him to say hello.

Maybe those patterns aren't as familiar as I thought.

I answer quickly, underneath the tray of my podium's computer keyboard.

Yes. Just nervous about lecture today. Talk later. xoxo

I stick on my lapel mic, take a sip of water, and I'm on.

"Good afternoon, class. Today we're examining child abuse and neglect—otherwise known in the broader sense as child maltreatment. Now you know at this point in the semester, that I was raised in foster care, and we'll be examining the foster care system as well, given that children subjected to abuse and neglect are typically placed within that system to ensure their safety."

I take a step away from the podium, and click to the next slide on the presentation.

At this point I offer my students a resigned and practiced smile. I know I'm making it look easy to talk about my past. "Of course, safety is not always found in foster homes."

I move to another slide and my students see a flow chart of the child welfare system, which looks like a multi-headed hydra vomiting agencies, acronyms, and abbreviations.

"By the end of today, I promise you'll understand how children come to harm." I expect to see grimaces on a few faces, and I do. "And I also promise. . ."

My phone vibrates again on the podium, and for a moment it breaks my concentration. Several students in the front rows of the auditorium seem distracted by it as well.

I should have turned it off, not just set it to vibrate.

"And I also promise that you will leave class today with the knowledge to prevent children from coming to harm."

I say this in a flourish to make up for my minor lapse. Students expect a certain level of theatrics to keep their attention. Sometimes I jump up and down and shake my hair side to side. Often I laugh at my own jokes when no one laughs with me —an occupational hazard. I'll even imitate the coos and babbles of babies so that students can understand how language begins. But today I only offer a swish of my arm from fourth to third position in ballet—Patty and Dave signed me up for classes. They were an older couple who gave me a room all to myself and wanted to keep me, until they didn't. Over the almost-year that I lived with them, Patty and Dave signed me up for whatever classes I showed interest in. Ballet and tap. Mandarin. Self-defense.

Sometimes those classes are useful in my life.

A few nights ago, while I cleared the table after dinner and Justin did the washing up—he'd made us spaghetti carbonara, my favorite—I caught him looking at me. He'd said that even when doing boring chores, like gathering up the dirty dishes, I carried myself like a dancer. It's not the most romantic thing anyone's ever said to me.

Except that it kind of was.

Today I'll tell my students about Patty and Dave. And the other places I was sent to.

As I'm talking, I hear the door creak open at the back and, careful to not give away my line of sight, I glance up to see who's arriving late to class, ready to tap at my watch and give them a well-practiced stink-eye. But it's not one of my students. Instead, I see Justin's dark shock of hair easing into the classroom, along with the rest of him. He's wearing his long, navy-blue peacoat, cheeks bright pink from the cold, and eyes focused only on me.

In an instant the static shifts; her voice inside my head.

"Speak of the devil and he will appear."

It shocks me, and I drop the remote mouse I've been using to advance through the slides with my students. For the next several seconds, I stoop over and try to clasp the stupid device in my fist again, but my hands don't seem to be working.

It's one of the few things I can recall about my childhood: her voice, and what she used to tell me when I'd ask for her help, her love. For money to get milk at the R & S market on the corner, for a kiss at bedtime, for her to sign the form that would let me get free lunches at school. My memories of life before care lie in strange and disconnected pockets inside my brain. Compartmentalizing. I learned about the phenomenon in graduate school. Although Dr. Koftura calls it something different. And sometimes, and only with Annie, it's my "Hot Pocket memory." "Better out than in," she'll bellow between slurps of root beer or the chaw of a Snickers bar.

If you can't make fun of brain damage with your best friend, then maybe you should rethink your life.

Dr. Koftura and I determined during one of our sessions that the scene that ran on repeat the longest was probably an amalgam of memories, stacked together and compressed like steel inside my head. In it, my mother calls out my name again and again, until I take the risk of going into her bedroom. She's lying splayed out across the dull brown comforter, the shades drawn and the smell of liquor and other things sweating out through her skin. Her face is blurry except for her mouth, which I can see with perfect clarity in my mind as her upper lip curls in on itself and she says it, that phrase that so often greeted me: "Speak of the devil. . ." Later, hurtling around from home to home because I was "a poor fit" or "unreliable" or even "dangerous"—because attractive pre-teen girls always are to some degree—I became convinced that my mother knew something about me no one else would admit. Even now, with all I've accomplished, it's hard to know if it's true or not—whether my mother thought of me as the devil.

And honestly, it'd be easier for me if she did.

It takes every ounce of my self-control to bring my mind back to my lecture, my students, my classroom, but I do it. I finally grasp the cheap plastic mouse, stand up, and smooth down the front of my skirt. I do so because the alternative of letting my life descend into a chaos of bad memories isn't an option. Not for me.

Because that would mean letting her win.

Justin stays at the top of the classroom, his back against the wall, while I handle the line of students waiting to talk to me after I dismiss class. He doesn't walk down the aisle until the room is empty.

I must give him a look, because the first thing he says is, "Is it okay that I came?"

He's worrying his hands by rubbing them together, a nervous habit I haven't seen before. "I hope I didn't intrude, or make you feel. . ." he pauses, apparently searching for the right word, and then rejects the sentence altogether. "I hope I don't seem like a stalker or anything."

He tries to laugh at his joke, and then gives up.

I work to rearrange my face, then give a little laugh back. I thought I'd recovered from earlier, but seeing Justin up close has me feeling upended. I give a silent "fuck you" to my mother for trying to ruin another good thing in my life, even though I haven't seen her for almost twenty years.

I'm too slow to react, and Justin goes on, growing more uncomfortable by the second.

"I'm just not doing well today, am I?" he says, chin tilted

down as he talks. His bangs fall over his right eye and he absent-mindedly brushes them away.

"It's no big deal," I finally manage to say. I give him a smile and reach to take his hand, hoisting my bag over my shoulder.

"I saw your text about your lecture today. I felt bad that I couldn't talk when you needed me."

That catches my attention.

All auditory hallucinations aside, showing up at my class like I'm too fragile to handle my job isn't the coolest thing he could have done. And that text earlier...

"Really, I appreciate the gesture." I give his hand a squeeze. "Next time, though. . ." I begin, but students for the following class start to pour into the room, all of them managing to walk and stare at their phones at the same time.

"What is it?" His eyes meet mine, those blue eyes like two pools I could happily drown in. He looks so earnest, like he'd do anything to make me happy—all I have to do is ask.

I decide to let it drop. I'm in no shape to pick a fight, anyway.

"It's nothing," I say, and we walk up the carpeted aisle, through the door, and out into the biting cold of December. Snowflakes are falling, and he offers to walk down to the student center and buy a hot chocolate for me at Starbucks. It's a little ritual of mine after rough lecture days. A warm sweet drink after the bitter lecture topic for today is exactly what I want.

When I'm back at my office, hot chocolate in hand, and Justin headed across campus to his office, I check my phone to see the text Justin sent earlier that day during my lecture.

I'm coming, he'd written.

After the police have confiscated my phone, I'll go back to the messages between Justin and me, replaying them over and over in my mind, and realize how they might read as something other than love.

J ustin lives in an apartment on the second floor of an old Victorian building, just a few blocks away from campus. I live within walking distance of the campus, too, but in the opposite direction in a young professional complex, housing other junior faculty at the university. My building looks like an IKEA catalogue manifesting itself in rust-belt Ohio—all straight lines and white edges—but Justin's apartment is different. It has, for lack of a better word, balls. There are spires and turrets, and one of the apartments on the first floor actually has a stained glass window. There are bats, literally, in the belfry. Well, technically it's an attic, but still.

Justin showed them to me one night as they headed out for dinner from under the eaves of the roof. You can tell they're bats, and not birds, he'd said, because they look like chaos in the sky.

The neighborhoods around Youngstown State's buildings were once all derelict and vacant, with pigweed and thistle growing taller than me, and walking to Justin's apartment I look for the winter carcasses of gargantuan rogue plants growing out of cracks in sidewalks and the broken asphalt of abandoned driveways. When I would run by them on the five-mile loop I followed religiously as an undergraduate at YSU, I'd have to dodge the swarms of bees that gathered around the weeds on warm days. Now, in the years since I'd left for grad school and had returned to teach here, most of the surrounding blocks have been razed and rebuilt with "luxury" student housing, new or renovated parks, and a few coffeehouses amidst other older, but renovated, apartment buildings. Likewise, my runs around the neighborhood have been replaced with a treadmill and a gym membership.

Walking the few blocks from campus to Justin's apartment, I see recently planted saplings and the skeletons of larger trees unburdened from their leaves. The harsh lake-effect snow that swoops in from Lake Erie hits just a few times in December, only to ratchet up further come the bleak midwinter of February.

When I look down the Fifth Avenue hill that descends into the vacant spaces of downtown Youngstown, the crumbling roof of the city's rescue mission shelter is visible, and next to it the red square tenements that makeup Youngstown's public housing. I count from the right end of the array of crumbling structures until my eyes rest on the fifth building. I haven't been back to my childhood home in years—not since Annie and I went searching for it during one of her visits after I started my undergraduate program at YSU, only to be met with a shifty, blissed-out twenty-something with track marks in his arm. He was sitting on the stoop claiming he didn't live there, but was keeping an eye on the house for a friend. We didn't stay long. Just being near it, seeing the windows where I'd peer in after school, hoping to see my mother making a sandwich, wiping the table, sitting on the couch waiting for me. Hoping to see her doing anything that told me she wanted to be my mother, but the windows were always empty when I arrived home. My mother was eternally in the back room, doing what she did best: taking care of herself.

The prick at the back of my skull comes hot and quick.

I turn around towards the way I came and decide to take the longer route to Justin's apartment, across the bridge.

When I reach the highway overpass that crosses from campus proper into the surrounding neighborhoods, I stop and look out over the buzzing traffic below. Deep breath. My eyes focus on a crow flying against the slicing December wind and the world reassembles itself. There's a buzzing against my leg and, when I pull my phone out of my pocket, it's hot in my hand, *Annie* insistently pulsing up from the screen. Below her name is her pixie face glowing with a smile I'd snapped before she realized I was taking the picture.

I hesitate a moment before answering, even though I want to hear Annie's voice.

"Hi there," I say breathlessly as the icy wind that's always whipping over the overpass for Route 680 slings itself down my throat.

"Where are you?" Annie asks, her voice slightly echoey on her side. She must have me on speaker.

"What do you mean?" I tease. "Just look me up."

Annie insisted we both download the Find My Friends app so we could keep track of each other. "There's a special place in hell for women who don't monitor their best friend's booty calls," she'd intoned like a public service announcement. I had to laugh. Not because what she said was funny or even remotely true—I'm not a one-night stand, swinging-from-a-chandelier kind of person—but because, if I didn't laugh, we'd have to talk about why we're really keeping an eye on each other. Or rather, why Annie needs to watch out for me.

So now we both keep track of each other.

There's a sigh of annoyance on Annie's side.

"Okay, fine," I say. "I'm just walking home—can't you hear

the wind howling over the overpass? What about you? Why am I on speaker?"

Annie lives with two other young professionals—Gloria and Paula—in order to make rent in Cleveland as she pursues her dreams (and talent—Annie is very, very talented) of being a painter.

"Don't worry, no one's listening in." Annie takes a sip of something, and I hear her sniffle a bit as the bubbles catch in her nose. She's pretty much addicted to Coke—the drink, not the drug. "So, how's that stalker of yours?"

She doesn't like Justin.

Annie and I met at a group home when we were both fifteen. I actually forget the group home's name—something like Storm Shelter or Day Spring. Sometimes when Annie and I were bored we'd play child welfare mad libs, where you'd have to pick a weather phenomenon and a synonym for i) home, ii) family, or iii) healing, and combine them together into one perfect moniker. It's amazing how many times we actually created names that turned out to really exist—afterwards we'd Google them to see if they were real.

Most of them were.

Raining Light. New Moon Transitions. Sunshine Smugglers.

Okay, that last one I made up. But still.

In group homes, you have to share a room with another ward of the state, and I was assigned to share a room with Annie. Tall, whippet-thin, with almost white-blond hair, Annie looks much younger than she actually is.

That was a problem when we were younger, because I could never seem to get her into R-rated movies unless she remembered to bring her ID, but now she can literally still get the kids' discount when we go to the theater because she passes almost as a pre-teen. Although Annie will often tell me she wishes she had tits like me, to which I remind her that she'd then have to wear a bra every day.

Annie and I had had to share a small barracks of a room at the top of an old Victorian house that had been converted into Storm Shelter/Day Spring/Flower Rebirth. The floor sloped east, and since Annie had already been there for a few weeks by the time I arrived (her previous roommate had turned eighteen and had been unceremoniously kicked out to fend for herself the day after she blew out candles on her cake, the same as Annie and I would have to do eventually), she had the bed that was positioned at the apex of the slanting floorboards.

When I showed up, coming straight from a home where the foster mother turned out to be milking the system and was stripped of her clearances, I just had a book bag with someone else's initials etched into it and a duffle bag with a broken zipper. Annie offered me a "Hello" when I found myself in the doorway, being shuttled in by another staff member whose face and name I'd forgotten before they'd even finished introducing themselves, and I responded by silently moving across the room and sticking my two cases of belongings under my bed.

"Aren't you going to unpack?" Annie said, gesturing with her eyes to what looked like a military surplus desk and dresser next to the bed.

I ignored her, lay down on the bed, and closed my eyes. If I'd owned headphones, I would have put them on, but those had somehow got lost two foster homes ago. I'd just learned the word *stoic* in school for a unit on Greece, and had decided that that was my new approach to life. I sat there, silently wrapped in my own world, carrying the burden of life like a pubescent Atlas.

When I opened my eyes, Annie's face was maybe two inches from mine, and I could see the inner ring of green surrounding the pupils of her eyes, flanked by an outer ring of lighter blue. Her nose touched the tip of mine as she moved her mouth to say, "So you're one of those girls, huh?"

In our world, that was the verbal equivalent of lobbing a grenade at my head.

"I think you mean *you're* one of those girls," I snapped back, pushing the tip of my nose into hers before suddenly sitting up and forcing her to move back onto her knees. She'd been crouching next to the bed that supposedly was now mine.

"Oh *really*," she said. "Let me guess—you don't make friends; you don't talk to people; but you probably write in a journal somewhere about how stoic you are as you navigate the system, right?"

Stoic, I thought. She had to use that word. It seared into my already burdensome chest, underneath the cheap training bra I'd grown out of last year but had yet to have replaced because I was too embarrassed to say anything.

"No, let me guess," I say back, standing up and pointing a finger at her. "You're the girl who makes 'nice' to everyone, helps clean up after dinner, always says 'Please' and 'Thank you' and starts calling everyone 'Mom' and 'Dad' as soon as you arrive because you think it'll make them keep you longer."

I'd find out later that Annie'd been in care since she was five years old, after her parents had died from simultaneous heroin overdoses. With no grandparents living and no "kinship" care options available, mainly because nobody in her family wanted a child tainted by her parents' addictions, Annie had already been in twelve foster homes by the time she and I met. She'd moved to the group home just a few months before I showed up.

It was not because she was a bad kid and the families couldn't deal with her issues. Despite all her trying to be a perfect ward of the state, Annie was still a normal kid with normal problems—talking back sometimes, forgetting to do her chores, having some trouble with grades in school. Annie kept getting kicked around from home to home because of the same hard truth we both shared. When you're in foster care, all your problems—even normal ones—become magnified until people see you as just another ticking time bomb of violence, mental illness, and promiscuity waiting to explode.

After I'd called her a "Miss Perfect," Annie's face went blank for a moment, and I thought I had her—I prided myself back then at being able to read people—until she burst out laughing.

"Are you *kidding* me?" she said. I had no clue what to do with that, so I ended up crossing my arms against my chest like a shield. Or a wall.

"You think I do those things because I think—even for one second—that it'll help me stay put longer?" Annie's eyes were wide and she kept moving her arms around as she talked, carving wide arcs in the air. For a second, I thought that maybe she was on coke. The drug, not the drink.

"Look, Morgan—that's your name, right?"

To which I just nodded my head silently, trying to avoid her spazzing out on me due to the cocaine high I assumed she was under.

"I do those things because everyone—the social workers, the teachers, the police, the parents, the foster parents, the judges— they all think that we turn into animals the longer we're in the system. And I don't know about you. . ."

Just then, Annie turned her head to the side while a maniacal grin spread across her face. I tried to back away further, but ended up stumbling across my feet as I missed the slanting floor's angle where it descended towards my bed. By now I was certain she was on something hard-core and twitch-inducing.

"But I'm no animal," she shouted, and then promptly began jumping up and down, making monkey noises and scratching her armpits like you'd see a little kid do—until she broke. When

Annie started giggling, it was so intense I thought the floor-boards would shake loose.

That's when I finally got the joke—Annie wasn't high; she was just crazy. In the best possible way.

Her whole weirdo routine cracked me up out of my "new group home" funk, and the two of us stayed like that for a good long while, big bellyfuls of laughter ricocheting around the room.

When we calmed down, Annie reached out her palm to help pull me up from the bed I'd landed on after I tripped over my own feet. Her hand was soft and warm and she was wearing a butterfly ring on her right hand index finger.

Annie paused to consider me for a moment, her face soft and quizzical. We kind of had a moment.

Until she snorted like a pig. A big, noisy intake of breath that scratched at the back of her throat and filled the room. I responded by barking like a dog, with ruffs and growls.

And then we were both laughing again so hard that we had to hold each other by the shoulders to keep the other from falling over with belly aches.

That's how Annie and I became friends. That's how I made the best friend I've ever had.

Neither Annie nor I say anything for a moment. The fact that she's used the same word to describe Justin that he did earlier today, after he just showed up at my classroom, bothers me.

Stalker.

People throw that label around way too carelessly.

Into the silence I hear her snap the top of another can of Coke. The fizz travels over the phone so clearly that I almost feel the bubbles under my nose as she takes a big, gurgling sip.

"That stuff isn't good for you," I say. It's an old argument between Annie and me.

I make artisan flat bread and quinoa salads. Annie eats Snowballs from the Unimart on the corner of her street and drinks twelve packs of Coke. I keep telling her it's going to catch up on her—not in a jiggly flab sort of way. Neither of us really care about that. For the last several months she's been looking pale and her eyes are red-rimmed and strained when I see her. I actually ordered a package of vitamins for her online, to which she quickly responded upon receipt by calling me and saying, "Why is my pee yellow, Morgan?" And that was the end of that. Now, whenever I visit her at her big city apartment in the Heights—which isn't as often as we'd like, but it's hard to get away with work and all, but still—I notice the vitamin bottles with another layer of dust added to them on the top of her fridge.

"Yeah, well Justin isn't good for you."

But there's no playfulness to Annie's voice. We both sit there, listening to the wind echo across the line, until Annie breaks in.

"I'm sorry. I shouldn't have said that." I know she's talking about the "stalker" part more than the "not good for you" comment.

"I hate that word," I tell her.

And even as I say it, I think to myself that it's my turn to apologize now, but I don't. Instead, Annie rushes back in, her explanation at the ready and, at least compared to the silence, familiar to us over these last few weeks.

"He's not normal. The two of you together isn't normal."

This is what she keeps telling me. "What's not normal, Annie? Huh? I don't understand how having a boyfriend who wants to spend time with me and who makes me feel good isn't normal."

"That's just it," she says, and I know we are heading towards an all-out fight. I consider avoiding it altogether—launching instead into the scene from my classroom earlier today, telling her about the blip in my mental armor. She'd listen; she'd make me feel better, stronger, but apparently my subconscious has an itch that needs to be scratched, and so I lean into this fight that's been brewing between us for weeks.

"What is?" I say, with sarcasm dripping.

"He's not real," Annie replies. "No boyfriend is like this in real life. No relationship is as perfect as you are making yours and Justin's out to be."

"Maybe you should date better people."

Annie stays calm, and I feel childish trying to get a rise out of her. She's had a string of lame relationships—boyfriends or girlfriends who always seem more interested in their work/video games/phones than her.

"I'm not talking about *my* dating life. I *am* talking about yours and about how you are around him. Eventually he's going to slip up and do something that isn't perfect, and how are you going to deal with that when you have him on such a pedestal? I mean, come on, Morgan—doesn't this seem familiar?"

"You haven't even met him yet," I argue. And it's true. Annie and Justin have never met, although I've tried to make it happen a few times over this last month. Justin doesn't like to drive long distances—he says the highway makes him nervous, as driver and as passenger. And Annie has been getting her exhibition together and just can't seem to get away. So I have to keep asking myself where all this is coming from for her.

"You've never even seen us together," I add. "How do you know how I am when Justin is with me?"

Annie blows her breath out. She takes another sip of her drink. Her voice gets quiet; her tone much more serious than it's been for this entire conversation so far. "Okay, maybe I'm being a little harsh towards Justin. But come on, can you really blame me for being defensive for you? I don't want it to happen again. You've been through this already..."

I don't let her finish.

"That was different, and you know it. I've worked really hard to get better." I don't try to keep the snark out of my voice. I know Annie isn't saying these things to be cruel to me, but that doesn't change the fact that I feel attacked. "Can't you see how happy he makes me?"

"No, I can't," Annie says. "I know when you're happy, and this is different. You're desperate. Weak. I don't know—those words aren't quite right." The line goes silent for a second. The wind whips up again and hurls itself across my face. "You know what it is," Annie finally continues. "Even when things were at their worst with Richard, you were still yourself. Messed up, sure, but yourself. Being with Justin is doing something different to you. Since you've been with him you seem like a version of yourself that's been copied a couple of hundred times, and the ink is wearing off."

Sometimes I forget that Annie is an artist—a real, legitimate creative person—and then she'll say something like that and I remember again. But today, I'm too much of everything—angry, hurt and exhausted—to appreciate anything that she's saying.

I just want to win the argument.

Annie goes on, "How much does he even know about you? And I don't mean the stuff with Richard. I mean the accident, your appointments with Dr. Koftura, the way your brain works sometimes?"

I ignore her.

"What happens when you let him see who you are? What happens when everything's not perfect?" There's a pleading edge as she asks, but I don't want to get into this. Not now.

"You know what it is, *Annie*?" I put extra emphasis on her name, and draw out the last vowel until it squeaks in the back of my throat. "You're jealous. You can't stand the fact that I have a man who loves me—"

Annie cuts in, "Has he said he loves you?" But I ignore it.

"—and who wants to spend all his time with me and take care of me, and you can't stand that I have someone else in my life besides you."

I don't wait to hear her response. I hang up on her, too embarrassed to deal with the aftermath of what I've said. Instead, I listen to the pounding of blood in my ears until I reach Justin's apartment. It's only after stepping inside, after Justin peels my coat off me and brushes the snowflakes from my face, when I remember I never found out why she was calling.

I hold office hours at 8am twice a week. It's a trick I happened upon early on in my career (I'm still early on, I suppose, so I guess I mean "earlier") to schedule office hours at the undergraduate equivalent of the crack of dawn. It helps weed out ambivalent students from showing up just to fish for extra points in the last exam.

Typically, I spend the hour reading the news headlines and checking my Google alerts for updates to developmental topics —the world is obsessed with growing our children healthier, smarter, and prettier—but today I can't help myself. I have to post something about last night.

I log into my Twitter account and scan the most recent trends before opening up a new tweet box.

Hah—that should be something, shouldn't it? Tweet box.

Despite my fight with Annie, I'm in a good mood this morning.

Today, at 6:12am, as he was handing me a cup of tea in bed, Justin said he loved me.

I almost dropped my cup.

Sure I deflected the whole question of "Did he say he loves

you?" when Annie asked me last night, but it burned me all the same. One thought kept skittering through my head. *Why was I talking about love when he wasn't?* To be honest, it felt a little sickening.

Growing up a ward of the state, love can be a touchy subject.

But then I wake up today and Justin is standing there looking at me with this expression on his face, and before I'm even fully with it he says, "I love you." Plain and simple. And then he kissed me, and so I found myself saying it back to him against his lips. And then, well—afterwards I had to rush into work this morning.

@NotThatKindofDoctor Good morning, Tweeties! Have a love, love, lovely day 😊

As I click "post," a thought shimmers in my periphery.

I log on to Facebook.

I don't use this account nearly as often, mainly because I prefer the snappiness of Twitter for posting pictures of my baking exploits or comments on academic life—that's what I post, usually. But Twitter doesn't have something Facebook does.

I click on "Relationship Status"—and then stop.

You're being impulsive, I tell myself. *You shouldn't be doing this.*

I haven't done any online searching yet, because back when things got bad, Annie made me promise not to fall down the same rabbit holes. She even made me sign a contract she'd drafted up—when she showed it to me, I tried to crack something witty, but ended up with something like, "Hey, who's the psychologist here?" while Annie gave me a watery frown and said I should take it seriously. And I have. At least until now.

I type his name into the field and wait for his profile to pop up.

The contract had three items on it:

- I will not Google the men I am dating.

- I will not follow or stalk the men I am dating.
- I will not use social media for anything dating-related.

God, it's embarrassing to list those out. But like I've said again and again—and Annie can confirm for me—I'm better now.

I look at the field and see several Justins appear, but no Justin McBride that is *my* Justin McBride. And just like that, a hard little seed settles inside my stomach.

My boyfriend isn't on Facebook. My boyfriend who's just said he loves me.

I sound like a teenager, don't I? Instinctively, I peer up from my screen and walk over to my office door, just to make sure that I don't have any students waiting for me. The hallway is empty, except for my colleague Maria letting herself into her office two doors down.

"Cue the music," she says, twirling her finger the way she always does as finals week lurches near. And she's right—things get a little wild with students manifesting all manner of ailments and excuses, and requests to meet with the dean about your refusal to accept a late paper.

But today I'm not game like I usually am, and only manage a brief smile before rushing back to my desk and logging back over to Twitter. Then Instagram. And finally—I'm not proud to admit this—even though I don't have an account, I create one for Snapchat just to search for his name.

No Justin McBride anywhere online.

The disappointment I feel shouldn't be a surprise to me, not if I'm being honest with myself. And it isn't a surprise—not really. What it is, as I carry it through my day, is something else, potent and raw.

Familiar.

The next day I force myself to read the research article on institutional privation I've assigned to my students for a maddening twenty minutes, and all the while compartments of my brain are ticking away at full speed. I have to read sentences two or three times before they make any sense, because every time *He loves me!* rolls across my serotonin receptors, *But why?* comes along to dampen any effect it might have.

I spent the bulk of yesterday prepping exams and grading, while Justin was busy with his own research. I wouldn't have minded us seeing each other in the evening, but Justin said he had a lot of work to catch up on, and asked instead if we could meet for dinner tonight.

Which is fine. Totally fine.

Except I keep repeating to myself, "How fine it is."

I wish I could call Annie, but things need to simmer down between us for a bit before I extend an apology. She's called and texted a few times, all seemingly checking in on me and ignoring the fight we had.

We'll makeup, I'm sure of it. Just not yet.

I also don't want to face telling her that I broke our contract. Or lie to her through omission by not telling her.

After a full read-through of the article, and some detailed notes added to my already hefty lecture packet, I finally decide to let myself call Justin.

He picks up on the second ring, and I swear my heart does a little somersault that borders on nausea when I hear his voice.

But something's off. All the dips and strokes of how he usually speaks to me aren't there.

"Morgan, what's going on? Are you okay?"

I pause for a second, a sharp stab of annoyance playing in my mind. *Why does he keep doing that?* I ask myself. *I'm not that needy.* But the reason for me calling sits at the edge of my tongue, taunting me.

"I'm fine. I was just calling to say 'Hi.' Hi." I give a little flourish to my voice on that final word, and hate myself for it.

Cringeworthy.

But I couldn't admit I was really calling because I wanted to ask him to sign up on Facebook so we could put our relationship status up. Not to Justin and not to myself.

"Oh . . . hi." His voice has an edge to it, and I start to worry about him taking back what he said this morning. "Look, I'm really busy here. I'm in a meeting with my advisor. Can I call you back?"

I tell him of course he can, and sorry that I interrupted his meeting.

I lick my lips, trying to dispel this bitter taste in my mouth.

My phone dings. Justin. Three hearts, each getting bigger than the last one. *I love you*, it says right after the hearts. And there it is—the first time anyone's ever said they loved me in writing.

If texting counts as writing.

I glance at my watch. It's time for office hours—I still have a set of afternoon times as well, just because I remember being an undergraduate and feeling that an 8am start time took herculean efforts. I open my office door and find a line of students waiting to meet with me. A few faces I recognize from my classes and a few are unfamiliar. There's the sonorous hum of rustling North Face jackets (every undergraduate's solution to our bitter Ohio winters) and the snapping of laptop covers closing for the next hour as I usher each of them into my office, one by one.

Some—the students whose faces I don't recognize—want to meet and review their grades to determine whether they should late-drop the course. Others are already prepping for final exams and have questions on Chomsky or sociometry, or any other of the topics we've covered. One young woman, who I think is the same one I shared a smile with at our last lecture, sits down and gives me a heartfelt confession of how my lecture inspired her to volunteer with foster children. She wants to know if I have any contacts with child and youth services.

Do I ever.

At the end of the hour, I swing my door closed and slump into my office chair, tearing into a granola bar before the lock even clicks.

I did a good job with each and every one of my students. I know I did. I was present, attentive, engaged. I was a boss. Even the students who gave me big dripping praises about how much they loved my class and "could they please have some extra credit so they could pass without having to actually go to class" received the same polite tone I offered to my students asking for clarifications on the difference between perceived and socio-metric popularity in childhood.

But I'm fighting myself. Because below my professional demeanor are a riot of thoughts pouring through my head, on a constant but mutating loop since yesterday.

- *Why isn't there a trace of Justin on social media?*
- *Why did he sound so weird when I called?*
- *Was he* really *in a meeting with his advisor?*

I wish I could say that I talk myself through it—that years of therapy and medical treatment and an encounter with the police have taught me to control myself.

What I do instead is gather up my purse, check the campus map to be certain, and then head over to the office of Justin's advisor.

Because, if there's one thing life has taught me over and over again, it's that love makes no guarantees.

6

A month ago I'd stood at my podium, reviewing my notes on Chomsky's theory of language development, and rolling my eyes to myself once again as I did every semester at how obnoxious his linguistic equations were, when I heard someone clear their throat. I hadn't noticed anyone coming up to my perch at the front of the class, but then again I hadn't been looking for anyone either.

In front of me was a man, shaggy, dark hair hanging over his right eye that he brushed away as my gaze met his. He was older than my students, with just the hint of a dark beard that I'd later discover was simply his way of skipping days between shaves, and a few crinkles at the corners of his mouth that I associated with smokers. I couldn't smell the nicotine and arsenic on him, though, as I often did with my students who seemed to arrive at my office for a meeting having just stubbed out their cigarettes on their boots before sauntering through my door.

The smell of cigarette smoke makes me nauseous, and my skin pricks up in beads of sweat when I'm around it. Not the most professional posture for a professor, I'll admit, but some things just can't be helped. Smell is one of the strongest memory triggers we humans possess.

"Excuse me, Professor Kalson?"

I roll into my best paper-shuffling "I'm busy" pantomime. I figured that either this guy was playing at getting a chance to announce some club event or blood drive, or he was trying to sell my students something.

I gave him a dubious look, which he seemed to be prepared for.

"I'm a Ph.D. student in anthropology, studying language diaspora," he explained, "and I saw from your online syllabus that you're covering Chomsky today."

I was, admittedly, caught off guard. After two years of full-time teaching, I'd never had someone voluntarily ask to sit in on a class. Especially language-acquisition-device, esoteric-to-the-point-of-incomprehensibility Chomsky. I think my mouth might have hung open a little, which is a bit embarrassing to own up to.

"Shall I just sit anywhere?" Justin continued.

"Isn't a sophomore-level course a bit below your training?" It was rude of me to say this, I know. All professional surliness aside, though, I couldn't shake the feeling that I should be nervous around this guy. And when I'm nervous, my defenses go up and I start to play offensively. After all, it's how I'd made it through my Ph.D. program in four years.

I glanced at my watch.

Justin laughed, ignoring my dig at him. And then he said something I couldn't dismiss. "When it comes to understanding Chomsky, nothing is too basic for me."

I couldn't dismiss this, because in academia it's rare to meet a man who's willing to admit what he doesn't know, or that he's anything other than brilliant. All the bravado can get exhausting, and I'd spent the last ten years—undergrad, graduate school, and two years of faculty life—immersed in it.

My shoulders relaxed a little.

"There are usually some open seats towards the back," I said.

Justin reached into the pocket of his coat, and to my surprise pulled out a pair of black-rimmed glasses. No case, no protective glass-cleaning cloth, just straight out of his pocket. He studiously put them on, and the heavy frames only served to highlight his chiseled cheekbones. Watching this reverse-Clark Kent process, it was impossible not to notice that this visitor of mine was actually pretty cute, and that perhaps my nervous vigilance was more butterflies than boundaries.

Then, with no sense of self-consciousness at his awkward formality, he extended his hand across the faux wooden threshold of the podium, knocking past the computer monitor and the desk light. "Justin McBride."

I took his hand in mine and gave it a firm shake. His skin was pleasantly warm.

"Morgan Kalson. Nice to meet you, Justin."

When he let go of my hand, the inside of my palm tingled for a few seconds afterwards. That's how I knew I was in trouble.

Again.

7

I lock my office door, wrap my scarf around my neck, and slip out the side stairwell and into the fresh, biting air of December. I avoid the elevator in my building. There's no need for forced, awkward encounters with faculty and students alike in the shoddy lift that threatens to reject at any moment its one purpose of moving up and down. Youngstown State's psychology department is still housed on the fourth floor of DeBartolo Hall, and the outer façade of the building remains a devotee to burnt orange coloring and smokers who attend classes in the English department on the third floor.

Justin's department, anthropology, is in Tod Hall, which is a short walk across the center portion of campus.

Youngstown State's campus is an odd mix of 1920s-era brick with Ivy League aspirations, 1960s angularity, and the gleaming starkness attributable to the new donor money that's been flowing in ever since our new university president, a local boy done good by way of a big league football coaching position, came on board. I don't recognize half the buildings on campus from my own undergraduate days, and I don't have much reason to frequent the new buildings anyway. Most of them are sports training facilities with the scope of a blimp hangar.

As I walk I hear a distinctive chirping in the trees, and look up to see a thuggish group of robins puffed out on an almost barren crab apple.

It occurs to me that they should have left for warmer climes already, and a flash of worry for the birds flits across my mind. We aren't even into the thick of "lake effect" winter yet.

Campus is barren today, save for a few bundled masses of students in their puffy winter coats in various shades of bruising. And then I spot her, in her iconoclastic bright red coat.

Maria.

I'm going past the large rock in front of Kilcawley Center, which students regularly paint over with different themes—this morning the rock is blue and white with a mixture of blurry Hebrew lettering from the university's Hillel group—and just when I think I can move behind it and avoid Maria's line of sight, it's too late. She's caught me with her big smile, a creamy Starbucks cup in hand.

"Morgan!" And she actually lifts her arm in the air, her hand flipped down at the wrist like she's the star of a romantic comedy come to commiserate with her best friend. Maria and I aren't that close, and although I don't know if it's my already anxious state, given the way my morning's been going, the hairs on the back of my neck prickle as my colleague gets closer to me.

Maria arrives where I'm standing, and I consider how it probably looked odd that I didn't move closer to her as she beckoned me over.

"I'm so glad I caught you." Maria's mouth does the impossible and opens even wider into a bright white grin, her red lipstick matching her coat perfectly. I glance at the lid of her cup, hoping that a scrim of lipstick would have worn off as she sipped it, but the entire top is pristinely white. Not even a speck of coffee that's whorled itself out of the drink opening. The woman looks perfect and I can't help but feel homely in contrast.

"I was just going for a coffee," I say instinctively, hoping this will speed up our interaction.

"Oh great, then I'll join you." Maria holds up her coffee in salute. "I was hoping to pick your brain on something." She scrunches up her face a bit. "I thought you only drank tea."

Even as I consider telling her that I have an appointment back at my office and was just grabbing a quick hot beverage, I know she'll maneuver through that as well and suggest that we walk back together and chat until my meeting appointee arrives.

"That's what I meant," I say, resigning myself to at least spending the next half hour trying to stay focused on whatever it is Maria wants my opinion—or support—on. A recent faculty meeting with her passionately arguing that the microwave should only be used by individuals capable of cleaning up after themselves comes to mind.

We walk over to the Starbucks embedded in Kilcawley Center—the same one where Justin and I went earlier this week for my hot chocolate—but the atmosphere of the café is entirely different with Maria as my companion. The soft lighting and tinkling sounds of coffee beans grinding and steam rising have been replaced today with a tableau of student workers sloshing around tepid coffee, their eyes hollow under the fluorescent lights and dark stray hairs poking out of their caps like wires.

Or maybe it's just me.

"Here, let me pay," Maria says, and when I try to object, she adds, "I'll owe you more after you hear the favor I want to ask."

She winks at me, which serves only to unsettle me further. *Does she want me to form a microwave hygiene committee with her? And exactly how long is this impromptu coffee date going to take?*

I thank her for my tall chai tea, and she directs me towards a small table with minimal sugar grains and only one creamer splotch at the very center. I notice Maria wipes it up with her finger before rubbing her hands on a stack of napkins she'd grabbed at the cashier stand.

"Filthy undergraduates, am I right?" Maria gives a little cackle from the back of her throat. "God love 'em, or else we'd be out of a job."

I decide that I am going to take back control of this situation.

"So, what's this about?" I ask. "And just so as you know, I have a meeting across campus in a few minutes."

This declaration does not appear to faze Maria in the slightest. She simply leans back in her chair, unwinds her scarf, and drapes her blaring-red coat across the backrest.

"You know I just got that new National Institutes of Health grant money?" she begins, and I cringe internally. This is much worse than any communal kitchen drama.

I nod. "Congrats. Do you need recommendations for research assistants or something?" Fingers crossed.

I take a sip of my chai tea, and the foam manages to burn my upper lip.

"No, no—nothing like that. You didn't happen to hear what the grant is for, did you?"

I had, and that gave me all the more reason to cut this meeting off at the jump. But then a tinge of guilt rises up my throat, because Maria has never been unkind to me. I take a deep breath.

"Just a little bit. It sounds really groundbreaking," I offer as my olive branch.

"Look, I know you're busy," she says, and her words are a small balm on my distracted mind. "But as you've probably already heard, we're looking at how termination of parental rights influences maltreated children's symptoms of PTSD."

Finally, Maria is speeding up her speech as she hurtles forward into what she and I both know is a sensitive subject. She continues:

"And you speak in your classes about your own history with child welfare, right?"

I nod, my eyes feeling beady even though I don't mean them to.

"Sorry, a mutual student of ours mentioned that to me earlier this week when we were meeting about a resident assistant position for the grant. And I thought, well, why don't I talk to Morgan about it? So here I am."

I don't say anything.

"Soooo. . ." Maria extends the word while looking down at the dirty table. "Do you think we could meet a few times while I get this data collection up and running, and you could help give me some insight into how I could ask kids about their experiences of leaving home and spending time in foster care?" Maria is getting nervous. Her smile strains at the corners and there's a tiny smudge of lipstick on her front tooth. "I want to make sure I ask the right questions, you see?"

Part of me wants to ease her discomfort, but a larger part wants to end this conversation as soon as possible.

"I don't see how I can help. I don't remember much about that time." I stare over her shoulder at a photo of one of YSU's former presidents hung on the café's wall.

Maria's mouth twists into a skeptical frown.

"Children's memories often fail during points of trauma," I add. And then I can't help myself, because I don't think Maria is being kind anymore. "Surely you know that?"

She flinches a little as my not-so-subtle jab registers with her. I can't have insulted her too badly, though, because she barrels ahead, undaunted.

"Sure, yeah—but you have to remember *something*. Don't you and your siblings talk about it?"

I let out an audible sigh, my patience spent. She's grasping at straws, and I just can't understand why she's digging around in my past.

"I don't have any siblings."

"Oh, sorry. I just assumed. . ." but Maria doesn't go on to explain herself.

"Like I said," and I stand up, "I can't really help you much. Except to tell you that removing children from the only home they've ever known, no matter how awful their home life might be, is traumatic, and one of the best tools humans have for coping with trauma is simply forgetting it ever happened."

"Is that what you did?" Maria asks, and her voice is so sincere that I almost decide to sit back down with her.

"I survived, didn't I?" And with that I thank her for the tea and head away from her questions and towards my own.

8

Outside again, and free from Maria's gaze scratching at my back, I shove my hands in my pockets and walk as quickly as the throngs of students switching between classes will let me. When I arrive at Tod Hall, the door opens with the suction of brand new construction, even though it's one of the oldest buildings on campus. There's construction plastic hanging from the ceiling in corners of the lobby and a note indicating that the main stairwell is unavailable due to renovations. I'm supposed to take the annex stairs at the back of the building.

I smell fresh paint as I walk, and the telltale printouts stating "Do Not Touch: Fresh Paint" are scattered on the floor in the odd way Youngstown State physical plant painters like to inform the general public that the wall has wet paint. Never mind that most people don't look for signage about painting projects by scanning the ground.

The back stairwell doesn't match the newly refurbished front of Tod Hall, and I almost trip on the stair guards that peel up like the tongues of thirsty dogs as I climb to the second floor.

Like I said, I never take the elevator.

Similar plastic draping decorates the walls when I arrive at the anthropology department, the stagnant air of the hallway mixing with the smells of wet plaster and the knocking sound of something being hammered. The doors lining the hallway are still in the old-fashioned style, with wood paneling and a large window in the center fitted with frosted glass with the professor's name etched across the top.

It's only then, as my eye scans down the hallway of faculty names, that I realize I don't know the name of Justin's advisor. I have no idea which office he was just sitting in earlier this morning. I have no idea where I'm going.

But instead of giving me pause and making me rethink my decision to come over and ambush my boyfriend, the state of my mind is such that this only makes me walk faster.

I assume the department is set up similar to psychology, where some communal office in a less than ideal corner is designated for graduate students' desks. The hallway carpet is worn down the middle and ripped at the edges where the baseboards have been torn out, but it still manages to muffle my footsteps as I walk down the hall. I don't pass a single door where the office is lit from the inside.

The department feels oddly abandoned, and I can't hear any of the ambient noises of academic life—typing, the whoosh of copies, fits of coughing, murmurs of conferences from behind doors, the odd crying of a grad student receiving mentor feedback for the first time. It is entirely silent. I pull out my phone and text Justin.

Where are you?

I go to hit send, and then reconsider. I add a smiley face after the question mark. Not because I feel it, but because I want Justin to reply and I'm beginning to think that perhaps his quick responses these first few weeks were a temporary delight.

The phone vibrates in my hand almost immediately after I hit send.

Thinking of you, it says, with three heart emojis. A brief instant of relief floods my synapses, but just as quickly it's gone.

He didn't quite answer the question.

So I ask again. *Where are you?* adding, *Want to grab lunch?*

This time my phone stays silent. As I'm waiting for Justin to reply I hear rustling coming from the door directly opposite me. I move closer to it, and although there's no etching on the glass door I find a handwritten sign in spidery script listing the names of five different people, with the heading of ANTHRO 260 Grad TAs.

And sure enough, the office sits next to an ancient-looking janitor's closet, with the men's lavatory on the opposite side. Of course this is the graduate student office.

I scan the names and don't see Justin's listed, but then again, I tell myself, he's never mentioned a teaching assistant position before. Just his advisor's existence, if not name, and certainly anthropology grad students are put on grants to fund themselves, just like psychology students. I force myself to knock on the frosted glass.

A woman with a short red fringe, freckles, and an underbite opens the door, and promptly scans me from top to bottom.

"You're not here for office hours, are you?" she asks. She offers a toothy smile.

"No, I'm looking for Justin McBride," I say, clipping my words to hide my growing agitation at the situation I've created for myself. "Is this his office?"

The redhead turns her eyes to the poster on the door as if to remind herself who the other students are, and I feel slightly reassured. Perhaps the department's grad student group is larger than I imagined.

"I don't think so." She pauses for a moment to consider, and then adds, "At least, I've never heard of him."

I can see into the office behind her, and the familiar settlement of desk carrels with ancient-looking computers takes me back to my own graduate school days spent in dusty, poorly lit offices, sharing half a desk with another student who you eventually came to loathe because of their penchant for Luna bars and garlic.

My phone buzzes, and it's Justin.

Great—where do you want to meet?

When I read it, my shoulders hunch automatically as if loaded down. I want to shout, *Just answer the damn question and let me stop being this person—this paranoid, nervous, desperate person.* But of course I don't, and instead ask my new redheaded friend if there are grad student offices in other parts of the building, or other parts of campus.

"I don't know," she says. "Maybe, but as far as I know, this is where they stick all of us. I've been here three years, and have yet to see a window."

And with this she winks and closes the door in my face.

I text Justin back.

Your office.

And then I wait.

9

I t takes Justin twenty minutes to show up outside the TA door. I feel like a moron waiting by it, staring at my phone and skulking around the darkened hallway. Thankfully, the redheaded grad student doesn't leave her office while I'm waiting, and my pacing of the hallway goes unnoticed by everyone except myself.

Just as I'm about to give up and call Annie for a reality check, Justin appears at the end of the hallway. At first I only see his figure through the plastic sheeting, and the effect is disorienting. He looks like a bloated, distorted version of himself, with mad shoulders and a sloping paunch. The shadow makes a menacing eclipse of the little light in the hallway before he slips through the plastic and emerges as his normal self on the other side.

"Here you are!" he exclaims. "I've been looking everywhere for you."

"Yeah, and now I'm going," I say, fully aware that I sound like a Real Housewife.

Justin stands in front of me as I try to move past him. His face is all concern. "Hey, what's wrong? You sounded strange earlier. Is everything okay?"

I take a step back. "*I* sounded strange?" I put a hand on my chest, feigning amazement. "*I'm* not the one pretending to be a grad student. *I'm* not the one sitting in on classes, pretending to have offices and advisors. *I'm* not the fraud."

The thoughts topple over themselves as they clamber to the front of my brain.

- *Justin isn't who he says he is. He's some sort of imposter.*
- *He's a liar.*
- *He doesn't love me.*

I look up, hoping to see comfort or at least irritation in Justin's expression—something to let me know I'm being as ridiculous as I sound—but instead I see something else, something alien and frantic working in Justin's features. I don't wait for an explanation and start to move past him towards the stairs. He reaches out to take a hold of my coat, murmuring, "Wait. I can explain," but before he can grip it with any purchase, I am past him and flying down the stairs, and then across the lobby to the outside.

I'm running now. Away from my boyfriend. Away from the mess I've made.

"Morgan," Justin calls from the steps of Tod Hall—he must have moved fast after I passed him—but I keep on running. There are footsteps behind me, and so I turn around and call back to him, "Leave me alone, you *liar!*"

I say it louder than I intend, and the faces of students and faculty traveling across campus turn towards me with looks of concern mixed with interest.

"I can explain. Wait." Justin runs towards me, and I decide to stop and face him. Because I don't want to become a spectacle, but also because a part of me knows I'm not thinking rationally —Dr. Koftura and I have gone over scenarios like this before—

what to do when I feel myself getting out of control. Or what I *should* have done. *Focus on your breathing*, I remind myself.

Justin and I are standing close enough to have a normal conversation, and when my eyes meet his there's kindness in them. I exhale.

"What's going on?" I ask.

"I could ask you the same thing," he says. "Why do you think I'm a fraud?" He tests the last word out on his lips, like it has no place in this conversation.

I take another full breath and feel it fill my chest. I don't answer until I've breathed out again.

"I talked to one of the grad students—they've never heard of you." My voice rises slightly as I say this, and I consciously try to shift it back to normal as much as I can. "And who's your advisor? You never even told me their name."

Justin actually laughs at this point. Looking at his face and how unworried he suddenly looks, I try to laugh, too, but all that comes out is a choked sort of sob.

"My advisor's name is Professor Farak. I don't have an office because there are no spaces left in the grad student room, and I said I didn't want to share a desk."

I let the information sink in for a moment. And another.

Justin looks expectantly at me, and then lets out a sigh of exasperation and moves to turn around and walk away. That's when it hits me—it's just exactly what I'm doing.

"I'm sorry," I call out. "I don't know what to say." The wind has kicked up and I reach up to tuck a loose strand of hair behind my ear. "I'm so embarrassed." I stare at my feet.

Justin turns back and comes closer to me. He puts his hands on my shoulders and squeezes a little harder than would be pleasant. He says, "Well, why don't we go make it better? Can I take you to lunch?"

And as I turn my body into his and join our steps together to head towards Kilcawley Center, my mind flashes back to that hallway and the names on the doors. The second door I passed read, in black embossed letters against the frosted glass of the door, "Professor Joseph Farak."

Justin would have seen the sign, too, as he came down the hallway to meet me.

Certainty comes like an avalanche. It's him that's doing something. Not me.

I break away from our coupling, and as I do so I shove Justin away. He stumbles into a bench along the side of the sidewalk and knocks his shin against the metal bar of its armrest.

"You *are* a liar. I went by your advisor's office—in fact I could see it the entire time I was waiting for you, and nobody came in or out. You weren't meeting with your advisor. You just made that up as you walked by it to meet me."

I want to stop, but I keep going. "Where *were* you?"

Justin has sat down on the bench, and he murmurs his answer so quietly I can't quite hear. I only catch the last word, which sounds a lot like "Bitch."

Something shatters inside my head.

I put my face next to his, a finger thrust at him, and say, "Don't you ever call me a bitch again, or you'll regret it."

Justin and I lock eyes, and that same expression that I saw in the hallway by the grad student office washes over his face. Watching it again, I recognize something I didn't before.

Disgust. He's disgusted with me.

I start to move away, appalled at my behavior, an apology again on my lips.

But before I can say anything, Justin sets his mouth. I watch as he clenches his fist.

"Get out of my face," he says, gritting his teeth so hard I swear I can hear the enamel grinding away. His face has turned red and a vein pulses in his forehead like it's about to burst. "You *bitch*."

I reel back, ready to follow through with my promise.

"Morgan?" A female voice breaks into the chaos. I turn reflexively, and my colleague Maria is standing a few feet away from me, looking perfect as ever in her red coat and matching lipstick. She must just be leaving the café. "Are you alright?"

Justin quickly stands up. "She's fine," he says. "It's just a disagreement we're having." He reaches out to touch my arm and I jerk it violently away. Out of the corner of my eye I see Maria startle back.

I look over at her. "I'm fine, Maria, thank you." I brush a few stray hairs from my face, self-conscious as ever of what I must look like to her.

"Are you sure?" she asks, but I don't reply. Instead I start to walk towards DeBartolo Hall, and after a moment Maria moves to join me. Justin stays where he is, and I only glance back once to look at him as Maria and I walk away. I don't catch his eye, though, because his face is buried in his phone.

Predictably, my phone buzzes a few seconds later. When I bring the screen up there's a text from Justin. *We were meeting at a coffee shop downtown because his office is under construction.*

Oh God, is all I can think. *What have I done?*

10

Maria and I are both silent on our walk back to DeBartolo Hall, but as soon as I am safely within the privacy of my office, I call Annie. She picks up on the second ring.

"This had better be an apology," she says when the call connects.

"I think it's happening again." The words rush out of my mouth and into the phone, and it's a relief to say them out loud to my best friend.

Annie doesn't need to ask what I mean.

"What happened?" she says, and the playfulness that's almost always in her voice is gone. "Are you okay? Is Justin okay?"

"Yes, yes," I assure her. "It's just . . . we had a fight," I offer lamely. I wait, trying to arrange my thoughts in my head before telling them to Annie. Part of me wants to leave out certain details, but ultimately I decide to give Annie almost everything. I talk in a rush, before I can change my mind.

"I talked to Justin earlier today and he sounded weird on the phone and said he was meeting with his advisor, but then he wasn't on Facebook or Twitter when I looked him up—" I leave out my new, now-defunct, Snapchat account.

"You did *what*?" Annie tries to cut in, but I barrel on.

"—and it just seemed weird, so I went to go find him at his office. Except he wasn't there, and then he showed up after I texted him and said he was meeting with his advisor, but his advisor's office was down the hall and Justin wasn't inside, so. . ."

"Morgan, what happened next?" Annie over-articulates the words, making my cheeks flame up and a lump form in my throat. This is how people, even best friends, talk when they think someone is losing their mind.

"I'm not crazy," I murmur the words, and even to me they sound unconvincing.

Annie doesn't say anything for a moment. "I know that. You know I know that." I hear a rustling against the phone and picture her rubbing her hand across her face, which is one of Annie's tells that she's working at keeping herself calm. On my end of the line I close my eyes and pinch my nose to keep a fresh wave of tears from welling too much.

"What else happened?" Annie asks again.

I tell her about the fight Justin and I had, and how I got in his face and that he then called me a bitch. I explain his message afterwards, and how I misread the entire situation—blew it all out of proportion. I leave out the part where I saw him clench his fist, because I'm not sure anymore what I saw and what I *think* I saw. And besides, people do all sorts of things when they're fighting.

Like threaten their boyfriend.

After I'm done, I wait for Annie to say something, and the silence on her end of the line is excruciating. Just like when I ask my class a question and everyone stares at their feet, hoping to get away with me answering it myself, I count silently in my head as a way of managing the awkward pause without filling it with my own blather. One one-thousand, two one-thousand. It works well with my students, because often what feels like an eternity is actually five or six seconds until one of them takes pity on me and raises their hand. Today, with Annie, it takes to the count of eight one-thousands before she says something.

"We had a contract. You promised."

Annie's voice isn't disappointed or mad. She just sounds worn down, and the realization that I am leaving everyone who cares about me in a wake of either frustration or fatigue makes my face burn hot with shame.

"I know I did." I scrounge around in my brain for something to hold on to, to show for myself. "I didn't Google him."

Annie gives a reluctant laugh, and I feel both of us relax a little bit. But there's no way Annie will just let this go.

She cares about me too much.

"This is exactly how you acted with Richard before *and* after he broke up with you," she says. "You remember? Stealing his phone and reading all his texts, searching for ex-girlfriends online and then pretending to be friends with them so you can get more information, following him to see if he was having an affair with his ex-girlfriend—and that all started because he told you that she called him to say congrats on his thesis defense. Because he turned out to have a past. To not be a perfect, unblemished, idol of a boyfriend."

I don't say anything because there's nothing to argue about. It's all true.

"Come on, Morgan. That's what I was so upset about the other night. You make these fantasies of what love is supposed to be, and then, when life doesn't live up to reality, well . . . we both know you have a history of being a little—" She stops for a second, searching for the right word to describe me, even though I already know which one she's going to choose. "Look, I'm just going to say it—*paranoid*. You see problems that aren't really there, and then you go off and make real problems that actually replace the imaginary ones." Annie pauses, and I hear her take a sip of something. She and I always need something to munch on—nuts and Trail mix for me, Ho Hos and Twizzlers for her. Don't read into that too much—orally-fixated, my ass. We both just run high metabolisms, and it's a small reassurance that my implosion this morning hasn't put her off her snack game.

Maybe this isn't so bad after all.

"I know it's not exactly the same," Annie goes on. "You haven't shown up at his house after he broke up with you, drunk, screaming that he was a liar and a cheat. Justin hasn't called the police on you because of a night when you got drunk and showed up and you wouldn't leave, and you started waking up his entire neighborhood. But that's just it—for every single example I'm giving I feel like I have to put a massive '*yet*' at the end, because if you keep doing this you are going to end up in the back of a police car again. Or worse."

Maybe it will be.

I let her words sink in. Part of me desperately wants to defend myself and say that Richard was ages ago—that I've changed—and that this whole thing with Justin is nothing like what happened with Richard. But another part, deeper inside, knows what I'm capable of.

"I'm just so embarrassed," I concede, and the echo of my words from earlier today with Justin—before everything *really* went to hell—unmoors me for a moment. "What am I going to do?"

An e-mail pings into my inbox. My eye catches the subject line. *Urgent Review Sheet Question.* I've received thirty-five e-mails since this morning.

"Do you want to keep seeing him?" Annie asks, her tone unreadable.

I picture Justin's face when I called him a fraud. How disgusted he was with me.

But then I picture all the other times he's looked at me and my chest almost bursts.

"Yes," I answer, my voice wavering just a fraction. "The good and the bad—I want it all. With him." I cough to cover up the pressure catching in my throat.

I'm terrified. It's not just that I've ruined everything, but that I'll *always* ruin everything. There's another pause on the line, longer and heavier than the ones before. And then Annie makes her decision. To let me try to love Justin.

"Alright. Okay, Morgan." Her voice is quieter than it's been this entire conversation. "You can't understand how much I want this to be true. For *you*."

I don't know what to say, so I just sit there, trying to read my best friend's thoughts across the line. When Annie talks again there's a hint of humor back in her voice, and it soothes the pulse that's been rioting inside my temple this entire conversation.

"In that case, you should *call* him and *apologize*. And then he should apologize to you for calling you a bitch, and done. The end. Then go have hot makeup sex and order pizza."

"It's good advice," I say, relieved at how simple Annie thinks it'll be to fix this. I absentmindedly reach out and play with a black Sharpie lying on my desk, twirling it between my thumb and forefinger. There's a bag of kale chips in my bag that I grab and rip open in one satisfying jag of my arm.

"I still haven't told him," I admit.

I don't have to tell Annie what that is. The accident. The brain damage. The episodes. Her voice. I almost add that I heard it again when Justin came to visit my class, but Annie cuts into my thoughts.

"You should," she says. "Maybe not right away; maybe not while you're eating something that's meant to give rabbits diarrhea."

That makes me smile.

"But you should," she goes on.

I take a sip of water to wash down a bit of chip stuck in my throat. I cough.

"That stuff will kill you," Annie chuckles.

I need to say it out loud.

"What if he decides he doesn't want me anymore?" I ask. "That he doesn't really love me." *What if I'm too damaged for any of this?* is what I really mean.

"He won't," she assures me. "*Because* he loves you. Telling him about your past doesn't change who you are."

I consider this for a moment. Only half teasing, "So does this mean you're on Justin's side now?"

"I'm on *your* side—I always am. If this is who you're going to love, well, then I'll just have to learn to love him too." I hear her take a quick breath in. "And then you need to follow the contract we set up." Annie chews on those last words. And maybe a piece of licorice. But there's an urgency there too.

"It's just. . ." My voice trails off because my mind is back on that conversation with him, seeing him clench his jaw. And his hand. Angry. Ready to strike.

Me, reeling. Ready to strike back.

But Annie is right to hold me accountable. "It's just *what*? Is there something you're not telling me?" She's instantly nervous, probing.

I push it aside, because—like Annie said earlier—I have a tendency to make imaginary trouble into real problems that have teeth. And so I offer up a problem I know is real.

"It's just that, this morning—" *God, was it only this morning?* "Justin said he loves me, and then the very same day I go and make this huge mess of things." An e-mail pings into my inbox. A forgotten Post-it note on my desk reading *Tech x 5692* glares back in bright fuchsia. I want to say goodbye and end this call. I want to avoid this thought that's been burning inside my head since I left Justin this morning.

"What if being in a relationship is just something I can't do? You know—what if this is just one thing that I can't get right?"

Annie doesn't hesitate.

"We aren't broken," Annie says, and the relief that floods my body is familiar and welcome. Annie knows me so well, knows what I need before I even do myself sometimes.

She's my best friend.

Annie's voice suddenly gets much louder. She must have the receiver right up to her lips as she says, "We. Aren't. Broken."

"I hope you're right," I say, feeling suddenly as exhausted as Annie sounded earlier.

"You might be the doctor," Annie replies. "But trust me. *This* I know."

A beat passes.

"One of these days, I swear—you're going to wake up and realize how much you're worth. And then all this other stuff will be like a bad dream."

I wait for her to go on, because I don't want to break the spell of what she's just said.

"Just keep trying." Annie clears her throat. The line fizzles as she takes a sip of something.

I crunch a kale chip into the receiver, and Annie fake gags at the sound.

Then briskly she adds, "Now, delete all your social media apps, call Justin, and . . ."

"What?"

"I think you need to make an appointment with Dr. Koftura. Just to check in."

I crush the chip bag in my hand until its edges prick at my skin.

"Way ahead of you," I finally say, because I know she's right.

11

I check my schedule for the remainder of the day after I hang up with Annie. One of the perks of being in the teaching faculty is the ability to work from home when not in the classroom or holding office hours, along with the apparent flexibility you have to make emergency doctor appointments if need be. I have a meeting with my boss, the head of the psychology department, Professor David Sothern, in an hour and then the rest of my afternoon is free. David had been a little cryptic in the e-mail, but then again that's always been his style. You never know whether you're going to get promoted or chastised.

A few months ago, one of the cognitive psychologists down the hall from me, Lance Jacobs, unsuspectingly went into a meeting with David, only to be told he wouldn't be receiving tenure. Lance had stormed out of David's office, yelling obscenities and insulting David's wife/mother/genitalia. The noise brought the entire department out from their little warrens, myself included, and we watched as David calmly waited for Lance to wear himself out. David never said a word, just put a hand gently on Lance's shoulder and led him out through the door to deposit him into the shifty elevator that was thankfully waiting to be boarded.

My thumb taps the home button on my phone, closing out my calendar, and I force myself to focus and do a mental scan through my job performance over the course of the semester. Aside from what happened this morning with Justin—and the meeting can't be about that, since David scheduled our appointment earlier in the week—I've been having one of the best semesters of my career: engaged students, well-prepped and delivered lectures. Before all this mess with Justin, I'd felt I was finally coming into my own as a professor.

I start composing a text to Justin, something along the lines of, "I'm so sorry, I know I have issues, please forgive me, I love you too." All one big run-on purge of remorse, but when I read it over I just can't quite stomach the desperation of it. Annie's words bubble up like indigestion. *We're not broken.*

I delete the message.

I answer a few e-mails (all of the "Will this be on the final exam?" or "I just decided to go to graduate school and need a letter of recommendation in seventy-two hours" variety). I empty my recycling bin on my desktop. The basket icon is now pleasantly empty.

I do a Google image search for no-knead bread recipes.

When I take out my phone again, I don't delete Twitter and Facebook (*Sorry Annie*), but I do finally send a text to Justin. Then I call Dr. Koftura's office and set an appointment with her for this afternoon. Before I leave for my appointment, I hold the button to power off my phone. As the screen turns dim, the imprint of my message stares back at me.

I'm sorry.

I figure it's harder to sound crazy when you limit yourself to two words.

My department head's office is hidden behind an imposing desk occupied by Sheila, his staff assistant. Sheila is the kind of woman who wears holiday-themed sweatshirts, and somehow manages to make them look good on her. She brings in cookies on a regular basis and walks them around to the faculty offices, each tasty morsel proffered from a perfectly nestled place inside her Danish butter cookie tin. Everyone, including me, thinks she's fantastic.

My boss, David Sothern, doesn't have quite the same effect.

Sheila spots me as I venture down the faculty hallways towards the main offices in the psychology department, and her hand instinctively reaches for a tin of what I'm assuming is something delicious.

Blueberry muffins, it turns out.

Before I can snag one, my mouth watering despite my earlier cruciferous snack, David emerges from the oak-paneled door of his office and sees me standing over Sheila's desk.

"Kalson!" he exclaims. For some indeterminate reason, he calls all the faculty members by their last names. Never a "Professor" or a "Doctor" preceding it. It's as though we're all members of some lacrosse team where he got last pick for his teammates.

I follow him into his office and find him already sitting at his desk, his computer screen off, and a stack of papers neatly laid out on the shining wood. I catch a glimpse of his family photos as I walk in, with his wife and three almost-grown kids smiling back at him every day while he works.

David waves me to a seat opposite his desk. I start to sit down, but he adds, "Close the door, would you."

It's not a request.

I do as I'm told and settle myself in the indicated chair,

which is 1960s style leather and oak, with a few cracks in the seat. The old leather catches greedily on the fabric of my pants as I settle in.

I wait for David—Professor Sothern—to begin.

"Do you know what we need to discuss today?" David asks.

Like I said, he's no Sheila.

I pull a thoughtful face and consider the question for a few moments to stop myself from saying something else. "No, I can honestly say I do not." I punch the "t" with my tongue.

"Hmm . . ." David leans forward. "I wanted to congratulate you once again on the op-ed you wrote for the *Plain Dealer* in June. You've garnered some great press for the department. And you were absolutely right in what you wrote—child protection is failing our children and, as you point out, it failed you too. I'd thought that could become an avenue of research for you as you work towards tenure. Your interest in child welfare could not only lead to groundbreaking science, but also hefty grants to help fund your work within our department. Maria's recently had some luck in this same area, and I see a lot of potential in you. . ."

A bead of sweat drips from my underarm into the band of my bra. I shift in my seat, trying to take in the compliment, and feel my pants snag on one of the leather faults. The scratch of a tiny rip sounds across the quiet space between David and me.

David interrupts himself. "Is everything okay? You look pale."

It takes me a moment to get the words out of my mouth. My ears are buzzing.

"I think I'm just hungry." I give a nod towards Sheila's desk behind the wall of his office. "Sheila's muffins. . ." I trail off.

I fold my hands in my lap and focus on the crease between wall and ceiling behind the withering ficus in the corner. I shape my mouth into a smile, and hope it doesn't resemble rictus.

David pats his stomach and smiles back. "They *are* delicious, although I may have overindulged a little." I force a chuckle, and somehow laughing with my boss about his midriff helps me feel better.

"Yes, well," David reaches up and straightens his tie. "Keep up the great work and you might be looking at preparing your promotion/tenure package in the next couple of months. I wanted to give you a heads up."

I have to wait a few extra moments, more than is polite, for the riot in my body to subside. I pause another couple of seconds, until the expected whorl of satisfaction at my boss's approval rises in my chest. "Thank you. That's great news," I say.

David turns his head back to the papers on his desk and I make a line for the door. He calls out a "Goodbye" to me, which I hear from Sheila's desk, where she's waiting with the muffin tin ready for me to tuck into as I pass by on my way back to my office. Even though I'm no longer hungry, I grab a muffin and take a massive bite before heading back to my office. Blueberries burst in my mouth.

Sheila smiles and holds the tin out again. "One for the road?"

12

St. Elizabeth's hospital sits right around the corner from Youngstown State's campus, and Dr. Koftura's office can be found in one of the extension buildings built a while ago onto the original hospital's structure. It's more than a little convenient that I can walk over for my appointment directly from my office. On my way out, I pass by Maria's office and catch a glimpse of her dark head bent over her desk, highlighter in hand. I rush past, too embarrassed to hash over what happened this morning.

It's bitter out today, and the wind chafes at my body as I walk over the freeway overpass and past the antediluvian street sign reading, "No cell phone use in this area." The burst of pleasure from my successful meeting with David—*Sothern!*—has leaked out of me and I have to arm-wrestle my mind into submission so it will stop replaying my weird spaz out in his office. By the time I enter through the staggered mechanical doors designed to keep the winter air out of the reception area, I am shivering from the cold and clammy from nerves.

I'm worried about what Dr. Koftura will say.

The receptionist is a young man in his mid-twenties. I hand

over my university insurance card and take in his dimples and wavy blond hair. I offer him a smile, trying to get out of my head for a minute, but he ignores me almost entirely, aside from mechanically asking for my date of birth and name of the doctor I'm seeing. He looks over my shoulder as he hands back my insurance card and tells me to take a seat in Waiting Room B.

Still got it.

Before I can warm my hands up on a well-thumbed *People* magazine (I just look at the pictures, I swear), a dark-haired nurse with huge hoop earrings calls my name. I follow her through the magical door that leads to the warren of exam rooms, and sit obligingly as she takes my blood pressure, weight, and height. The nurses do this every time, and every time I think what a waste it is to measure my height, seeing as I haven't grown since I was fourteen and I've been coming here for biannual exams for the past umpteen years.

As the nurse leads me further into the tributaries of exam rooms, we pass by Dr. Koftura's office, emblazoned with the embossed nameplate of Jana Koftura, M.D., and Dr. Koftura herself. She's on her knees, wiggling the lock on the door to her personal office. I have a few seconds to gaze inside as the nurse and I walk towards her, where I glimpse a pristine desk with papers in neat stacks and a computer screen sitting on one side. There are two chairs in soft brown with leather seats across from the desk—new additions from the last time I was brought into Dr. Koftura's inner sanctum. After all these years of care, I've only been inside her office twice. Once when we first began treatment, right after the accident, and then a few years later, when Patty and Dave decided I couldn't stay with them any longer and I needed to go to another foster family.

I hadn't taken the news well.

"Do you need some help?" I offer by way of introduction.

As she turns her head towards me, her dark hair is so

lustrous that it catches light from the industrial fluorescents and creates a corona around her face.

Dr. Koftura's gaze fixes on me for a moment, scanning for something—*Does she not recognize me?* I think for a split second —and then offers me a smile.

"Morgan, it's so good to see you." She gestures to her office, still crouched on the floor. "This door won't stay shut. I keep closing it, locking it even, and then when I walk by again it's open."

"I can call maintenance," the nurse offers, with an edge to her voice that makes me wonder what Dr. Koftura is like to work for.

Dr. Koftura turns her gaze back to the door and its lock. "That's not necessary. I've already called several times, and they have yet to send anyone to fix it." She mutters something under her breath as the screwdriver in her hand slips.

"Do you have other tools here?" I ask. In foster care, making myself useful made it more likely for me to stick around a home. Usually. I can plunge a toilet like nobody's business. Or pick a lock.

"I brought my entire toolbox in." Dr. Koftura stands up and lets out a sigh. "But it's no use. It really is quite ridiculous. I have private files in there—the lock should work."

"I can try and fix it," I offer, and I reach my hand out to grab the screwdriver from her, ready to impress her.

More than once in grad school I had professors compare the human brain to one big electrical circuit, and each time I heard that, all I could think was, "I wish." If that were the case, we'd all be easy to fix.

Dr. Koftura gives me a complicated look, and then shakes her head. "This can wait."

She asks the nurse to take me over to the exam room.

"I'll see you in a minute," she says, and heads back into her office.

It's only a few minutes when I hear Dr. Koftura's gentle knock on the door before she enters. Her long, silky hair is tied in its usual braid at the nape of her neck. Over the years, streaks of gray have been added to her plaits. One dark wisp falls in front of her eye as she swings the door open, and she tucks it behind her ear as she greets me once again. I feel like a five-year-old, fidgeting on the exam table with my sweaty palms.

"Morgan, how *are* you?" She does the full double-hand hold that few people can achieve genuinely, but Dr. Koftura is certainly one of them. There's a comfort in seeing the same doctor for most of your life.

"I'm okay." I give a watery smile before asking after her two kids, who are almost as old as me now. I can remember when they were younger, and I was younger, too, and how Dr. Koftura's skin would look ashen, her eyes sunk from the fatigue of raising her children on her own—her husband died when they were young—but even then she'd still be glowing in that way she has.

Sometimes, when I was younger, I'd pretend Dr. Koftura was my mother.

"Oh, you know—these millennials have their own unique formula for navigating the world, don't they? And parents aren't usually a big part of it." She smiles again and sits down, clipboard turned over on top of her knee, and looks at me intently.

"What's going on? I have a few notes from the intake nurse, but I'd rather hear from you directly."

I'd been rehearsing what to say to her on the walk over, but now my mind seems to have gone blank. I take a deep breath and try to remember how I wanted to explain my shitstorm of a morning.

"My boyfriend and I got into a fight today. After I couldn't find him online—not even on Facebook, and I mean everyone and their grandmother is on Facebook—" I glance up from my hands, where I've fixed my eyes while I've talked, but Dr. Koftura doesn't shift her expression at my lame joke. She stares at me intently. "So I searched for Justin—that's his name, Justin—and when I didn't find anything I started getting suspicious, thinking that maybe he'd been lying to me. I ended up trying to follow him on campus, and things just spiraled from there."

I blush because all my "prepwork" has resulted in an incoherent babbling fit.

She's going to take my shoelaces, I think.

I raise my eyes expectantly. Dr. Koftura frowns at me, but not in an unkind way. Finally, after a few more moments of consideration, she speaks.

"I see. What do you mean by 'spiraled from there'?"

I sigh. I might as well finish the job.

I tell her about my fight with Justin. I tell her everything.

Dr. Koftura listens calmly, nodding intermittently as I talk. Active listening. Normalizing.

I know what she's doing, but from her it reads as genuine.

When I'm finished, she says, "Morgan, these are patterns that you and I both recognize."

I shrug my shoulders, eight-years-old again, and waiting for my Band-Aid and lollipop. "I know," I say. "That's why I'm here."

She nods again.

"You had several episodes during your graduate training, and we discussed how that was possibly due to the stress of your program. I've been worried about your transition to your full-time position at the university, especially now that you'll be coming up for promotion soon. Do you see any connection between your behavior this morning and potential stressors at work?"

She doesn't glance at her clipboard once, and I try to remember if I mentioned four months ago at my regular check-

up about the possibility of promotion, but can't recall. Dr.
Koftura adds, brushing the same dark strand of hair behind her
ear again, "You've been at the university for two years now,
correct? When Jawinder had just begun working, his first tenure
assessment also came at two years."

Her eyes scan the ground for a breath or two. She doesn't
usually talk about her husband.

Jawinder was a medical doctor—an internist, according to
one of the nurses who clued me in a few years back during an
extra long wait in the pre-screening room—who went down the
academic route and became a faculty member in YSU's biology
department.

I think back to my earlier meeting with my department
head, push away the weird hot flash that sent me rushing out of
his office, and focus instead on what he said. That jolt of satisfaction I felt at his compliment barrels through me again. It only
lasts for a moment, though, because I know what I need to tell
Dr. Koftura.

"It's not work." I swallow. Hard. *This is so embarrassing.*
"Justin said he loves me."

Surprise flashes across Dr. Koftura's face, followed by relief.

"Well, that's wonderful," she says.

"Is it?" I steel myself to go through with this rehashing. "The
same thing happened with Richard." I point out the obvious. "I
don't do well with vulnerability."

"You know that's not entirely true," Dr. Koftura says, her
voice gentle. "We've been monitoring your health for a long
time, because when you were a child—"

I cut her off, parroting the words I've heard so many times
before, here in this office. "I sustained a massive head trauma
after being struck by a moving vehicle, which resulted in
episodic amnesia and perceptual distortions."

"That's correct," my doctor chimes in. "And because the

brain can sometimes not show the effects of injuries until years and years after the trauma occurred, we check in with you at least twice a year. You know I'd prefer," and here she touches her hand to her chest, just above her heart, in a gesture I'd dismiss as cheesy if it were anyone else. "I'd prefer to see you at least four times a year, but you've never agreed to that since you were old enough to decide this on your own. But I'm glad you're here today talking to me about your concerns."

"I don't know." It's the best I can offer.

She nods thoughtfully but doesn't say anything. We know the same tricks: silence is really just opportunity.

"I've been feeling fine, otherwise," I add. "No blips in my memory. No weird déjà vus."

"No re-emergence of memories?" Dr. Koftura asks. "I know in the past this has been difficult for you."

I decide not to mention hearing my mother's voice the other day in my classroom. I'm convinced it was a fluke—a remnant of stress given the lecture topic. And besides, my mother has nothing to do with love.

"Just the normal background noise," I say.

Dr. Koftura's brow furrows slightly. "No changes there?" she asks.

"No," I reply.

Dr. Koftura raises one eyebrow slightly, but I hold firm.

She continues, "Tell me more about why you think Justin saying he loves you caused your behavior today."

"Because, like you said earlier, it seems to be a pattern with me. And that's what scares me, I guess. I know about the effects of trauma on the brain." She and I share a measured look at each other. We both know the data is not in my favor. "What if I'm destined to always get paranoid whenever somebody starts to care about me?" I want Dr. Koftura to tell me it's going to be okay. That I'm okay. Because, unlike Annie, she knows how trauma changes a person, down to the cellular level.

"That hasn't happened with Annie," Dr. Koftura offers.

"That's different." I say it almost automatically.

"How?" Her face is expectant, like she's leading me somewhere important.

"Because Annie and I are just friends." Being with Annie is like breathing. I don't need to think about it, and it keeps me alive.

"But you care about her, and she cares about you, right?"

I nod in the affirmative, although I can picture Annie blowing me fake kisses from Cleveland. *You are the love of my life,* she'd deadpan.

And we'd both laugh.

But it'd still be true.

"So, what makes you think that you are incapable of loving someone in a romantic relationship? Both involve trust, vulnerability, care, and compassion. Clearly you've developed these skills, despite the challenges you've faced."

"Because I always mess things up. Like this morning on campus with Justin—I was totally out of line." I rake a hand through my hair. "Irrational. Don't you think?"

Dr. Koftura doesn't say anything for a moment. Instead she levels her eyes on me and tilts her head to one side. I suddenly feel exposed and cross my arms over my chest.

"I think your behavior today was problematic for your relationship, but not something that should frighten you." *Well, she has me pegged.* "It's a manifestation of past behavioral patterns, not of the brain damage you suffered as a child. And not as a result of any sort of adaptation to trauma from your childhood, either. This is your first relationship since Richard, correct?"

"Yes."

At least that's easy to admit.

"And that ended quite dramatically as I recall, but you were in therapy for an extended period of time afterwards and you took full responsibility for your actions. You and I have worked on these issues for a number of years as well. In other words, Morgan," and Dr. Koftura leans towards me and puts her hand on my arm for emphasis. "You've worked hard to overcome your past and, as a result, you are not bound to repeat it."

I swallow hard again. I clear my throat and grab a tissue from the box on the side counter. It feels smooth and soft in the palm of my hand as I start to shred it into thin strips.

"Now, I still want to do a full examination of you, but the fact that you called me so soon after your fight with Justin shows how much progress you've made. You are aware of your patterns; you have the tools you've built over all these years to break those patterns; you have a strong support system in Annie; and it appears in Justin as well."

"So, you don't think I'm going crazy?" I croak out. God, it has been a day.

Dr. Koftura laughs. "I wouldn't use that term to begin with, but no, I don't think your mental health is at risk. I want you to think of your actions today as habits, not symptoms."

"Do you think Justin's good for me?" I ask the question impulsively and then inwardly cringe. I study a poster detailing the signs of stroke that's fixed to the opposite wall of the exam room, waiting.

She motions for me to take a seat on the exam table. "I don't know enough about him, although the little you've told me suggests that he seems to have good control of his emotions, even in provocative situations." She cocks an eyebrow at me, and I give a nervous half-smile in return.

That's one way of putting it, I think.

An image of his clenched fist flashes up, the white of his knuckles beckoning me, but I shove it away.

Dr. Koftura continues, "You deserve to be loved, Morgan. I hope you remember that as well." She turns her back to me in order to set down her clipboard, and it gives me a moment to compose myself.

"Let's get started, then, shall we?" She turns back towards me as she begins to run through her standard list of assessments, starting with my eyes and working her way downwards. Then she shows me the same set of photographs, pictures that have been in my file since I was a child, and she helps me retell the story we've knitted together over the years to fill the blank spaces in my memory. Thirty minutes later I leave with a clean bill of health.

On my walk back to my apartment I turn on my phone and hold it in my hand, the cold air searing into my skin as I wait for the screen to come to life. At first nothing appears on my home screen, and a rush of disappointment threatens to swallow me, before I feel my phone vibrate as it registers three notifications. Two are texts from Annie, asking if I made the appointment with Dr. Koftura, and one is from Facebook.

It reads, *"Justin McBride has sent you a friend request."*

A little yip escapes before I slap my gloved hand over my mouth.

I quickly text Annie back to tell her my appointment went well and that—of course—she was right. I do feel better after talking to Dr. Koftura. Then I log into my account.

I'm at the intersection of West Boulvard and Wick Avenue, and looking up before I cross the street I see the Youngstown State stadium looming like a massive UFO over the entire campus. With the athletic training center next to it looking like an oversized lozenge with its slick red siding and windowless exterior, the effect on the landscape is anything but picturesque.

It makes me think of my old foster parents, Patty and Dave, bringing me to campus as part of a special campus outreach program. We'd gone to a few seminars on college life, geared specifically to intrigue middle schoolers. The three of us had had lunch at Noodles café, which was the best on-campus dining at the time, and then we'd wandered around the campus buildings until finally ending up in Maag library, where they let me roam around the stacks for over an hour, just admiring the books. I lost count of how many times Patty or Dave told me that day that I could go to school here when I was done with high school. That I was meant to go to college.

It was the first time anyone had told me that I had potential. And then a few months later, Dave was diagnosed with lung cancer, Stage 4, and although both he and Patty cried and cried, I had to find a new place to live because Patty said she couldn't take care of both Dave and me.

However hard it was leaving them, what was even harder was knowing that if they'd really wanted me, they would have found a way to keep me.

On that day, a little over ten years ago, I thought Youngstown State's campus was the most magical place I'd ever been to. In all honesty, even after four years of undergraduate classes and two years as a professor after graduate school, I still think it's beautiful. (Although I learned a long time ago that magic is something reserved for middle-aged virgins and Disney—it has nothing to do with me.)

Safely across the street, and dodging cracks in the sidewalk as I make my way back to campus, I open up Facebook and see Justin's profile pic gazing back at me. It's a selfie, taken outdoors somewhere with a tree and a bench in the background. Dark hair, brooding eyes, wicked sexy smile. There's no mistaking him. I push the button to accept. Once we're connected, I start to navigate into his profile, curious to see who he's friends with. I know I must look like one of my students, bent over my phone like some trendy hunchback, but I never do this otherwise and figure the generational police will forgive me one millennial moment.

It's clear to me, as I scroll through, that Justin had just created his account a little while before messaging me. He only has two friends—me and, surprisingly, Annie—and just his profile pic. I'm about to like his profile photo when a notification pops up again for Facebook. When I click on the little red flag, it reads: *Justin McBride has sent you a relationship request.*

I hit the confirm button.

By now I've passed campus and am almost at my apartment. The building is in good shape for a structure built in the 1980s and the landscaping is always neatly prim, as though the apartment complex had hired a compulsive gardener to trim down any rogue growth on the yew bushes surrounding the apartments' building and parking lot. It doesn't have much character—not like Justin's apartment—but it's comfortable, cheap, and close to campus. It's the triple crown of junior faculty housing.

A huge elm tree sits in the center of the parking lot, with a little island of grass around it to protect the tree's trunk from rogue tenants parking too close to it. As I traipse across the parking lot, my peripheral vision catches a swath of yellow from behind the elm tree.

A shadow moves from behind the tree and towards me. It's Justin, holding a huge bouquet of yellow roses.

I'm so surprised to see him I stumble on the railroad tie encasing the grass around the elm tree. I trip and am just about to face-plant onto the asphalt with my phone crashing screen down when Justin manages to catch me by the crook of my arm and hoist me up. I am a walking—née tripping—Internet meme.

"Are you okay?" he asks, adjusting the roses in his arms to

keep them from scratching me on the face as he helps me steady myself.

"What are you doing here?" I actually shout this at him, like I've recently contracted relationship Tourette's. "I'm sorry," I continue, this time at a normal volume. "I mean, I'm sorry for saying that just now, and I'm sorry for earlier. I was totally out of line."

"No, you weren't," he begins to say, and I try to barge in again with more apologies on my side, but Justin's voice is stronger than mine. "I was acting like an asshole. I know I can sometimes be evasive, for no good reason. Or maybe for good reason—my dad was always kind of distant with me. I think I learned it from him."

I've never heard him talk about his father.

He looks down at his hands. "Not that that's an excuse or anything—I just keep thinking about how I acted and I'm trying to reconcile it with who I think I am, you know? If I'd just told you where I was, all of this could have been avoided."

I'm tempted to mention that my little excursion across campus to track down his office would still have happened, because his evasiveness didn't begin until I was already searching for his office and texting demands for location updates from him, but I don't. Instead, I ask, "Does this mean we're okay then?"

"If you forgive me for calling you a bitch, then yes—we're fine."

"As long as you forgive me for getting all thuggish in your face," I add, trying to make a joke out of it and hoping I'm succeeding. I keep thinking of what Dr. Koftura said, and Annie before that.

He seems to consider my comment for a second, and then bursts out laughing. "Yeah, you did kind of look like someone who might walk around with a tire iron, back there at the bench." He reaches out to pull me into a hug, and I let him. "I guess I like my girlfriends tough."

"Well, you're in luck then." I smile up at him. I am, more than anything, relieved. It's a relief to have this morning behind us. It's a relief to know that I'm okay—that I'm not falling apart. And it's a relief to be able to trust what Annie and Dr. Koftura have told me.

That I can do it—this whole love thing.

Speaking of. . .

"I'm sorry about your dad," I murmur into his wool coat, chafing at my own selfishness a few moments ago.

Justin gives an infinitesimal shrug. "I'm sorry too."

He pulls away from me and offers the bouquet shyly. "These are for you. I almost got red ones, but the yellow ones just seemed to fit you better."

I take the bouquet and nod my head, giving into the change of topic. "They're perfect."

I can't smell them because they're wrapped in a plastic bag to protect them from the cold air. Which reminds me that at this point my hands feel like frozen meat hooks. "Want to come inside?" I ask, and Justin doesn't even have to answer. He takes my hand and we walk into the warmth of my building together.

14

J ustin and I are lying in bed at my apartment. We'd ordered in a pizza for dinner, I graded some papers while Justin caught up on some reading, and then spent a decent chunk of time making love. Or, as Annie would have put it, having hot makeup sex. He's just returned from the shower with warm skin that's pinked up under the hot water and the smells of Irish Spring soap. I'm feeling especially cozy and relaxed, and before I can stop myself I ask him,

"So how come you weren't on Facebook?"

I'm tracing the tiny bones of his ribs that barely protrude through his skin, and the fragility of his body washes over me.

"Why are *you*?" he teases back, and I roll over to enfold him with my bare stomach and breasts pressed against him like a body lock.

"Answering a question with a question is what got you in trouble in the first place," I say, and laugh to let him know that we are past that whole misunderstanding. Although I still want to talk about it, apparently. "Seriously, did you go on just for me?"

"Of course I did." He squeezes me back with his long arms,

and I can see that he must be getting cold because the dark hairs on his arms are standing up. "I knew it was important to you. You know, you kind of mentioned it when you were accusing me of being a fraud."

I look up, worried that he's not quite over our fight, but find Justin's mouth twisted into a grin. I slap him playfully on the chest, to which he exclaims, "Your interrogation tactics won't work on me!"

"So, what did you do this afternoon?" he asks lazily, his hand tracing circles on my spine. I'm tempted to tell him about my appointment with Dr. Koftura. To let this be the moment where I unspool everything, while our bodies are thrumming and we're just so damn happy.

Justin knows I grew up in foster care, but I haven't told him about the accident. Or my mother. He definitely doesn't know that I see a neurologist on the regular. And I'm pretty sure—read, dead certain—I haven't told him about the whole police-Richard-restraining order situation.

A thought skims across my mind.

Maybe I'm the fraud.

I kiss him hard on the mouth and feel the air rush out of me. "You," I say. "I did *you* this afternoon."

"Hang on," he replies, his mouth muffled against mine as we kiss. "Should we put a picture up of us? Isn't that what people on social media do?"

I blush, happy for the distraction. "It seems to be part of the process," I offer. He kisses me again, and then holds up his phone. Justin touches the little camera to flip its viewpoint and suddenly he and I are up on the screen, looking clearly sex drunk and overused.

And naked. No nipples or anything, but still clearly unclothed.

Click. Justin takes a picture with his phone and starts to review it before I can protest.

"We can't have a picture of us—clearly in bed together—for your profile picture." I'm serious, but trying to sound playful at the same time. I don't want to ruin our little love bubble we've made for ourselves here tonight.

"It's too late," Justin crows as he gets up from the bed to avoid my reach and presses the upload button on the Facebook app.

I'm up out of bed, saying, "No, you didn't."

Justin comes back up to me, wraps his arms around me, and says, "I want the world to know that I have this beautiful woman in my bed. And that I love her!"

And I'll admit, at that exact moment I was kind of okay with it.

"Fine," I say, and kiss him again as I reach for his phone. "But let's check your privacy settings."

"Hang on," Justin says, backing up in mock outrage, his hands up in the air like I've asked him to hand over a weapon. "Fair is fair." And he extends his hand out towards me.

I think for a moment, wondering if this is a game or something else, and try to read Justin's intentions: raised eyebrow, sexy smirk.

It's been a long day, but I'm determined to have it end well.

"I'll show you mine if you show me yours," I say.

He breaks out into a laugh as I hand him my phone, and so I try and laugh too.

That evening Justin is asleep in bed and I'm full of the pizza we ordered in and ate while watching old costume drama movies, which Justin insists are not his favorite but also that he doesn't hate them either.

I'm having trouble sleeping, despite the fact that my body should be exhausted and deep into REM cycles by now, given all the physical activity and bursts of serotonin it got tonight. I'm trying to read a book—I'd grabbed *The Age of Innocence* by Edith Wharton—which should put me to sleep because I've read it so many times since I was a teenager, but my mind is still electric with unspent energy.

My phone vibrates against my bedside table and I pick it up to see a text from Annie.

How's it goin'?

I pause for a second, and then text back with the picture Justin took earlier.

She writes back immediately.

Hah! Already saw that on FB u love-addicted weirdo

He brought YELLOW Roses!! I type back.

Well no wonder u fucked him

Hey!

Just kidding / Seriously tho everything's good?

Yeah, just can't sleep. Reading Wharton

<3 Wharton Annie writes back.

Annie and I have been obsessed, collectively, with *The Age of Innocence*, both novel and movie, since we first met in our group home. We even watched it together a few months ago, Annie in her loft in Cleveland and me in my little faculty apartment, and live tweeted it to keep each other entertained as Newland fell in love with May Welland, and then Countess Olenska. Annie and I continue to have the whole debate about whether May deserved the yellow roses originally sent by Newland to Countess Olenska, instead of the boring day lilies he always ordered for his fiancée. Annie says yes, and I adamantly argue no. May Welland is a timid milquetoast, whereas the countess fights for what she wants. End of story.

The Twitterverse, as it were, seemed to not care about our debate, but Annie and I had had fun all the same.

What r u doing?

Annie's reply comes back a minute later.

Sorry, just making dinner ;) / Stir-fry and skittles tonight

I write back, but as I do so I notice the glow from my phone is casting itself on Justin's face. I check, but Justin is still sleeping soundly on his side, although his breathing seems shallower. I shift the light of my screen down, careful not to wake him up.

Sounds yummy

There's a brief pause, the dots moving on Annie's side, and then disappearing, and then starting again.

So you guys talked? About everything?

I think back to my conversation with Annie. Her assurance that Justin would love me, no matter what slippery dark things lurked around in my past.

And then I think what it would mean to never tell him any of it.

Yeah, we did. You were right.

Texting makes lying to your best friend so much easier.

I'm always right. Get used to it.

I don't text back. For a moment, I can't.

A few breaths later my phone lights up.

Luv u she writes.

Luv u too / gnight

I hit send before I add something snarky to lessen the weight of it all.

I click off, turn my phone over, and go to spoon myself into Justin's arms. Except that his arms are stretched out in front of him now and I can only manage to touch his left arm with my fingertips. The rest of his body is too far away for me to hold. A shiver runs through me, and guilt seeps in. I resolve to tell Justin everything in the morning. All the pieces of my past I've left out.

The next morning, though, I wake to Justin looking intently at my face.

"Let's go away together," he says. "Let's leave today, just for the weekend."

My mind is still on the edge of sleep, but the words are there, willing to be true.

I'm. Not. Broken.

15

I think I'm awake, but I can't open my eyes. They are swollen, or glued shut somehow from sleep. Or is there a bandage over them? My mind is awake at least, and my impulse, when I can't open my eyes, is to reach my hand out to touch Justin. Or Annie. But instead my hand won't move beyond what feels like some horrid claw.

My mind whirs itself further into life, and I swear that if someone had the MRI scanning me right now they'd see my hippocampus stutter into action. Because I can remember it all. The accident, Justin's face unreadable, my hand on the wheel over his as I try to save us, the sickening squeal as metal collides with wood, collides with soft tissue and bone. And something later on. A rustling outside the car that sits around the edges of my consciousness.

That voice, inside my head.

My heart falls deeper into my chest when I think of Justin unbuckling his seat belt. Deliberate and steady in that motion, despite the chaos swirling around us.

"Where is he?" I try to ask, but there are tubes connected to my nose and gauze packs my cheeks. My tongue is desperately dry and feels swollen and brittle at the same time. I can't seem to move it without feeling a thousand pinpricks of pain. I'll learn later that my mouth was full of windshield glass where it fell while I was screaming. They'd had to pick out the pieces, one at a time.

I can't be alone, because I feel hands on me now, gentle and soft, which I recognize later is partly due to the rubber gloves everyone wears before they'll touch me.

"Ah, let's get these off, now. I can see they're making you skittish."

It's a woman's voice, and sounds vaguely Irish, which isn't something you often hear in Youngstown. Most of our immigrants came a few generations back, at least.

My eyes start to focus, and the dimmed lights of the room I am in come through the haze of my vision.

"We put this on to keep the swelling down, but it seems to have slipped while you were sleeping."

I can still feel a stickiness in my eyes, and think for a moment it's dried blood, but after removing the covering bandages the nurse dabs at the corners of my eyes with a wet piece of gauze and the cloth is barely streaked with dull yellows and beiges. No blood, dried or otherwise, I determine.

"Airbags didn't deploy, apparently." She says this conspiratorially, as if I'm not supposed to know this piece of the puzzle.

I start to ask again about Justin, but my nurse—I'd glimpsed the name "Deborah" on her uniform as she turned away from me—is bustling about with a tray near my bed, clanging instruments and unwinding what looks like gauze from a large roll that's just emerged from a ripped paper packet.

"Ah," the nurse says as she leans over my prone body, her rather voluminous breasts pressing against my arm as she tries to adjust other bandages that blanket my head and neck. I want to reach up and touch my scalp, wondering in an unconscious act of vanity if they've had to shave my head, but she clucks her tongue in disapproval and gently presses my arm down with her left hand. "There we are. Best not be touching these, now. Listen to Nurse Debbie and you'll be right as rain soon enough."

I try to make eye contact with her, but I hear the door to my room gasp open and she's already moving away from my bed.

"Dr. Holdren, how are you?" Nurse Debbie inquires of the slim blond woman who's just entered.

"Don't worry about me, nurse," Dr. Holdren says, a bite to her tone. "How's our patient?"

I turn my head towards my doctor and try to catch her eye and explain that I can't seem to talk, but her eyes are drawn to the chart that sits in a basket at the foot of my bed. Even after she raises her eyes they train themselves on the blipping machines surrounding me, rather than on my body.

I make a noise somewhere between a grunt and a cough, and then again, until finally Dr. Holdren turns her gaze over to me.

"Please don't try to talk," she says, and goes on to explain about the glass she extracted from my tongue last night. "You've encountered severe head trauma, internal bleeding, three broken ribs, and various abrasions and bruising. Overall, I'd say you were very, very lucky. But you must be gentle in your recovery, and *no talking* until I do a full examination of you, including the wounds to your mouth."

I sit dumbfounded. *Why is no one talking about Justin?*

Dr. Holdren puts her hands to my neck, just beneath my chin, and begins to press her fingertips against my skin, with the boundary of her gloves' latex between us. I wait like a docile child, which was never my style even when I *was* a child, as she moves her hands and her eyes down the vertebrae of my neck. She examines the cuts and bruising to my arms and legs, murmuring to herself or perhaps to Nurse Debbie—who waits nearby, chart and pen in hand—and I breathe obediently when

Dr. Holdren tells me to, her stethoscope pressed to my chest, and then again when the cold metal disk touches my back.

Finally, after what seems to be an eternity of prodding, she asks me to open my mouth and extends a wooden tongue depressor to the right side of my cheek first, followed by my left. Her face is so close to me that I see the line of makeup foundation she's left between her forehead and her hairline, the two tones of beige just not quite matching. And I'll admit, as she manipulates my body like a doll, seeing this small imperfection in her makes me feel a spark of power inside the deep hole of fear that's been growing inside me since I woke up.

Dr. Holdren pulls away, apparently satisfied with my current physical state, and murmurs something else to Nurse Debbie, who promptly scribbles into my chart. Looking at me, Dr. Holdren offers a wan smile.

"You seem to be in one piece. The wounds inside your mouth should heal nicely and I haven't found any remnants of glass remaining, which is a testament to the surgical team on duty when you came in."

I nod as emphatically as possible, trying to express my gratitude, and hoping that this will speed along the process of my being permitted to ask where Justin is.

Dr. Holdren moves away from the bed and towards the door to my room, and I realize that she's done with me for now. I lurch forward, focusing my brain on every single muscle in my mouth as I try to get them to work together to make the words I need to say.

"Wah 'bou Jushin?" I manage to push out past the swelling in my tongue and cheeks.

My doctor turns, her blond hair brushing over her right shoulder in a waterfall of honey-colored highlights. "What's that?"

She's asking Nurse Debbie, not me.

"She wants to know about her boyfriend," Debbie answers, and then gives what seems to be a meaningful look. "The man in the car accident."

I watch a mask go down over Dr. Holdren's face as Debbie's words register. The corners of her mouth inch towards her chin and her eyes narrow into a look of tense annoyance.

"He's not my patient," she replies, before heading through the door and on to the next poor soul awaiting her care. "Anyway, he's not a family member."

I see starbursts in front of my eyes, and I don't know if they're from the head trauma Dr. Holdren has just described, or from the intense anger pumping through me like adrenaline. Poor Debbie is left with me, and I am done with this shit. I sit up in bed, my balance swimming a little as I find my level, and shift my torso close to Nurse Debbie's position at the foot of my bed. Tubes and medical tape pull against my skin, the one connected to my nose becoming detached. A machine beeps frantically.

My face is as close to Nurse Debbie as I can get. As I start to speak, tears of frustration and fear, and whatever else my body is churning up inside, begin rushing down my cheeks in an unfamiliar torrent, and the words I'm saying dissolve even further into an incomprehensible blather. It hurts to feel my shoulders shaking up and down, and the pain in my ribs is so intense I think I might actually pass out, but I can't stop crying.

Dr. Koftura's words come back to me. *You deserve to be loved.*

Through the blur of my tears I make out my nurse's eyes, nose, mouth, and if there is an opposite to Dr. Holdren's resting-asshole-face, then that is what Nurse Debbie looks like.

"There, there, little one," she says, and her hand, still swathed in the gloves she has not taken off, comes to rest gently on my back. Her touch feels entirely different from Dr. Holdren's, and I'm so relieved to have just the smallest bit of compassion that I don't even knee-jerk grimace at her endearment.

I am like putty at this point, so physically and emotionally drained that I mold to her every suggestion, and willingly let her nestle me back onto my bed and replace the tube in my nose. Nurse Debbie moves away from my bed, but as I start to protest she gives me a soft look and indicates the chair sitting next to what must be the bathroom door. She pulls the chair over in one swoosh of her strong arms and settles herself into it next to my bed.

I watch her adjust her smock, and twist her wedding ring around her finger twice. She smooths the blanket where it's bunched up next to my knees.

She is going to tell me.

I know it will not be what I am hoping to hear.

Finally she looks up at me, and her blue eyes are almost like Justin's, wide and swimming.

"Justin is dead, love."

My hand on top of his. Steering us towards safety.

I thought.

My chest rips open. I clutch at the hole in my body I'm sure that Nurse Debbie can see growing, and growing.

But if she can, she doesn't make any sign. Instead she says, "I'll stay here with you if you want." And she holds my hand in hers, the rubber glove finally stripped away.

16

I must eventually have slept, because when I wake up Nurse Debbie is gone and I'm alone in my room. A machine glows with a green haze that colors the room, and since there is no clock I have no idea what time of day it is. The light coming through the partially closed blinds of the one window is anemic, like it always is this time of year, and there's no way for me to tell from the sun whether it is morning, twilight, or already the next day.

There's a tray next to my bed with pink plastic covers, hiding, what I assume, is some sort of meal. I shift my body weight over towards the tray, hoping that whatever beige wonders are hiding underneath might give me a clue about the approximate time of day, but my ribs shriek in pain as I do so, and I fall back against my pillows.

For once in my life I'm not hungry.

And then I remember, like a freight train crashing into my brain, still fuzzy from drug-induced sleep.

Justin is dead.

Dead.

I see his face—not the face of the Justin I first met, when we traded jabs about the drollness of Chomsky, or his face when he'd bring a cup of tea for me in the morning after we'd spent the night together. It's his face as he hit the accelerator, my car shrieking into the hulking mass of that ancient tree.

The face of a stranger.

What happened?

The pain is so intense I want to shed my skin and become someone else.

I think back to our fight earlier this week, and the nasty things I'd called him. "Liar." "Fraud." *Is that why he did this? Why he wanted to hurt himself?*

Or both of us?

No. The answer surges up from my gut with such force it knocks the breath out of me. We were happy. We were in love.

None of this makes sense.

Something scratches at the back of my brain.

It's there, lurking after the shattered glass and the squeal of metal. I reach for it—try to hold on—but I can't. The hole in my memory after impact is like a cut filmstrip. Just a black nothingness.

Not again.

I want to scream, and I start to open my mouth in an expression of sheer grief and frustration, when someone else—in fact two people—come through my hospital room door, tailed by Dr. Holdren, who's wearing a different set of earrings and a fresh shirt from the last time I saw her.

At least one day has passed. If not more.

The room is full of women now, and it's clear to me from the start that my two new visitors are not medical staff. The first, a squat woman with a short brunette crop and huge hoop earrings, wears a leather jacket that seems to be more of a blazer, jeans, and a white button-down shirt. Her partner, because I'm assuming, given the gun holster I see on the hips of both women

beneath their business casual attire that they are law enforce-
ment officers in some capacity, is tall and willowy, with high
cheekbones and with her hair in miniature braids that are
pulled back into a chignon at the nape of her neck.

The tall one speaks first.

"Ms. Kalson, I'm Detective Ormoran and this is Detective
Miller." She gestures to the brunette, who gives me the tip of her
chin and an aloof stare. Detective Ormoran's voice is lilting and
honey-toned.

Even in the state I'm in, I make a note that she's the good cop
in this duo.

Detective Ormoran goes on, "I believe you've already met Dr.
Holdren. She says we can come and talk to you for a few
minutes, if that's alright..."

Dr. Holdren cuts her off. "Just for a brief time, and don't
excite her too much." My doctor keeps her eyes on the detectives. She wanders over to the foot of my bed and pulls up my
charting, the paper scratching against the cheap plastic of its
holder. "I'll be outside if you need me." She leaves with my chart
in her hand.

Even though I never said it was okay for them to come in, the
detectives settle themselves in the two chairs available. Ormoran
glides her long frame into the chair Nurse Debbie had used—
when was it, one night, two nights ago?—and her knees bump
into the side of my cot. She sits closer than is comfortable. I
cross my arms over my chest—gingerly, since my ribs keep
shouting at me to stop breathing—and wish that I had more
armor against the world than a faded blue hospital gown.

Miller pulls her chair towards the foot of my bed and settles
herself, like she's getting ready to read a cozy book and wrap a
blanket around her shoulders. A pad of paper and a pen are
poised on her knee.

All three of us sit, waiting for someone to begin talking, all of us accustomed to uncomfortable silence. I force myself to swallow the questions tumbling around inside my head. Because as soon as they stepped inside my room, I knew. They're not here to help me.

Finally, Ormoran speaks.

"So, you're a professor?" It's a question, and I wonder if she's testing me, because technically I'm not a professor. I'm an instructor, a lecturer. Tenure-track, not tenured.

Miller says nothing and stares at me.

While I'm weighing my answers, Ormoran moves on, not interested, it seems, in my confirmation of the fact she's tossed out. "I went to YSU, you know. I played in the women's rugby team."

"Okay," I offer. My voice comes out clearer than it did when I last tried to speak, which makes me guess that time has marched ahead quite a bit since Nurse Debbie was here, holding my hand. My mouth is dry, but the gauze has been removed and I don't taste blood anymore.

"Yeah, we were State Champions a few years ago—maybe you saw the pennants hanging in Kilcawley?"

I have no idea why we are talking about sports, but I'm certain I should play along.

Good cop.

"I remember reading about it in the *JamBar*." Half the student newspaper at Youngstown State is devoted to campus sports, so I figure this is a safe bet.

Miller is solemn; her head is poised over her notepad as she scratches something down on the paper. "There's no women's rugby team at YSU. She tells that to everybody, trying to sound like she's some star athlete." Her voice is pure Youngstown city proper, with the nasal Os and dropped Gs that mimic the way my students speak. The way I speak too. And Justin.

I correct myself. *The way he spoke.*

That knife in my ribs again.

Ormoran gives a quick glance at her partner, and offers the air between Miller and me an embarrassed smile. "It's true. I just like to try and put people at ease, you know. People—like you, dear—see two cops coming into their room; they've been through a trauma, and they're just hoping to come out alive from it. I don't want you to be nervous."

Ormoran shifts forward towards my bed, and I think she might be about to reach and hold my hand, but her hands stay primly folded in her lap.

"I'm so sorry about your friend." She says this with her eyes fixed on mine, her hand hovering again above her knee as if she might reach out to touch my arm in an act of comfort.

But she doesn't.

"What do you remember about the accident?" she continues.

I tell her about the winding road, and about the oncoming car that Justin seemed to try and shift into, and how I pulled the wheel back. When I explain the call from "Mom" coming in on Justin's phone, Ormoran murmurs something to Miller that I can't quite catch.

"Do his parents know?" I ask, desperately. Justin wasn't close to them, and I never met them, but still—the thought of his mother learning that she was calling just as Justin drove us off the road, sends a dense shot of pain through my chest.

"One of the first steps in any investigation like this is notifying next of kin," Ormoran explains to me. "Can you tell me what happened after the phone call? What happened next?"

"How are they doing? Do they want to talk to me?" My voice sounds warped and reedy. A dull throb starts to ache inside my head.

"Right now, we need you to focus on telling us what happened." Ormoran's tone is kind, but a new firmness has crept in.

I remind myself who I'm talking to, and do as I'm told.

I pour it out for both detectives.

The phone call, the look on Justin's face, and the tree looming up in front of us. The churning chaos of the crash. And then nothing.

When I'm finished, Ormoran meets my gaze, her face creased with concern.

"That must have been frightening," she says. Miller just sits there, taking notes in her little pad.

I nod, because there's nothing else to do.

"Why didn't you take over the driving?" Ormoran asks.

"How could I?" Someone pokes an ice pick behind my right eye. I sound like a child who is already bored with this conversation. I look over to the tubes connected to my arm, and wonder what kind of drugs they're pumping into me right now.

"Of course, of course," Ormoran nods obligingly. "But I'm sure that you told him to pull over, right?"

"Yes. I thought he was having a panic attack. At first."

"Why would you think that?" Miller this time.

"Because he was afraid of driving."

The two women look at each other, their faces surprised.

"Well, if that's the case, why was he driving?" Miller asks, her pad of paper forgotten for a moment.

My mind scrambles back to the day we left, but I don't know how I can explain Justin's insistence to the detectives, other than to state the obvious. "Because he wanted to."

Ormoran raises her eyebrows, and Miller gives a soft "huh," and scribbles something in her notebook.

"He didn't trust you behind the wheel?" Ormoran's face puckers in disapproval.

"No," I correct her, and try to force my brain to stop whirring so I can pluck the memory back. "No, he was being considerate." *Was he?* I think.

"So, he was trying to be a gentleman? Trying to take care of you?" Ormoran asks.

I nod in confirmation.

"But, here's my thinking," Ormoran shifts her body away from the bed as she adjusts her position in the rigid hospital chair. She crosses her legs and is careful to tuck her foot underneath the bed. Her long legs leave her little room to get comfortable in the cramped quarters of my bedside. "There were better ways to show that, weren't there?"

I give her a blank stare back. I'm not sure what she's getting at.

"Where were you going? There are a lot of fancy resorts right around there. Not too much else, though."

"Justin wanted to go away for the weekend. We were heading to the Wolf Mountain Lodge when—" My voice trails off. I don't know where to look, so I stare at my hands folded in my lap.

"Wolf Mountain Lodge." Miller repeats, her voice almost monotone. Whereas Ormoran is like a walking stick of empathy, Miller seems like an imprint of a person. She keeps fading into the background, and I almost forget she's there until she interjects with her listless voice, notebook shoved in front of her face.

"And he'd made reservations?" Ormoran chimes in.

"I guess so," I say. "I just assumed he had." I hadn't asked Justin, because he'd planned the entire trip. Spur of the moment. I wasn't supposed to worry about a thing. "I really, I just. . ." A fist of grief clenches at my throat.

Dr. Holdren must have been just outside my door, because as soon as I start sobbing she is in my room, fanning her arms and making it clear that the detectives' time is up.

"We were just about to leave, anyway," Ormoran says, and gives a heavy glance in my direction.

Dr. Holdren returns Ormoran's look with an icy stare.

"We'll come back later, Ms. Kalson. Get some rest." As she

leaves, Ormoran taps the foot of my bed twice, as if to confirm that she and Miller haven't caused any harm with their interview.

Miller stands up and packs her paper notebook into a garish pink purse I hadn't noticed when she came in and sat down. It strikes me as odd, because such a colorful purse seems to clash with her persona.

"We called all the resorts around there, hoping to figure out where the two of you were headed," she says, "including the Wolf Mountain Lodge, but there were no reservations anywhere. Not under McBride. Not under Kalson. In fact, when we called Wolf Mountain Lodge, we were lucky to get hold of anybody. It seems they're closed for renovations until further notice." She finally looks at me, and her beady brown eyes scan me up and down like she's surveying a horse that's just been discovered to be lame. "You take care."

The door brushes against the linoleum of the hospital's floor as it closes.

Dr. Holdren is still there, actually looking at me for once.

"Thank you," I say, and I mean it.

My doctor says nothing, but she does nod her head slightly before putting my chart back into its holder and walking through the door herself. I'm left alone. Thoughts scramble to the surface, trying to make sense of what just happened.

Which is when I understand why Ormoran asked me about the rugby team.

She wanted to see what I looked like when I lie.

17

W hen the detectives leave, I am too anxious to sleep. My legs twitch from nervous energy.

Suddenly I'm desperate to get online and read the news reports about Justin's death. I want to meet his parents —he said they didn't have the greatest relationship, but still I want to see them, say how sorry I am. And, yes, go looking for answers.

I want to call Annie.

And that's what my mind fixes on, sitting there in my hospital bed with a gown that opens backwards and with no one to give me information, grieving and terrified that the detectives will be back soon and that they think I had something to do with Justin's death.

I need to talk to Annie.

I hit the button by my bed, which I think must call the nurse because that's what I'd seen on the television doctor shows I watched as a kid, and sure enough a few minutes later Nurse Debbie bustles in, calling me "love" and asking what I need. Today her hair is pulled back into a sleek bun, and her scrubs have tiny white and brown dogs on them.

"Do you know where my personal effects are?" I chide myself for sounding so goddamn formal, and then recover. "I really need my phone to call my friend."

Nurse Debbie furrows her brow. "I don't know where it might be. But, I tell you what, I was just about to come in and get you up for a walk around the hallway. Doctor says it's good for healing your ribs and muscles. We can ask around while we walk, okay?"

I nod as I start to lift myself out of the bed.

"Whoa, whoa there—let me unhook these." Nurse Debbie rushes over to get my IV adjusted for traveling, and then puts my arm around her shoulders to help lift me up. We walk gingerly to the doorway, and as we do, the need to use the bathroom comes on with sudden urgency.

What the hell have I been doing this entire time? I wonder. I'd know if I had a catheter. But then I recall the crinkling of the sheets. I should have known as soon as I shifted in bed and heard the telltale scrape of cotton against plastic. Rubber sheets are fundamental to the group home experience—they come standard with each bed so mattresses don't have to be switched out each time a kid has a nightmare.

"Um—can I go in here for just a moment?" I ask, waving my hand towards the bathroom door as we pass it on our journey around my bed and towards the hallway.

"Of course." Debbie shifts her weight to help me change direction and enter the extra-wide doorway that leads to the bathroom. "Here you are." She holds onto my IV and lifts the lid of the toilet for me.

She doesn't want to leave me alone in the bathroom.

"Can I just have some privacy? You know?" I try to give her a meaningful look that says that I don't want to pee in front of her, but the swelling in my cheeks makes it difficult to control the muscles in my face.

Nurse Debbie clucks her tongue. "I'm not supposed to let you in here unsupervised."

"Oh, really?" I imagine this is standard hospital policy, and start to work up a reason that it wouldn't apply to me, when she adds, "I shouldn't tell you this, but it's because they're worried you might hurt yourself." Nurse Debbie whispers the last part, as if she's embarrassed to admit the hospital has such a poor opinion of me.

I don't know what to say.

"How about I just stand by the door, and you leave it cracked while you go?" Although I'm thankful for her compromise, and as soon as she is on the other side of the door I sit down to relieve myself with an urgency I hadn't quite known was there, I'm also starting to wonder at how good of a nurse she is. At least, I mean, it seems as though she takes the hospital rules as guidelines more than rules—and that can't always be good, right, can it?

As soon as I flush, Nurse Debbie is back inside the room and busying around me like a mother hen, helping me adjust my robe before I make my way over to the sink to wash my hands. There is a mirror above the sink, and it's the first time I've seen myself since the accident. My two eyes are turning from purple to yellow, making my entire face look jaundiced. My hair has been shaved in random patches where stitches or sutures—I realize I don't know the difference between the two—were needed. Like I used to joke with Annie after I finished my doctorate and she'd call me with some random medical question that was burning a hole in her mind. "I'm not that kind of doctor." To which she'd inevitably reply, "What good are you, then?" and we'd both bray like some middle-aged insurance salesman with a drink. After the stress of defending my dissertation and having to convince my review committee that I was worthy of finishing my degree, it felt good to treat my Ph.D. like it was no big deal. It took the pressure off, which is something Annie's always been good at doing for me.

There is a wide band of purple bruising, running from my right shoulder, between my clavicles, and down towards my sternum. The coloring is so deep that I see it through the slightly transparent fabric of my hospital gown.

Debbie notices the expression on my face—one of horror and anxiety and disgust all mixed together, because that's exactly what I'm feeling—and says, "Not to worry. Most of this will be gone in a few more days, a week at the most. Seat belts are wonderful, aren't they?"

She nods her head towards the band on my shoulder and chest.

I touch the skin gingerly, and watch myself flinch in the mirror.

Nurse Debbie moves to turn me around and back out into the hallway. "Just imagine if you weren't wearing yours, and count your blessings."

In my mind, I see Justin unclicking his seat belt just before I grabbed the wheel and we swerved off the road. Snippets of color creep into the black of my memory. *The sound of crunching gravel. Shadows and glass. Movement where Justin was, on my left.* But Justin wasn't there, because I'd heard him crash through the windshield. *Or had I?*

I bend over and retch, but there's nothing in my stomach. Nurse Debbie pats my back, and murmurs something soothing. "Let's get you back to bed," she says, steering me towards the cot and the waterproof sheets.

Think about something else, I tell myself. I will myself. *Get your phone.*

I stand back up. "I'm fine," I say. "Just a little woozy." I pat Nurse Debbie's arm, willing my fingers to feel warm and sturdy on her skin. "Let's keep going."

She gives me a skeptical look, but turns our direction back to its original path.

We are at the door to the hallway now, and I hear the bustle of the hospital outside for the first time. Where my bed is, the din of the working hospital never reaches me.

Nurse Debbie holds the door open and I shuffle out into the hallway, taking care to not bump any of my body parts on the doorframe. I'm already exhausted, my body ready to give up, but I need to talk to Annie. I need some connection to the outside world. I lift my chin up and straighten my back as much as I can without visibly wincing.

"Come on now, love. Just down to the nurses' desk and back. We can ask about your belongings there."

The concrete goal helps, and the two of us begin to make slow progress down the hallway, with faster moving men and women careening down the hall with a purpose and charts in hand, shifting their paths around us without so much as a word.

We find ourselves at the nurses' desk after what seems like an eternity of right foot-left foot shuffling. I can't remember putting them on, but look down to see a set of paper slippers on my feet. Nurse Debbie stays by my side, holding me and the back of my gown, making encouraging noises with each step I take, and I feel guilty for thinking earlier that she wasn't good at her job.

There is a man in pink scrubs sitting at the nurses' station, and as we make our slow arrival, Nurse Debbie leans her huge bosom over the counter and calls out, "Tom, love—how're the little ones? And Sheila?"

Tom turns towards us and, glimpsing Debbie, gives her a broad smile. "They're just fine. Thanks for asking." He looks at me next. "And who's this?" Tom smiles again, this time less vigorously as he clocks my bruises.

"This is Morgan, from over in 223B. She's been in a car accident..."

"Ah, poor thing," Tom offers, and his eyes crinkle in concern. "But you're healing up, I see?"

I don't have a chance to answer as Nurse Debbie barrels on, which I'm learning she tends to do as a rule.

"And see, Morgan's a professor at the university, and she needs to see what's going on with her students, but she can't because her phone was in the car, along with her purse and other things."

I haven't told my nurse any of this, but don't feel the need to correct her.

Tom's eyes brighten up. "Ah, I see." He swivels his chair around and shoots himself, feet planted on the floor, across to the opposite side of the circular desk area. "Let's see what we have for 223B."

He begins shuffling through a stack of cubbyholes seated underneath a computer kiosk, with plastic bags containing shoes, keys, and various items of clothing. It only takes him a second to pull out a plastic bag with a flourish, and I know it's mine because inside are the black Doc Martens I was wearing Friday night and my bright red wallet. I also see my phone, which has a zebra-striped case.

"Here you are, dear," Tom says, handing over the bag. There's a bright yellow slip lining one side of the bag, with the words "Evidence Release" printed in bold black across the top. A series of signatures follows a paragraph of fine print that I can't seem to focus my eyes on to read. The bag itself has a dusting of black powder clinging to the insides of the plastic.

I mumble a thank you and look away, cowed by the evidence slip.

"You are most welcome," he replies cheerfully, not phased in the slightest it seems by the contents of my bag. "Enjoy your walk back."

Nurse Debbie thanks Tom and gently turns us around to start the long trek to my room. My legs feel more wobbly than they did on our way out to the desk, and without thinking I reach and take hold of Debbie's elbow. She puts her hand on top of mine, and when we are several steps away from the desk and beyond earshot of Tom, she says, "He's a real sweetheart. But don't go losing your heart to him, love. Gay as a songbird, that one." And she gives me a wicked smile that I can't help but return.

I've decided—for better or worse—Nurse Debbie knows what she's doing.

As we make our way down the hallway, I spot Dr. Holdren standing outside my door, her head bent towards another, smaller figure with dark hair and huge chandelier earrings. As I see the woman's hand reach up to brush a strand of stray hair that's fallen from her braids, I know who's waiting for me and Nurse Debbie.

Dr. Koftura has come for a visit.

18

I resist the urge to call out to Dr. Koftura, her face being the first familiar one I've seen since the accident, and instead wait patiently for her to look up and notice Nurse Debbie and me approaching, my IV pole in tow.

"Morgan," and the way Dr. Koftura says my name makes me let out a small yelp of a sob. She is the exact opposite of Dr. Holdren.

I sense Nurse Debbie give me a glance, and then look over at the two doctors waiting for our arrival. "You know her?" Debbie asks, under her breath and with her hand brushing at her cheek to cover her mouth partially.

"I do—she's my doctor."

"No, not her—the other one." Debbie must have thought I was being droll, pointing out Dr. Holdren as my doctor.

"I mean the other one—*she's* my normal doctor."

Debbie drops her hand from her face and offers a smile to Dr. Holdren and Dr. Koftura as we come up on them.

"Just going for a stroll," she chirrups. "Come for a visit, then?" She directs the question to Dr. Koftura, who offers a warm smile in return.

"Yes. I wanted to see my patient. Dr. Holdren and I were just consulting for a few moments about Morgan's condition and plan of treatment."

I'm still clutching my plastic bag of belongings. Dr. Koftura's arrival—however welcome—makes my phone feel like an unexploded bomb in my hand, waiting to be disarmed.

After some slight resistance to Dr. Koftura's insistence that she was perfectly capable of settling me back into my room, Nurse Debbie leaves with Dr. Holdren close behind. Dr. Koftura takes my shoulder and elbow and guides me into my room, and then onto my bed. Before I lie down, my arms and legs still feeling like shredded electrical wires, she fluffs my pillows for me and smooths the bottom sheet with the flat of her palm.

It's obvious she's a mother.

"I'm so, so sorry," she says, once my sensors are all attached again properly and she's settled herself into the chair next to me. No foot-of-the-bed chart glancing for her.

I have no words, and so I just nod. The bag with my belongings sits on the little table, where the plastic-covered dishes have been cleared away by some invisible hand. The sun slants vaguely through the window of my room and the black dust in the bag stands out in the beam of light like little fleas. Dr. Koftura notices me glancing at them.

"It's just standard procedure, right?" I ask, but she says nothing.

A thought occurs to me. "Have the police been in touch with you?"

I watch as a shadow crosses her face.

"Yes, they have. And, Morgan, you have to understand that I am here to care for you as your doctor. My only intentions are to ensure your health and safety." She has her left hand up on her chest, her palm pressed flat against her sternum. The diamond of her wedding ring winks at me from the fluorescent lights above. "And the safety of others too."

A hard seed starts to form in my stomach. I pull at the neck of my gown. .

"I see," is all I say. It feels strange, seeing her outside her well-appointed office. For the last almost-twenty years, we've only ever met each other inside those walls. But now she's here, trying to apologize for something she's done because she thought it was for my own good.

"When I saw you last week, I had a few concerns about your condition."

Last week—what day is it?

"My condition?" I roll the word around on my still-healing tongue, and it leaves my mouth bland and tasteless.

"Yes. You know that there are certain indicators we are always looking for. After your initial trauma when you were a child—and then the later incident." Dr. Koftura looks apologetic when she says this, and I almost stop her to say *It's okay. You can say I stalked my ex-boyfriend. I know.*

But I don't. I sit and listen, because I'm starting to understand why she's here.

"Your interactions with the police have been rare and fairly minor, granted, but they are of record. And you know as well as I do the signs that would cause concern. Erratic behavior. Changes in personality as expressed by behavioral choices. Hints of violence."

My eyes search her face for reassurance. "I know. But at our appointment you said there was nothing to worry about. You said they were habits, not symptoms."

A lightning flash of protest surges through my mind. *You said I was safe.*

She nods her head, but her eyes are defiant. "I know that's what I said—" And her voice catches. She shifts in her chair and brushes the same strand of hair behind her ear again. All her fidgeting makes Dr. Koftura seem like a child called to the principal's office. She takes a moment to smooth out the fabric of her black pants on the top of her thighs. "—but then I received a call from the police, saying that you'd been in an accident and that your boyfriend was dead. They asked about your diagnosis and symptoms."

There's a moment of weighted silence before Dr. Koftura lurches on with it.

"They think you killed Justin. That you ran the car off the road."

"I didn't," I protest. "You know I didn't."

A scratch at the back of my mind. *Did I?* I look at Dr. Koftura, who I've trusted for so many years. With all my secrets.

Did I?

No, I answer myself. I force my mind back to those seconds stretched into timelessness. *I was trying to save us. I know I was.*

Dr. Koftura lets out a long breath. "You grabbed the steering wheel right before the car crashed?"

My mind is ping-ponging, too agitated to land on anything.

Mom on the screen. Justin's mother. *Does she even know yet?*

And I'm suddenly very, very angry.

"What did you tell the police about me?" I ignore her question.

"Memory is a strange thing," Dr. Koftura says quietly. She's been staring at her feet, but now she looks up to meet my gaze. I can barely look at her. It hurts too much.

"You didn't remember your mother throwing you out of the house when you were seven, and wandering the streets until you were hit by a car in the middle of the road. In fact, you still don't —not really."

I stare back at her, willing myself to not look away.

"I'm so sorry," Dr. Koftura offers again, and this time she's not talking about the accident. She's apologizing for something else.

"I could have prevented all of this." Her hands wring each other, until finally her fingers find her wedding band and start to worry it around in circles. "I should have called you back in for another follow-up. I should have known this would happen."

She thinks I killed him.

A thousand pounds of pressure slam onto my chest. I can't breathe. I need fresh air. I need to get out of this room. I strain to pull air into my lungs, and I hear beeps urgently signaling from the machines my body is still tied to.

"Why don't you believe me?" I'm shouting, my voice too loud in my ears. "Why don't you believe me?" I repeat.

She looks at me with her cool, dark eyes. "Why do you believe yourself?"

A twitch at her jaw. A slight curl to her mouth.

Dr. Holdren rushes into the room, yelling something at Dr. Koftura, who moves meekly out of the way so Dr. Holdren can inject something into my IV.

And then I'm gone.

19

I wake up, in the same blue polka-dot hospital gown, to the opening strains of "Cornflake Girl" by Tori Amos, and I know it's my phone, and that Annie is calling me. The dense chords of the song keep insisting as I flail around, looking for where they're coming from. I finally see the rectangle of my phone lighting up from the side table, which has been pushed up against the edge of my bed. I rip open the bag, and the fingerprint dust puffs out in a black cloud and catches in my throat, making me cough.

The screen of my phone glows back at me, telling me it's Monday. Monday morning.

I've been in the hospital for almost three days already.

I retrieve my phone from the bag and press the green button, my desperation to hear Annie's voice causing me to fumble around. That, or the damn meds they have given me as a sedative have had side effects on my motor control. Still, I manage to pull the phone to my ear, wiping my other hand on the sheets, which leaves a black smear on the white fabric.

"Annie?" My voice breaks as I say her name, and I feel a swell of fear mixed with relief rising in my throat.

"*Oh my God—Morgan!* I didn't know if I'd be able to get through to you."

However glad I am to hear from Annie, I'm surprised my phone still has any battery left, let alone 45 percent power, like the indicator on my screen tells me. I haven't charged it since Friday morning, before Justin and I left for our trip. It should be drained by now.

The realization snaps into my mind with a metallic click.

The police must have charged it somehow. While they were doing something else with it.

"It's so good to hear your voice," I choke out, and it absolutely, truly is. But inside I'm wary. Dr. Koftura's visit, and detectives before that, cling to the edges of my sleep.

Annie charges ahead, like she always does.

"The cops called me—apparently they got my contact info from your phone, the bastards—but I told them all to go fuck themselves and that I'm not talking to them without a subpoena."

The vise stretching across my chest unspools just a little. Annie never curses, unless she is atomic-bomb-level pissed. And when Annie's angry she won't stop until the world bows down.

Annie tells me that the cops didn't give her much information, which is partly why she's so furious. "They wouldn't even confirm that you were okay. I was going out of my mind!"

She gives me twenty questions next. *Am I hurt? Where am I? How's Justin? What happened?*

I steel myself and tell her about the accident. About Justin.

"I can't believe he would do such a. . ." She stops herself, and then says, whisper quiet, "I'm so sorry." Neither of us knows what to say next. And then something must jump to the front of Annie's mind, because she asks, "Have the police interviewed you yet? What did you tell them?"

I can picture her, pacing back and forth and running her

hands through her short spiky hair as she talks to me. I hear her rummaging around in her kitchen, working off her nervous energy by cleaning the dishes or rinsing out the sink, and the normalcy of the sounds feel like they're coming from some alternate world.

I try to remember my earlier conversation with Ormoran and Miller, but my memories from after the crash keep coming in and out of focus. "They came for just a few minutes. I didn't even realize I was being interrogated until afterwards."

"Fuckers," Annie says under her breath.

"Dr. Koftura came to see me."

"Did she set the cops straight? Did she tell them to leave you alone?" Over the years, Annie's come to admire Dr. Koftura almost as much as I do.

Did? I don't know.

"Annie, she thinks I did it." I do know that.

Annie's quick intake of air slices across the phone line. "*What?*"

"She thinks that she should have seen this coming, after my fight with Justin and my emergency appointment. She's blaming herself for not seeing the signs."

There's a pause at Annie's end. My heart is becoming more insistent, pounding against my chest, and I worry it'll set off another slew of beeping in the machines I'm hooked up to.

And then Annie's voice comes across loud and clear. "What signs? There aren't any signs. You've never hurt anyone. Ever. This is ridiculous."

The knot that's been tightening in my chest since I woke up starts to unthread. I take a deep breath, and my pulse slows down. Because Annie knows about Richard. She knows about my past. And she still believes me.

"I don't know what she's told the police, but I'm pretty sure she thinks I'm unstable. And that I'm capable of hurting some-one." *Breathe, Morgan.* "What am I going to do?"

Asking it out loud makes the chasm of what I'm facing spread out in front of me. *Justin. Dr. Koftura. The detectives coming back soon. Any moment now.*

Annie pauses for a moment, and I almost hear the cogs turning as she sorts through this disaster that's become my life. "You are going to say fuck all to the cops, because you don't have to tell them anything. You are going to stop seeing that quack of a neurologist. You are going to call Dana. And we are going to figure this out. Together."

I'd forgotten about Dana Vasquez, and tell Annie as much. She'd been the legal representative for both Annie and me as we navigated through the child welfare system and into adult life. She's brilliant, and actually cares more about the clients she works with than charging $200 an hour, which is why the myriad social workers of Mahoning County direct their child charges to her when in need of legal advice.

"Dana is our best bet. I'll look up her contact info and call her as soon as I'm off the phone with you," Annie tells me, and I'm relieved that I won't have to hold Dana's name in a to-do list in my foggy brain.

A wave of fatigue washes over me, as sudden as the wave of anger I felt earlier.

"What am I going to do?" I ask her again, and this time I'm not talking about the police, or lawyers, or doctors.

"I'm so sorry," Annie repeats. And unlike Dr. Koftura, I know it's for what happened to me, and not for what she thinks I've done.

Annie told me that the detective she spoke to—she thinks it was Ormoran—didn't want her visiting me. Or rather, they told her that I was in recovery and wasn't allowed to see visitors yet. I gave her Dr. Holdren's name, hoping that Annie could get permission from her. In the meantime, Annie has my room number and the name of the hospital—Conneaut Medical Center—along with my location (at least until my phone dies) on our tracking app.

"I have no clue where that is," she'd said, her voice growing fainter as she started putting the name into her mapping app.

Where am I?

I check the battery on my phone—30 percent left. And the charger was in the suitcase in the trunk of the car, not in my purse. Shit.

However much I want to search for clues, the thought of looking at Justin's old texts—or worse, hearing him speak out from old voice mails—twists my stomach into a knife-edge of pain. I tell myself I should save the battery for when Annie might call again.

I need to focus. I need to get out of this hospital.

As if conjured, Dr. Holdren walks through the door of my room, wearing a baby blue shirt in some sort of silky fabric and her hair hanging loosely over her shoulders.

"You're healing nicely," my doctor tells me. She looks at me with my chart held open in her hands. "How are you feeling?"

It is the first time that she's asked me this since I became her patient, and it takes me a moment to respond. *I need to get out of here.*

"Better," I answer, my voice as clear as I can make it. I move my tongue around in my mouth, and only feel small ridges where the windshield glass found its way inside me.

"Excellent. The results of your MRI scan. . ." Dr. Holdren frowns slightly as she reads something over in my chart. "They indicate that the swelling on your brain—which was surprisingly minor to begin with, given the trauma incurred on your car during the crash. . ." She pauses. *Incurred on my car. And on Justin.*

But neither of us says this, and Dr. Holdren moves on like a well-trained robot. *ASD disorder*, I think involuntarily, well aware that there's a surprisingly high prevalence of doctors on the autism spectrum. Brilliant attention to detail, but terrible bedside manner. "The swelling is reduced to the point of being minimal at the most. You've been stable for over twenty-four hours now, and the only reason you weren't stable for longer was because of that quack who came to see you."

My mind snags on the insult. She's talking about Dr. Koftura. *Maybe I can. . .*

"She's been my doctor for years—since I was a child, really," I say.

Dr. Holdren offers a guttural noise from the back of her throat.

"That's unfortunate," she says.

"Do you really think so?"

Dr. Holdren is still standing at the foot of my bed, and she stares at my forehead. "Yes. Otherwise I wouldn't have said so."

"I've always trusted her," I begin, but Dr. Holdren cuts me off, her face buried in my paperwork again.

"That was your first mistake."

"She thinks I did this," I gesture to my broken and bruised self, but Dr. Holdren isn't looking. And then I go for it. "She thinks I tried to kill my boyfriend."

Dr. Holdren snaps her head up from my chart. "*What* did you say?"

I explain again what Dr. Koftura accused me of. I start to tell Dr. Holdren about my work with Dr. Koftura, to which she waves her hand impatiently.

"I've read your case history. Conneaut and St. Elizabeth's are in the same network, so your records are already in our system. Even if they weren't, I would have followed-up until I had access to them. What kind of doctor do you think I am?"

I don't answer that.

"There is no reason to think that your condition," she points emphatically in my chart at something I can't see, "would contribute to any sort of violent tendencies. Particularly after decades of behavior that has shown no aggressive symptoms."

She's lecturing me, probably envisioning Dr. Koftura, not me, in front of her, listening obsequiously to her brilliance, and I don't care. She thinks Dr. Koftura is wrong.

I think of Richard and involuntarily glance at the small white scars on my knuckles. I think of the contract Annie made me sign. I see Justin's face, right before we crashed.

"Did you tell the detectives. . .?" I start to ask, but Dr. Holdren interrupts me.

"You'll need to sign a few forms, and I have a prescription for some extra-strength Ibuprofen for your aches and pains. As you may know, we're moving away from opioid painkillers—so sorry, but no Oxycontin for you."

I'd never said I wanted any to begin with.

"Do you have someone you can call to pick you up?" she asks, and it takes a few moments for me to answer because I'm just registering that I'm leaving.

"Annie. My friend Annie can pick me up."

"Good—how quickly can she get here?"

"I'm not sure—she lives in Cleveland."

"About an hour or two, give or take which side of Cleveland she's on. That'll do. Now," Dr. Holdren levels her gaze on me for the first time. She looks confident, but uncomfortable. "I can't guarantee that those detectives won't be back before your friend arrives, and since I'm discharging you I can't really say that you're unfit for questioning. But if you want my advice—and I'd certainly say you should want my advice—then I'd recommend talking as little as possible to them until you have a lawyer and are being officially questioned."

It's good advice, but I have something else on my mind. "Did you tell the detectives what you think—about Dr. Koftura?" I rush the words out, worried she'll leave before I can get an answer.

"Yes."

A fist unclenches in my chest.

"And I'm smarter than your other doctor. I'm smarter than most people. They should listen to me." Her eyes narrow. "And so should you. But I don't know if either of you will."

She snaps my chart closed, slips it into its plastic holder, and makes as though to leave. But she stops herself, and I watch uncertainty play out across her face. Then she walks quickly over to me, pushes the table that still holds my belongings to the side, and reaches down to hold my hand for a few seconds.

"Good luck," she says to the floor, and then squeezes my hand once before letting go.

She rushes out the door and calls over her shoulder, "Don't forget to call your friend."

20

After I call Annie with the news that I'm being discharged, and confirm she'll be about two hours before she arrives, I decide there's no need to save my battery.

I open up my text messages first and scroll through them. The vivid colors of the emojis Justin sent to me light up my screen. Our relationship is full of smiley faces, hearts, cute puppy and animal gifs, and so much tenderness that I don't know whether to let the ache of grief rip through me or to fuel my anger that perhaps all of this—whatever it was we had—was a lie.

I move through the list of messages until the very bottom. His last text to me was sent just before we met up Friday afternoon to leave for our weekend away.

Cannot wait to see you and spend an amazing evening together. I love you.

How could anyone misread that? I'd written back, *I love you too.*

We were happy, rolling through the snowy hills and pointing

out beautiful scenes for the other person to look at. I remember he had me look at a pony that was nibbling on crab apples under a tree—the pony had on a little blanket for warmth, and the only parts of its body to be seen were its shaggy head and perky little tail swishing as it munched happily on its snack. That had been—what? Maybe fifteen minutes before Justin ran us off the road.

It just doesn't connect. Not one single bit.

I only have a few voice mails from him, and don't want to listen to them. Not yet. Instead, I open up my Facebook app.

His face flashes up onto the screen, and I see that he has twenty new friends since we'd uploaded his photo. The picture of the two of us together, in bed, looking so goddamn happy, still sits as his avatar in the small circle in the corner of the screen. I click over to the notifications icon and scroll down to his friends list from there. All of them are my friends (mostly online friends shared from Twitter), who must have added him after our relationship status updated. Annie's profile stares back at me from Justin's list of friends, and I remember how she was friends with him on Facebook even before I was.

There's a rustling in my room, and I look up from my phone to see detectives Ormoran and Miller standing in the doorway. Ormoran's braids are loose today, with a pussy-bow tie shirt and black slacks. Miller is wearing what seems to be her standard white shirt, black pants again, with the same leather jacket. And the pink purse too.

"So, you found your phone," Ormoran says. "I'm sorry about the fingerprinting dust. It's standard procedure, unfortunately."

"Where's Justin's phone?" Miller asks, settling her laconic self in what seems to be becoming her favorite plastic chair again.

I stop dead in my tracks, picturing his phone on the dashboard and that name, "Mom," calling just before Justin spun out of control.

"What do you mean?" escapes my mouth before I remind myself of Dr. Holdren's advice. Perhaps she's right—she *is* smarter than me.

"I mean," Miller says, her face buried in the notepad she's pulled out of her garish purse, "the two of you are heading out on a romantic weekend, and Justin doesn't bring his phone at all to—what do they call it, Ormoran?"

"Story," Ormoran chimes in, her face impassive. *Miller must be good cop today.*

"Right, even though 'story' isn't an actual verb." For the first time I hear Miller's voice take on some tenor of emotion: revulsion. For the grammatical pirating, or the millennial need to document our lives, I can't tell. She goes on, "People your age like to post the stories of your day online. So why wouldn't Justin bring his phone with him to do just that?"

A small part of me is tempted to point out that Ormoran, Miller, and I are all approximately the same age, and that Justin was actually older than me. But, per doctor's orders, I bite my tongue. Instead, I do my best to say nothing by saying something. "That makes sense."

"What makes sense?" Miller asks, not at all confused.

"What you just said. I see your point."

"Oh, really?" It's Miller again, but Ormoran cuts in.

"Ms. Kalson, you're not really helping yourself here. You're just giving us gibberish."

Maybe they're smarter than me too.

"It might be better if you didn't say anything at all," Ormoran adds, to which Miller cuts a sharp look in her partner's direction.

"Why don't you tell us what happened in the car right before the crash?" Miller says, with more urgency than I've yet to see in her.

I don't say anything.

Miller looks at her partner, and Ormoran sighs, then says, "It'd help us immensely if you could go over those last few minutes with us. I know it will be hard for you, but we're asking for your help."

That didn't last long. I cast a look at Miller, who is still staring at her notepad.

I can't avoid it. My mind is back on that winding road, watching Justin cut the car across the lanes in quick switch-backs. I see myself reach my hand out to the wheel, and feel the stiffness of Justin's hand under mine as I try to steady my grip. I remember myself trying to turn the wheel to the right, trying to steer us away from danger. From that car barreling down on us. But then I think about Dr. Koftura saying, so many times over the years, the same mantra she gave me as I sat and watched her weep over her own guilt in this hospital room. Memory plays tricks on us. What we remember is not always the truth.

Why do you believe yourself?

Even though I haven't said anything, Ormoran urges me on. "You can tell us." She reaches out her hand and puts it just an inch or so away from mine—her signature move—and part of me wants to tell her everything. But the other part knows that really she's just very good at her job.

I want to glance at my phone and check the time to see how much longer until Annie arrives, but I'm worried what that might prompt Ormoran or Miller to say.

After a minute of silence, Ormoran seems to decide to take a different track. "Where's your mother?"

I look up at her, startled by the question.

"I was seven when I went into care. I never saw my mother again after that."

"What led to you being taken away from your home?" Miller asks, scribbling in her notebook.

"Why do you need to know about my childhood?"

"It helps us get some context," is all Ormoran offers.

Context forgives everything. Psychology 101.

So, I make a decision to tell the detectives a little bit about my life. For context. And maybe forgiveness.

"I was out in my neighborhood after school. We lived in the public housing over on Midlothian Boulevard, in Youngstown. It wasn't the best neighborhood, but it wasn't awful either. I had friends I played with. Our house was always full of people coming and going. I remember that. I don't remember much else about my mother—I can't picture her face. Sometimes I can remember her voice." I pause, slow myself down. *Be careful.* "But that's it. My doctor—" I avoid saying Dr. Koftura's name "—told me this is probably because of the trauma. After trauma, it's not uncommon for children to lose their memories, especially if it involves brain injury."

I feel like I've been talking forever, but Miller and Ormoran just sit there, quietly listening.

"One day, after school, I was playing in the neighborhood and I fell in the street. A car was going way too fast and smacked into me. It was a hit-and-run, and they never found the driver. My body flew over twenty feet, I guess—that's what the doctors told me afterwards." *At least that's what Dr. Koftura told me.* "I was taken straight to the emergency department of a hospital after somebody called 911, and I guess when the police went to inform my mother they discovered the type of mother she was."

"By this doctor, you mean Dr. Koftura, right? Your neurologist?" Ormoran interjects.

"What did she tell—" I start to say, but Miller interrupts me.

"What type of mother was she?" Miller asks, her eyes finally torn from her notepad and searching my face for something. "*Your* mother," she clarifies.

"I was just asking about what Dr. Koftura told you—" I try again.

"Please answer the question," Miller presses, still looking at me.

I let out a sigh.

"She was a terrible mother." I go on. "She was filthy, with men coming and going, never paying any attention to me. I fed myself, washed myself, took care of myself. The only time she noticed me was when she needed me to run an errand for her, to another house or someone on the corner of the block. Otherwise, I was just a nuisance." These aren't my memories; they are pieces of information I've gathered from listening in on the conversations of foster parents, social workers, and doctors for the remainder of my childhood. Adults love to talk about how other parents failed their children.

"So they took you away after that, and you never saw her again? Foster care for the rest of your childhood?" Ormoran asks.

"And a group home for the last part."

"Doesn't it seem a little extreme?" Ormoran looks at Miller. "I mean, we've got all sorts of cases where kids go back to their parents, and their families have done much worse than just being a neglectful mom. I mean, it doesn't sound all that bad, does it?"

"You didn't live it," I say, my voice icy.

"Yeah, well, it sounds like you don't remember much of it, either," Miller contributes. "Maybe it was worse than they've told you?"

Miller's observation hangs in the still air until Nurse Debbie arrives.

She bursts into my room, a whirlwind of energy, to check my

vitals and give me instructions for discharge. Today her scrubs have green frogs on them, and when she sees me eyeing them up, she explains, "I'm going to pediatrics later today." She glances down at the frogs dancing across her huge breasts. "D'you think the little ones'll like them?"

"Of course they will," Ormoran jumps in. "What kid doesn't like frogs?"

Nurse Debbie gives the detective a withering look. After she finishes measuring my blood pressure, taking out my IV tube, and rubbing the spot with a special concoction of alcohol and lotion to remove the sticky tape remnants, she pats me on the shoulder, leans down to my ear, and whispers, "Don't let them fuck with you, love. If they were here to arrest you, they'd've done it already."

With that, she gives a professional nod to the detectives and saunters out the door. Despite everything, I hadn't even considered they were here to arrest me, and Nurse Debbie's words of comfort only serve to stoke my growing fear.

I'm a suspect.

And the next words out of Ormoran's mouth confirm it.

"Ms. Kalson, we have had to run your name through the system—standard protocol—and we got a hit. Granted, juvenile files are sealed, but your adult file has one report. Drunken and Disorderly Conduct. And a restraining order against you on behalf of a Richard Mueller. We have to follow up on something like that." She shrugs her shoulders in apology. "So Miller and I dig a little deeper and end up reading Richard's statement. It seems he tried to break up with you—it doesn't state why—and you show up at his house drunk, mad as hell, and cursing him out. When he tried to calm you down, you took a swing at him, and even though you didn't hit him, you did end up breaking one of his windows and needing several stitches."

Or were they sutures? I think wryly.

Ormoran looks down at my hands, and a wave of shame floods my senses as I take in the tiny white scars dancing across my knuckles. I never wanted to hurt Richard, and I didn't even try to hit him. His pretentious stained glass window on his front door was another story, though.

Miller adds, "You have to admit there seems to be some striking similarities here."

There are bursts of light in front of my eyes. *Thoughts creeping out of dark corners.* Suddenly I feel so, so tired. And then I do it. I yawn. It can happen, when your sympathetic nervous system kicks in—it's a sign of intense anxiety. But I doubt Ormoran and Miller know that.

"Are we boring you?" Miller offers, giving me a weighted stare in the wake of my yawn. "Or are you able to answer a few more questions? For instance, you mentioned the phone call Justin received from his mother just before the accident, but we didn't recover his phone from the crash. In fact, we haven't been able to find it at all. Do you know where Justin's phone could be?"

"Can you help us, Ms. Kalson?" Ormoran adds for emphasis.

As I register what they're telling me, alarm bells ring inside my head.

I wait a second, waiting for the pounding in my temples to slow down, and just as I'm about to parrot phrases I recall from *Law & Order* re-runs, like "Am I being charged?" "I want a lawyer," or something similar, Dr. Holdren rushes in, her cheeks pink from running down the hallway. *Thank you, Nurse Debbie,* I think.

Behind her is a smaller figure with spiky blond hair.

"When did you get here?" Dr. Holdren demands of the two detectives. "Never mind, it doesn't matter. Ms. Kalson is being discharged, effective immediately."

Ormoran holds up her hands, as if in surrender. "We were

just leaving." Then she turns to me. "Think about what we said. We'll be in touch." And the two detectives head through the door, Miller holding it open for Ormoran to exit through first.

Annie doesn't wait a beat. She rushes over to me, grabs me in her wiry arms, and hugs me until I can't breathe. It feels wonderful.

21

We are flying down the highway, away from the hospital and the detectives, heading towards home. I let myself pretend, for just a few seconds, that I'm hurtling away from the disaster of my life, instead of heading back to it.

Before we left, Annie helped me send an e-mail to my boss, David, to notify him of my accident. I couldn't manage to type the words out without my hands shaking, and so Annie wrote while I dictated. Since it's still Monday, and my classes meet on Tuesdays and Thursdays, plus my large seminar on Wednesdays, I haven't missed any lectures yet, although I saw my inbox had fifty-four messages from students waiting to be answered. There are over thirty-five notifications on Twitter, some from my online friends asking where I've been. And several messages on Facebook.

One thing at a time, I tell myself.

At least I'm wearing real clothing again. The clothes I was wearing that night were too ripped and bloodied to give back to me—or the police are keeping them for other reasons and just not telling me—so Annie brought an approximation of an outfit from her closet for me. She dresses much more punk artist than I do, so I don't feel quite like myself in her ripped black jeans and a nubbly neon orange sweater. Then again, I wouldn't feel like myself in my favorite about-home outfit of slippers, sweats, and my chenille robe.

Because I'm not myself anymore. I left the hospital as someone different.

I know Annie is dying to talk to me, but I'm just too tired to handle more questions right now. I asked her to put on some music, and the strains of some indie band I don't know the name of are floating around in the heater-scorched air of her car. Outside, the highway is a bleak scene of gray snow and skeletal trees, mixed with the odd silos of factory smoke and industrial equipment storehouses.

We are *not* taking the scenic way home.

"I'm going to stay with you for a while," Annie announces into the heavy guitar lick that just spun out into some more emo-piano chords.

"Your music sucks," I comment, which she knows really means, "Thank you." We both laugh, and Annie says, "Well, you'll have to get used to it for a while."

"It'll be just like old times," I say, still trying to pretend that where my life is heading is different to what I know to be true.

"Hungry?" A huge sign is looming up in front of us for Davidson's Family Style Diner, boasting "24 hr Breakfast" in flashing lights. I actually don't know the last time I ate, and Annie's jeans—she's shaped more like a greyhound with long limbs and a willowy frame, whereas I'm a solidly built petite— gape off of me at the waist and thighs.

"I am famished." I say it like I'm surprised to discover this after having not eaten anything of real substance for almost three days. Annie gives me another laugh.

"That's a first." Sarcasm drips off her voice, and having this pseudo-normal banter with my best friend is a balm to my heart. Besides, Annie's right—I've never met an all-day breakfast I didn't love.

The parking lot is full of pickup trucks and beat-up Chevy sedans, which bodes well for the quality of the diner food. My stomach growls involuntarily when I catch a whiff of grease and frying meat.

Annie and I sit down in a booth amidst lots of flannel-clad men nursing coffees and steak-and-eggs plates.

"What time is it?" Somehow I hadn't even glanced at the clock in the car. I'd been grasping at straws, trying to stay rooted to the ground, despite the tumult constantly rumbling through my head. I remember learning in grad school that trauma victims cope by focusing on concrete needs. Food. Sleep. Touch. From what I can remember through the watery images of my childhood, those techniques didn't work for me when I was a trauma victim the first time. Dr. Koftura had preferred other techniques.

Quack. That's what Dr. Holdren had called her.

What did she do to me?

"Two hairs past a freckle," Annie answers, but then she looks at my face. "Sorry." She scrambles for her phone. "2:30 in the afternoon."

"What do you think all these guys are doing here?" I ask as we open our menus, sticky to the touch, and survey the horde of men surrounding us.

"GM plant," Annie offers in return. "B-shift switching out."

"What, seriously? Are we that close to Youngstown already?"

Annie shrugs. "I drive fast when I want to get somewhere."

I want to ask her what took so long for her to arrive at the hospital from Cleveland, but know that I actually have no idea how much time had passed. Talking with two detectives who suspect you of murder stretches time in odd ways.

A waitress wearing a blue smock with a pink ruffled shirt underneath comes over and takes our order. Black coffee and chocolate-chip pancakes for Annie. Hot tea, the Lumberjack Special (two waffles, five strips of bacon, three eggs, and fruit) and a side of whipped cream for me. The smells of non-hospital food have made me ravenous. After the waitress leaves, Annie decides it's time.

"So, when are we gonna talk about it?"

"Talk about what?" I say, because there's so much I don't know where to start.

"Right. Where to even begin," she says, and whistles just a bit between her teeth.

Annie taps her nails on the table in a syncopated rhythm, which apparently annoys the bearded guy sitting at the booth adjoining our table, because he turns around in his seat and politely asks her to stop. Annie blows a huge stream of air out of her mouth, whistling again, but stops nonetheless.

"I don't know what to do next," I tell her, because that seems as good a place to start as any.

Annie looks me over, and I can just imagine what she sees. My bruises are lightening, although they still cover my face, neck, and arms in a mottled palette of blues and indigos, with random splashes of yellow mixed in. I haven't washed my hair in several days, and my shoulders slouch from the pain of my healing ribs and the weight of everything that's happened.

I watch Annie's eyes as she sizes me up, and then says, "You are going to keep living your life. You are going to meet with a good lawyer—I called Dana once I knew you were getting out of the hospital and we've already scheduled an appointment for tomorrow morning. And you are not going to let anyone—not Justin, not the police, not Dr. Kandy-Ass—nobody is going to stop you from doing what you are meant to do. Which, by the way, in case you've forgotten, is not just to survive, but thrive."

"That's quite a speech," I say in return, and Annie promptly knees me under the table.

"Yeah, well, you've given it to me plenty of times."

And it's true. We've traded the role of cheerleader and support system—and, if I'm perfectly honest, drill sergeant—enough over the years to know the common tropes we play out for each other. That phrase—not just survive, but thrive—was one I learned from an evolutionary psychology professor at Youngstown State when I was an undergrad. At the time it felt like it fit my life post-group home, and post-foster care before that, like a well-worn T-shirt, because there I was in a college classroom learning about it rather than rutting around in a gutter somewhere. Or some deadbeat's trailer. Or huffing whippets behind the Giant Eagle after Rock'n Bowl on a Friday night.

I was thriving. I had pretty much been thriving ever since I'd stopped being a victim and become a survivor.

Pretty much, I think, my mind tracing back to Richard and the night that led to the restraining order.

But now here I am, sitting in a diner across from my best friend, trying to figure out which of those I was again.

In the past, I'd always been able to decide that for myself. Now, with what Justin had done, I'm not so sure.

Our waitress brings our food over, with my meal taking up over two-thirds of the table. I'd been desperately hungry when I'd ordered, but with the food set in front of me, suddenly my stomach feels leaden. Annie takes a sip of her coffee and nods approvingly.

"It wouldn't be such a sausage-fest here if the coffee sucked," she declares, and gestures to my plates with her fork that I should start eating before digging into her pancakes, which have surprisingly come with fresh whipping cream and a dusting of cocoa.

"Eat," she orders when she sees me just staring at my food.

She lowers her voice, "I know you may not be that hungry, but you need to eat something so your brain will work and we can figure this out together. One thing at a time, okay?" I have to look away for a moment, before I nod my agreement.

I pick up my knife and fork and start cutting away at my stack of waffles, which are delicate and fluffy. Gingerly, I open my mouth, wary of the pinprick cuts healing inside, and slide a bite into my mouth. As I close my lips around my fork, the butter and syrup rush in and put my taste buds on notice. In spite of everything that's happened in the last three days, the mix of sugar and fat in my mouth pushes down my creeping nausea and throbbing pain, replacing them with a ferocious hunger.

I eat the entire meal, while Annie looks on with approving silence.

Twenty minutes from my apartment, though, Annie needs to pull into a Sheetz. I can barely make it to a toilet before throwing up every last morsel.

22

We arrive at my apartment by 4 o'clock, and I am half-expecting to see yellow police caution tape draped around my door—which is ludicrous, I know—but instead my door looks perfectly normal. Just like it did when Justin and I left it on Friday afternoon.

I fumble with my keys as I try to get them into the lock, so Annie takes them from me and lets us both inside. The air smells of familiar rituals: tea, shampoo, and laundry detergent. I try to remember what Justin and I did in the final few minutes we were together here.

I remember zipping up my case, and Justin carrying it out from the bedroom for me. Inside were way too many lacy, sheer pieces of clothing. I blush when I think of the police rummaging through and seeing what I'd packed. A feeling of sick rises at the back of my throat again, but there's nothing left for me to throw up and I manage to push the urge to vomit back down.

Mind over matter. That's another mantra Annie and I both live by.

"I'm going to run you a bath, and then I'll pop out and get us a few supplies." Annie bustles around my apartment like it's her own place. From the bedroom, where I've sat down, unsure of what to do with myself, I hear her start the tub running, shortly followed by tinkling sounds in the kitchen.

Her head appears around the doorframe of my bedroom. "Come on, in you go."

We've seen each other naked plenty of times over the years, to the point where we're like an old married couple.

I start to take off my shirt, but wince at having to raise my arms above my head.

"Here," Annie comes up and helps me get her borrowed clothes off my shrunken frame. I'm not paying attention, working on raising my feet to get my socks off, when I hear a sound come from Annie. She's standing there, towering above me on her whippet legs, horror hollowing out her eyes. As soon as she notices me looking at her, she turns away and works on folding up my clothes/her clothes, which are littered over the floor next to my bed.

I stand up and make my way over to the full-length mirror I have in the corner of my bedroom. I'm a creature, a Hieronymus Bosch painting in the flesh. Fully naked, I can see the pattern of impact working its way across my body. The crisscross of the seat belt from my chest to my abdomen, the cuts from shattered glass across my face and neck in various stages of healing, depending on how large the glass was and how deep it cut into my skin. And scratches on my left arm, along the inside of my biceps muscle moving down towards my forearm. I hadn't noticed those before, but then again that was the arm I'd had covered in IV tape and tubing while I was in the hospital. Maybe the scratches were from my trying to pry them off while I slept—Nurse Debbie had said something about that during one of her visits. She'd called me a "Naughty Nelly," of all things.

There's a hand on my back, and Annie gently guides me away from the mirror and towards the tub.

"Honestly, it's not that bad," she says.

And for a moment of inexplicable mirth, we burst out laughing. Because we both know this is absolutely not true.

Annie helps me step into the tub. The warm water feels extraordinary on my skin, and a shiver of automatic pleasure works its way up my spine.

Annie explains that she's set out soap, a fresh washcloth, and shampoo for me to get at easily. "You look like a mongrel, so make sure to wash yourself up," she says over her shoulder, her smirk just a little too forced. "I'll be back in a few minutes with provisions."

I stop her as she makes her way through the now steamy air towards the door of the bathroom. "Annie?"

She turns around, and the familiar lines of her face are more soothing than anything else she can offer me.

"Are you sure you can stay?" I ask a little too desperately. I can't imagine Annie leaving anytime soon, but I know she has an exhibition she's working on and that I can't expect her to put her life on hold indefinitely just to play physical and emotional nurse to me.

She smiles at me. "Artist's life. I'm here as long as you need me."

"But what about your exhibition?"

"Don't worry about it," she strides back over and sits on the edge of the bathtub. "Seriously, I've got everything under control. My paints and canvases will be there when I get back. Besides," she splashes a little water in the air towards my face, but her mouth turns downwards, "I could use a little time away from it. I've kind of hit a wall. Some space will do me good."

She stands up suddenly. "Anyway, enough of that. You enjoy your soak." Her voice is bright again, but I force my brain to pay attention and remember that she needs me too.

"Anything you need in particular from the store?" she asks, now on her second way out the door.

I think for a moment, my mind trying to conjure up the normalcy of going to the grocery store, but nothing comes to mind. Except...

"A newspaper," I say.

"How terribly old-fashioned of you," Annie calls out, her tinkle of laughter louder than normal. "Back in a jiff."

I hear the door close and then Annie locking the knob and deadbolt with my keys. I'm left alone for almost the first time since I woke this morning. I lather up the washcloth and start to scrub at my body, beginning with the points that have bruises and working away from them. Because I've always found that starting where it hurts is better than leaving it to the end.

I'm out of the bath, dressed in flannel pajamas, my chenille robe, and real slippers with my hair wrapped up in a towel, beauty queen style, when Annie returns with an assemblage of overflowing carrier bags.

"I bought every good thing," she announces. I fumble over to help her with the bags, but Annie shoos me away like a babushka, all flappy hands and guttural disapproval. She's not exaggerating—she's bought the whole store. And then some. Chocolate bars, wheels of cheese, fresh bread that is still warm to the touch. Microwaveable pizzas—a soft spot for both of us from our group home days. Cookie dough in a tube—again from back when we were still living under the same roof. Strawberries and blueberries. Two bottles of wine: One fizzy, one not. A twelve-pack of Coke, for her. And four newspapers.

The local *Vindicator*, the *Plain Dealer*, the *Akron-Beacon Journal*, and the *Town Crier—Canfield*.

Annie must have guessed why I asked for a paper, and so she's brought me all of them.

"Where did you get the *Town Crier*?" I ask, sitting down at my kitchen table and thumbing through it first. The masthead reads, "Your Weekly Hometown Newspaper." Each of the suburbs of Youngstown have their own *Town Crier*, and with Canfield being at least a thirty-minute drive away, I'm surprised any store nearby had this specific version. I flip the paper open, and the lead headline for today promises details on the new zoning ruling for a bank of new condos set to break ground in March. Under the fold is coverage of the regional 4-H club competition with a picture of a huge Holstein cow and its child-size owner.

"It's called driving around to different news boxes until you find one," she deadpans. "I have my ways," she adds with a serious look on her face that I'm not sure how to interpret, until she gives me another smirk, this one as natural as they come. "Don't worry, I didn't hand out blow jobs to get it or anything. The gas station down the road actually had it next to *USA Today*. Oh, and there's one other thing." Annie goes to my door, unlocks it, and grabs something from outside in the hallway. I glance up in time to see her haul in a huge white marker board.

"What's that for?"

"For us to brainstorm," she answers. "Isn't this what you did all the time in grad school?"

It's true. I'd map out my experimental designs, Institutional Review Board deadlines, and critiques of my writing and how to address them. Now that marker board is in my office at Youngstown State.

The thought of work sends a wave of anxiety through me that I push down.

I thank Annie for her thoughtfulness, and for all the items she brought back. She refuses to take any money for them, and instead settles herself down in a chair opposite me and starts thumbing through the copy of the *Vindicator*.

"So, what am I looking for, specifically," she asks, her eyes just reaching mine above the broadsheets.

"Anything related to the—accident," I say. I can't bring myself to say "Justin's death."

On the ride home I'd already scoured the news online from my phone and knew that nothing had been posted by any of the nearby papers, so I was banking on the obituary sections and local news that often get skimmed over in the online presence of a newspaper. I figured my best bet was to go through the print copies for any clues. When I tried searching online for "McBrides" in Canfield, Ohio, the results turned up twenty different names, none of them linked with a Justin.

"And what are you hoping to find?" Annie asks from behind the *Vindicator*'s Valley Life section.

"Before Justin steered us off the road. . ." *God, that was a euphemism if ever I've heard one* ". . . he got a call on his phone that said, 'Mom.' The police say they've been in touch with Justin's parents, but they wouldn't tell me anything beyond that."

"So, we're looking for any information about his parents," Annie finishes the thought for me. "Did he ever say anything about them?"

The question makes me pause. "He always wanted to talk about me, you know." A hot flush of embarrassment rises up my neck. "I did try and ask about his childhood, about his family, but he'd always turn it back onto me. He was really interested in what it was like for me, growing up in foster care and group homes." I keep talking, working through what I was saying in my mind as I'm saying it aloud to Annie. "It was like he wanted to know every detail so he could hold on to it for me."

Annie doesn't miss a beat. "I'm sure that was a nice change. Most guys just want to talk about their dicks and their moms, hopefully in separate conversations."

Something occurs to me.

"How did you know to get the Canfield paper?" I ask Annie. Justin's family is from Canfield, but I don't remember mentioning it to Annie.

"You told me that's where he was from," Annie says without hesitation. "Right when you first started dating, remember? You yelled at me for eating Pixie Stix at 11 o'clock at night—don't ask me how you knew over the phone that that was what I was eating—and then you told me he was from Canfield, which meant he had to be a decent guy."

Growing up in Youngstown, Canfield was always seen as a luxury suburb of the city, right after Poland. Only rich people with houses and acreage could afford to live out there.

But I can't remember telling Annie any of this.

I have to shake myself, because there's no reason for Annie to lie. *I'm being paranoid*, I tell myself. *Just because you couldn't trust Justin, or Dr. Koftura, doesn't mean you can't trust Annie.* I change the subject.

"The police didn't find his phone in the car," I tell Annie.

"They are fucking morons," Annie responds. "Where do you think the phone is?"

"I don't know. Either the police have it, and are just using it to trick me into revealing something. Or. . ." Something shapeless in the back of my mind starts to shift. After the crash. . .

"Or. . .?" Annie prods.

"Or someone came to the accident and took it." I glance at my left arm, at the bruising and scratches running down it from my bicep to my wrist. "Annie, what if someone was there, at the accident?" My voice trembles a little, because I honestly don't know what this means.

"Then we'd better find out who it was. And we will," she says, her voice steady. My cheeks flame up with shame from my earlier doubts, and I pretend to be fascinated with the electrical warning tag on my toaster.

"Now start reading again." Annie taps the top of my paper.

We sit quietly for a while, the only sounds the rustling of the newspapers in our hands as we turn the pages and the crinkle of a chocolate wrapper as Annie trades between feeding pieces into her own mouth and passing some to me.

Almost a half hour passes while we comb through the newspapers, but ultimately find nothing referring to the crash or Justin. As I turn the last page of the *Plain Dealer* and confront a full-page ad for a mattress outlet, I let out a deep breath.

"Nothing on my end either," Annie concurs. She looks thoughtful for a moment. "Aren't there back issues that we can look through?"

Before I can protest that this wouldn't be helpful in finding info on the crash, she holds her hand up and continues, "Not for what happened to you and Justin, but just to find information about his family. Especially in the local paper—they post info about graduations, local competitions, sports games. There's bound to be something about Justin's family. If we can find out names, we can narrow down who they are from the white page searches online."

It takes a moment for what Annie is suggesting to click into place.

"I know where to go," I say.

Annie feeds me another bite of chocolate, and the taste floods my mouth.

23

The next day finds me on YSU's campus for the first time since the accident, while Annie stays back at my apartment, trying to catch up on some work related to her upcoming exhibition. This morning I had an e-mail waiting for me from my Department Head, explaining that my class would be covered for today, which was a relief given everything else I'm trying to sort out.

Walking across campus feels surreal, and it's strange to me that the familiar landmarks all look the same. Part of me wants to call out, demand an explanation for why people are buying coffee and going to class when my entire life has turned inside out.

Another larger part of me already knows that indifference is the world's status quo.

At least the meeting with Dana had gone well this morning. Annie and I had driven to her office, which sits next door to the rescue mission shelter in downtown Youngstown, just a few minutes from campus. Inside her beige office that smelled faintly of Murphy's oil soap and the rotting wood of the old Victorian house that had been transformed into offices decades ago, Dana was matter-of-fact. She'd take my case, she told me, but she had a few conditions. Her dark hair was pulled back into a sleek bun at the nape of her neck, and it wobbled back and forth when she shook her head from side to side, as if she were recalling all the clients before me who'd disappointed her.

"I haven't served as defense counsel in a criminal case for a few years now," she'd said. "But you and I know each other well, and I know you can follow instructions." She cast a shrewd glance at both of us. "When you want to, that is."

Annie and I had both been in family court with Dana enough times to understand that she was basically a bulldozer who set a path and went for it. As long as you stayed behind her, you'd be fine. That's how she'd managed to emancipate me legally from my mother—termination of parental rights, in fact —despite all bureaucratic red tape to the contrary. It's also how she'd managed to keep Annie and I together at the group home for so many years, instead of having one of us cast off into the abyss of foster care again when beds became scarce.

The air outside is warmer than usual for December, and the sun actually makes an appearance as I walk past DeBartolo Hall and head further into campus. I'm not going into my office today. I can't bear the kind faces and probing questions of my colleagues. There's too much of my old normal waiting for me at my desk, and so instead I'm heading to a place less familiar.

I pull the collar up on my coat and silently wish I'd worn a hat today. Despite the sun, a bitter wind still manages to work its way through the trees growing in the center of campus.

"Here's what you need to do," Dana had said towards the end of our meeting, after I'd explained everything that I knew about Justin, me, the accident, and the two detectives. "You do not—I repeat, do not—speak to the police unless I am present. If they try to ambush you again, you call me straightaway. Secondly, you need to avoid the press. It's not likely unless you're actually charged, but there's the possibility of them catching wind of this case and coming down hard on you if it's made known that you're a suspect."

Dana had taken a pause to take a sip of water from the Nalgene water bottle sitting in pride of place on her desk. Despite all the years I'd known her, she still looked like an ambiguous thirty-something. Her caramel skin was pristinely smooth, her eyes a vibrant golden brown, and it seemed obvious that she still ran marathons in her spare time given her compact and toned figure.

The woman is a powerhouse.

"Finally, you need to refrain from undertaking your own investigation. We don't need you getting into trouble because you're trying to beat the police to the punchline." Dana had leveled her gaze at me then, locking her eyes onto mine. "Do you understand?"

Over the years, Dana had come face-to-face with the initiative Annie and I both possessed when it involved making our lives a little less PBS-after-school-special. The wheels of justice and child welfare turn at a glacial pace, and so Annie and I had often tried to extract signatures, paperwork transfers, or guardian *ad litem* assignments ourselves. That is, until Dana made it clear we were only gumming up an already disabled system.

"Yes," Annie and I said in unison. It wasn't the first time we'd lied to Dana, despite all our best intentions.

Dana had given both of us an almost imperceptible nod, and had dismissed us with an, "I'll be in touch," followed by a repeated command: "Remember, don't talk to the cops without me."

By now I've made it to Maag Library, which sits on YSU's campus like an ode to 1960s architecture. A tall tower of a building with floor-to-ceiling glass windows interspersed with aquamarine paneling, it was admittedly an ugly addition to campus, although I still love it. It's a library, after all. YSU's collection of books is pretty phenomenal, ranging from precious historical pieces to the most up-to-date best sellers. Today, though, I'm not interested in the stacks holding shelf after shelf of books. I'm heading to the basement, where the microfiche machines can still be found.

The online archives of the *Town Crier* are practically nonexistent, but a quick search on Maag Library's site revealed that they carry decades' worth of microfiche for the *Town Criers* of all the surrounding suburbs of Youngstown. The librarian working the basement information desk is an elderly man in a burgundy sweater vest and fragile-looking bifocal glasses. When I ask for film of the last ten years of the Canfield *Town Criers*, he smiles. Scanning the basement level of the library, I'm the only person on this floor besides my friendly librarian. I'd bet my lunch most of my students don't even know what microfiche is.

The librarian returns with a wood box housing the microfilms and asks if I need help using the machine. Although I wince a bit as I take the box from him, the pain in my ribs duller than it was in the hospital but still an active reminder that my body is less than healthy, I shake my head in response to his question. I do not. Back when I was an undergraduate student here, I found myself regularly seeking out ancient research articles that seemed to be available only on microfiche.

As I load up the film, I decide to start with the present and work my way back, scanning for any reference to Justin or a McBride family that might fit the little I know about them. Justin's an only child, so references to siblings would rule them out. His mother and father are still married, so divorce filings wouldn't be relevant either.

And that's all I know, aside from their home being in Canfield.

I've approached today with a clinical precision. I have a to-do list, ready to check off each of the boxes as I complete the task. When everything else is chaos, a detailed checklist can make or break you.

- Meet with my lawyer. *Check.*
- Find the microfiche. *Check.*
- Look for Justin's family. *Working on it.*

But as I scan through the happy headlines of prom kings and queens, newly engaged couples, weddings, birth announcements, and high school sports teams winning some regional or state championship, the truth of my situation coils itself around my body like a snake.

Life hacks are for ripening avocados and decluttering your kitchen. Not dead boyfriends and police investigations. And, however much I don't want to admit it, Justin's made me partner in his own self-destruction. It puts everything between us under suspicion, because how could you love someone and at the same time try to harm them?

My mother used to say she loved me. Between the booze and the men and the fits. And calling me the devil.

I'm nearing the end of the stack of microfiche by the time my eyes scan over an image where a face strikes me as familiar. It's Justin, much younger but still as handsome, standing in a cap and gown with a man next to him. The headline reads "Canfield High School Graduation Ceremony 2006." I work the wheel of the machine to zoom in on the caption, which reads: "Ronald McBride stands next to his son, Justin, at the annual Canfield High School Graduation ceremony held this past Saturday, June 3, at the High School stadium. Justin McBride graduated as salutatorian for the class of 2005–2006."

A lump grows in my throat as I stare at Justin standing next to his father, both of them looking so happy and healthy in the bright sunshine of early summer. Still, I manage to take out my phone and take a picture of the photograph and caption, and text it to Annie. My message to her is more confident than I feel.

Found them, I write.

On my way back to the kind librarian with his delicate glasses, I manage to stumble only twice as I try to steady myself.

24

Walking back to my apartment brings me to the steps of Tod Hall and, not quite ready to face Justin's parents, I find myself opening the door and climbing the stairs once again to the anthropology department. Nothing much has changed in the days that have passed, and the plastic taping remains at the end of the hallway, although the signs announcing fresh paint have been removed. At first I think I might stop by the graduate student office again, in the hope of finding someone besides the redheaded girl I spoke to last week. Searching through the archives of Justin's hometown has left me feeling ripped open, and the knowledge that I barely knew anything about him stings like a fresh wound rinsed with salt.

In the ill-lit hallway, I pass by the door marked Professor Joseph Farak. And stop. *It's a safer place to start*, I think. The glaring *"Mom"* filling the void of the car just before impact—I know it won't be easy to talk to Justin's mother.

I knock on the door to Professor Farak's office, and the sound echoes down the lonely hallway. There's no light on behind the door, and after another round of knocking I turn around and set my sights on the grad student office. As I turn, though, I almost trip over a small man wearing a grey suit jacket, a full beard streaked with grey, and a tonsure of similarly grey hair cropped close to his scalp. He's at least six inches shorter than me.

Instinctively I offer an apology and notice, thankfully, that I haven't dislodged the mug of coffee the man is carrying in his right hand.

"It's no problem at all," he offers, his blue eyes twinkling until they take me in. Annie spent a long time this morning applying makeup to make my face look relatively normal before we went to our meeting with Dana, but my cheeks still burn under his scrutiny. Professor Farak's voice has a soft lilt to it that I can't place. It sounds vaguely South Asian, but I'm not sure. "I was just out for a coffee break."

"I'm looking for Professor Farak," I say, wanting to explain why I'm hanging around in this deserted section of campus.

"Well, you're in luck," the man says, as he moves past me and unlocks his office door. "That's me."

He sweeps his arm forward as a means of ushering me in, and I find myself inside an airy office with beautiful oak book-shelves, a pristine desk with a closed laptop at the center of it, and two ancient wooden chairs opposite the desk. The office certainly doesn't look like it's been under construction as Justin had claimed, and the heartache I felt coming into the building starts to build into something else. Beads of sweat break out at the base of my neck.

I take a seat in one of the chairs and rush in to explain why I'm here.

"I'm a professor in psychology," I explain. "A student of yours has been attending some of my classes." At this, Professor Farak looks up intently. He's seated himself in his office chair on the opposite side of the desk, his coffee cup set in the exact center of a coaster to the right of his computer.

"You must be speaking of Brady," he says.` "She's the only undergraduate I'm working with currently."

I'm not sure at this point if Professor Farak knows that Justin is dead, and because I don't want to blindside him I decide to avoid the topic and just focus on Justin's work with him.

"No, not Brady. The student I'm thinking of is a graduate student. His name's Justin. Justin McBride."

There's a pause, and I watch as Professor Farak furrows his brow. "You're speaking of an undergraduate student, I'm assuming? Unfortunately, I don't know the names of all my students."

"No, not an undergraduate student. Justin was a graduate student of yours."

"Was?" Professor Farak chimes in, picking up on my slip.

"I mean, he was this semester, I believe—but he's been killed in a car accident." I say the last few words quietly, with as much self-control as I can muster. "I wanted to stop by and offer my condolences."

"I'm so sorry to hear that," the man says. He'd been reaching for his coffee mug just before I mentioned this piece of information, and now he sets his arm down limply on his desk. "But, as I said, I don't know this Justin McBride. Perhaps he worked with a different professor?"

Professor Farak is still sitting, willing to speak with me for as long as I want to, it seems, but I'm desperate now to get as far away from this kind man as possible. I stand up too quickly, and my vision swims with bursts of white fireworks. I sway a little, and then feel the man's small hands gently grip around my arm and keep me upright.

"Are you alright?" he asks, and I'm able to focus my eyes again and take in the look of concern on his face.

"Yes, yes, I'm fine. I just forgot to eat breakfast this morning." Which is not true at all—Annie plied me with scrambled eggs and French toast, claiming I was wasting away and needed to keep my energy up—but it is the most believable excuse I can muster.

"Would you like to sit for a bit longer? I have some cookies in a tin—here." Professor Farak retreats back to his desk and starts rummaging around in one of the drawers.

"Really, I'm fine," I say, and make a meager attempt at a smile. "I'll head over to Kilcawley Center now and grab a bite to eat. Thank you so much for your time."

I rush out the door, not even waiting to hear his goodbye or well wishes. Despite my disorientation earlier, I take the stairs two at a time and soon find myself outside again in the fresh air. I breathe in huge gulps until I feel my body relaxing, even as my mind twists itself around the hard fact I've just confirmed.

Justin *was* a fraud.

I pull out my phone to call Annie, but as I'm about to dial a notification appears.

Text from Justin: *What are you hoping to find?*

I stare at the screen for a long time, trying to process what this might mean. When a second text appears on the screen, I take off running, ignoring the pain streaking through my body. Towards home. Towards Annie.

What are you waiting for? it read.

Speak of the devil, my mother's voice says from the dumpster fire of my memory.

25

Two hours later, Annie and I are in the car again, driving down Route 11 to Canfield, which sits just at the southwest corner of Youngstown city proper. We are going to talk to Justin's parents.

It only took a few minutes searching online to find their address and phone number, once we had a first name to narrow down the McBrides that came up in our search. Jean and Ronald McBride, residents of 2957 Palmyra Road.

After I'd told her about the two texts from Justin's phone, Annie wanted to scrap the entire plan, until I explained to her that this was the best way to figure out whether Justin's mom had any part in the accident, or the messages I was getting.

Rather than go as Justin's ex-girlfriend, Annie and I decided to play the part of reporters investigating the accident. I couldn't guarantee that Justin's parents didn't know what I looked like, but this option seemed more likely to get us the info we wanted rather than us showing up at their door as the injured girlfriend and her sidekick. We're dressed up like the door-stepping reporters you see on TV in those police procedurals. When I looked in the mirror in my apartment, my subconscious must have been playing tricks, because my outfit was a dead ringer for Detective Miller's. White button down, black pants, black leather-ish jacket. At least my purse was a brown messenger bag instead of Miller's pink gorgon. I pulled my hair back in a tight bun, grabbed a notepad and pencil—Miller 2.0—and we were off.

Neither of us wants to listen to music on the way over to the McBride house, and after I try to check in with Annie about her exhibition work, which she brushes off by assuring me everything's fine, we both just sit and keep our thoughts to ourselves.

It's only a twenty-minute drive from my apartment to the McBride house, and as we pull off Route 11 at the corner with an Arby's restaurant and a BP station, my phone vibrates. Annie and I both flinch—each of us expecting another text from Justin's phone—but it's just a notification from one of my apps that it's been updated.

Soon we're pulling into the McBride's driveway. The house is all gingerbread and sunshine—a split level with a large picture window and huge pine trees littered through the yard. Christmas lights are already hung around the bushes in front, and when we walk up the sidewalk to the front porch, we're greeted by a wreath on the front door with a wooden snowman holding a cardinal bird and a sign that reads: *Snow Days Are My Favorite*.

Jean McBride answers the door almost as soon as we knock, as if she were standing behind the curtains of the huge front window waiting for visitors, and when she opens the door, the smell of baking sugar and butter wafts over us. Jealousy sparks inside me, because Justin had all of this once.

I introduce Annie and myself as two reporters from the *Plain Dealer*, and hold up my faculty ID from YSU quickly as if it's a press badge. "I'm so sorry for your loss," I say, almost choking on the words for so many reasons my mind has lost count. "We were hoping to ask you a few questions about your son."

Justin's mother stares blankly at us for a few seconds, and the thought races through my mind that she didn't know Justin was dead. That I've made a terrible mistake with this woman, this mother.

But then she speaks.

"I have nothing to say about my son." Jean McBride moves to close the door in our faces, but I blurt out what Annie and I practiced, just in case she didn't want to talk to us.

"It's our understanding that your son suffered from untreated mental illness." *Understatement of the century*, Annie'd murmured when we first came up with the idea. I couldn't disagree. I go on, "We're working on a larger piece for the paper about the stigma of mental illness and roadblocks to care. We want to feature your son's story in it."

"You shouldn't do that," Jean says, and gently moves my foot out of the doorway with one of her own slippered feet before turning to close the door again.

Just as the door is about to shut, I call through the crack, "We're going to run Justin's story with or without your help— don't you want him to be an inspiration for others who are struggling with their mental health to get treatment?"

The door stops in its motion, and Annie and I both watch as it's swiftly swung back, revealing Jean McBride at the threshold to her home, the expression on her face unreadable.

"Why don't you girls come in," she says.

I look over my shoulder at Annie as we walk inside, and she lifts her eyebrows in return. *No turning back now*, they say.

"You can leave your shoes by the door, over there," Jean says, pointing to a tiled patch leading from the front door into what seems to be a living room.

Annie and I slip our shoes off, Annie's big toe poking

through a hole in her right sock. I nudge her with my shoulder, and she pulls her sock out to try and hide it, which just makes the hole bigger.

I sigh. *Here we go.*

Jean walks us into the kitchen and indicates that we can sit down at the island. She proceeds to bustle around in the refrigerator, and it becomes clear she's making us sandwiches. Neither Annie nor I speak, both of us afraid to break the spell that caused Jean to let us into her home. A few minutes later, Jean sets two plates in front of us, each with a ham sandwich, a pickle spear, and a glass of milk. She lays a fork and knife neatly on a napkin next to each plate.

"I wasn't sure what you'd like, but I figured everybody likes ham," Jean says, and gives us a wan smile.

For the first time, I really look at her. She's petite, with closely cropped blond hair that's almost white, dark brown eyes, a small, bird-like body that she's dressed in a blue cardigan and jeans. No jewelry except for a gold wedding band on her left hand. She looks very, very tired, with dark circles under her eyes.

I keep searching her face for hints of Justin, but I can't settle on anything that's similar. Walking into the kitchen from the front door and through the living room, I'd searched for family photos, maybe some childhood glimpses of Justin. But there were no photographs, save for a large portrait of a golden retriever sitting underneath what I assumed was one of the large pine trees in the yard out front.

"What did you say your names were?" Jean asks, looking between Annie and me.

"I'm Janet Smith and this is Abigail Locke," I say, remembering the "journalist" names Annie and I had selected before leaving for the McBride's. "We work for the *Plain Dealer* as freelancers and, like I said earlier, we're working on a story about mental illness and lack of treatment."

"We're so sorry for your loss," Annie jumps in. "We're hoping you can give us some details about Justin's life before the accident."

I forgot how good we both are at this. It might as well have been a skilled trade certificate that comes with "graduating" from foster care. We're all fabulous liars.

"It wasn't an accident," Jean says in response to Annie's condolences. A fresh knot clenches in my stomach. "Eat your sandwiches, girls," she adds, with a quick motherly nod.

"What do you mean?" I say before I can censor myself. The anxiety in my voice seems to make the entire room vibrate.

Jean gives the same look she did at the door, but continues, "I said, it wasn't an accident. My son did this."

Her words hang in the air while the three of us consider what they mean.

"Are you aware there was another person in the car?" Annie asks next.

Jean recoils at Annie's statement. "Yes, of course we are. The police told us right away that Justin had a girlfriend and that they suspected she was the real cause of the crash." Even though I'd guessed as much, hearing Jean say out loud that I was a suspect triggers something at the base of my neck, and the damp seeping of stress moves from my temples, down my spine, and under my arms. "Ronnie and I tried to tell them how unlikely that was—we tried to tell them about Justin—but they didn't want to listen. They dismissed Justin's past as young kid's antics; teenager stuff."

She goes on. "The police were adamant when they spoke to Ronnie and me that we shouldn't have any contact with her—they wouldn't even tell us her name. Any contact could taint the investigation, they said." Jean levels her gaze at me. "Still, I keep hoping she'll reach out to us at some point."

"What did you try to tell them?" Annie cuts in, bringing us back to Jean's earlier point. She quickly taps my bag underneath the table, and I take out my pad and pencil from it and start writing, trying not to wince from the flash of pain that runs up my ribs as I bend over to grab them. I have no idea what the words are that I'm writing down, and afterwards I'll look at my notes and see they are entirely illegible.

"You have to understand, Justin can't be an inspiration for anyone. You can't write about him that way, convincing other people who are struggling that they should try and learn from his life. He was a bad person." Jean's voice is pleading, trailed with a razor's edge of anger. "When we adopted our son, we knew that he had—*difficulties*. But we were getting older and we wanted a child. We had no idea, though, what that word could mean. What 'difficulties' were." Annie and I watch as Jean stares out into the distance.

Another word whirls around in my mind as I continue to parrot some form of shorthand with my shaking fingers. *Adopted. Justin was adopted?*

"Lots of kids have problems when they're younger," Annie offers. "Lots of kids grow out of them."

"Not like this," Jean quietly folds her hands and sits down across from us. "Eat up, girls—you're both skin and bone. Don't they pay you at the *Plain Dealer*?"

"What did he do?" I ask, my voice sounding in my ears like it's coming from miles away.

"Our son was twelve years old when we adopted him. He'd been removed from his birth mother years before, and then bounced around in foster care for years after that. At the time, he insisted that he wanted a family, otherwise—and you have to believe us—" she looks emphatically at Annie and me— "otherwise we wouldn't have adopted him. We weren't looking to bring a child into our family who didn't want to be there. But Justin said he wanted to come live with us. Looking back, I don't know why he said that."

I do. With a chance of a family, any kid would run from the shithole that is foster care. Or group homes. Annie and I just never had the option. Nobody wants damaged girls. Unless they do so for all the wrong reasons.

"So, was he argumentative? Did he sneak out and get drunk?" Annie asks, trying to bring Jean back to the question at hand: *Why did she think the accident was Justin's fault?*

"No, no, nothing like that. Trust me, we would have welcomed something like that. That at least would have been normal. With Justin, it was behavior you'd never dream of dealing with as a parent. God, we were so naïve." She lets out a long breath, and then seems to decide something.

"Look, I don't care if you publish this, just as long as you promise that you will show Justin as he truly was. My husband, Ronnie, he wants to protect Justin even now, after he's died, but I don't want that. I want people to know who my son was. I want them to know how, sometimes, people are just cruel."

That last word lands with a thud on my chest, and for a second my mind clings on to the possibility that maybe we're at the wrong house. That it's the wrong Justin. The wrong mother.

"Do you have any pictures of Justin," I ask, absurdly hoping that she'll show us a photo of her son and that it won't be Justin.

"We keep one in the den," Jean says. "We barely use that room." She leaves the table for a moment. While she's gone, I return to the checklist in my mind and quickly pull out my phone and hit a reply to the text messages I'd received earlier from Justin's phone. Annie and I had planned to send a message while in the McBride's home, just in case we'd hear a ding or a vibration that would help us determine if Justin's phone was back with his family.

I type *Who are you?* and hit send just as Jean returns with a small 4 x 6 photo frame in her hands. "Here he is."

Annie and I hold our breath for a moment, but don't hear any telltale sounds that make us think Justin's phone is close by.

I look at the photograph Jean is holding in front of us. Her son is my Justin. Was. The same lanky frame, the same dark, brooding eyes. Justin is dressed in a high school cap and gown, holding a diploma and smiling next to a man that I know from the microfiche is Ronald, his father.

"That was a good day," Jean says wistfully. "That's why we kept that photo." She leans over to me and grabs my wrist. I lurch back, startled. "You have to understand. Our son wasn't right. He wasn't normal."

"Can you give us examples?" Annie is looking thoughtfully at Jean, and I poise my pen over my pad of paper, trying to focus the way I need to. Jean lets go of my wrist.

"Look at him—he was so handsome. And he could make himself so likable—his teachers; his classmates. He had everyone fooled. Even Ronnie and I—for a time. Just the day after that photo was taken, Justin pushed me down the stairs. Later he said that it was an accident, but it wasn't. He'd done it on purpose, because I told him he needed to get a job if he was going to stay at our house after graduation. He couldn't just bum around. He'd already failed to apply to colleges."

I think of the look on Justin's face the day we had our fight. How I'd thought he might actually hurt me.

Which, of course, he did. Just not that day.

A shiver runs down my back, despite the sweat seeping through my shirt. I work to stay focused on what Jean is saying.

"Did Justin ever go to college?" Annie asks. I've gone mute, apparently.

Jean arches an eyebrow. "I wouldn't know anything about that. After he pushed me, Ronnie told him to leave. We tried to get in touch with him several times, but it was like he'd disappeared. Until three days ago, that is."

"Doesn't it seem a bit extreme, to kick him out after just one incident?" Annie seems fine pushing the issue, and I'm too invested in hearing more to give her any signal to back off.

"It wasn't the *first* incident. It was the *last*. After years and years of tormenting Ronnie and me." There's so much pain in Jean's voice. Both Annie and I hear it, and I stop writing my fake notes and look up at her face. She isn't crying. Her face is burning up.

She's furious.

"We gave him love, attention, shelter, safety, but it was never enough. We were never the 'right fit' for him. No, we deserved to be punished, apparently. Do you know how many nights I woke up to find Justin standing over me, a baseball bat in his hand? Just tapping it, up and down, and staring at me? We started locking the door to our bedroom after I woke up and his hand was on my shoulder, the bat above his head."

"Oh my God," I say...

... just as Annie says, "Didn't you try to get help?"

Jean laughs. "Our son had the most expensive therapeutic education of any child in the Tri-State area. Therapists, behavior modification specialists, psychiatrists. You name it; we tried it with Justin. But nothing worked. And he would always, always punish us afterwards. So eventually we just stopped. We gave in to our little tyrant we'd willingly brought into our home."

"Punish?" Annie asks it quietly, as if saying the word might make it too real.

"Did you notice the photo of Max in our living room? Our golden retriever?"

We both nod. How could we miss it?

"Max was a perfect family dog. He loved going on walks, he listened to our commands, and *loved* snuggling with Justin on the couch. The two of them were thicker than thieves. We all adored that dog, Justin included. Ronnie would take him for long walks in the morning. When we got Max and saw how much Justin liked having a dog, we let ourselves think for a second that maybe things were getting better.

"But then we took Justin to an appointment with a specialist who had extensive experience treating children like Justin—I remember there being some argument among the doctors we went to about personality disorders and children, but then this doctor told us she was confident she could help Justin. We'd been waiting for months to get that appointment. Afterwards, we tried to get Justin to take the medication the doctor prescribed. It was supposed to help him with his violent outbursts and his—what do you call it? His emotional storms, or something like that. But Justin refused. So we took away his Playstation for a week. The next day we found Max in the back-yard with a steak knife through his chest."

As soon as she says it, Jean cries out in one short bark of a sob. "I can't imagine what Max must have thought, seeing Justin turn on him like that. Justin was fourteen then."

"What did you do?" I ask, my hands too shaky to even pretend to write now.

"What *could* we do?" Jean says. "*Nothing*. That's what. We lived in fear for four more years, until finally he was old enough to leave and we could get him out of our lives." Jean wipes at her face. "I still love him, you know. Or maybe I love the idea of who he could have been."

"I'm so sorry," I say. "I'm so sorry for what your family has gone through." My head is swimming again, with bursts of bright lights flashing around the edges. Annie puts a hand on my leg, squeezes.

"All I ever wanted was to be a parent," Jean says, talking to herself more than she is to us. "When Ronnie and I found out that I couldn't have children it nearly killed me. And then we found Justin, and you know what? I was wrong. It was Justin who nearly killed me."

She rises from the table, and it's clear that our time with her is over. Our sandwiches are still sitting there, untouched except for a small crescent-shaped bite out of Annie's.

Jean walks us over to the front door, and as we put on our coats and shoes, she stands there quietly, looking at the huge photograph of her dog hanging in the living room.

"Thank you for your time, Mrs. McBride," Annie says, and holds out her hand.

Jean takes Annie's hand, squeezes it, and lets it go.

"Just one more question," I say, and it surprises me how composed my voice sounds when inside my mind is rioting. "The police suggested that you may have called your son on the day of the accident—close to the time it occurred, actually."

Jean tilts her head to the side, considering what I've just said.

"Yes, they asked me about that. I wasn't aware they'd disclosed that to the public."

I scramble for an explanation. "We're just going on what our source in the station told us." It's the best I can manage, and it seems Jean believes it.

"Ah. Well, like I told the police, I haven't spoken to my son in almost twelve years. I wouldn't even know what number to call."

Just then, with Jean standing empty-handed in front of us, I hear my phone ping a text in.

I don't know what makes me do it, but I feel like I need something else before we leave. Justin had lied to everyone. Justin had almost killed me. I need to know more. She'd mentioned all the doctors Justin had seen, and part of me wonders if any of them might be able to help me understand what happened. "Can you help us connect to any of the doctors who treated Justin?"

She turns to look at me, her dark eyes lucid and emotionless. "There were so many. I can't remember all of them. I do know that Justin's favorite, though, was a Dr. Koftura. He was a patient of hers for years and years. Not that any of it helped him." Jean's voice cracks on the last word.

My doctor's name is an electrical current burning through the air. Annie and I exchange a glance with each other. *What the fuck?* she mouths as we step through the door.

I want to get back to the car so I can check the text that just came into my phone.

Jean ushers us through the front door, out back into the cold December. It's evening now, and the lights on the front porch twinkle in the inky black that's descended while we were inside.

Jean McBride stands in the front doorway and watches us walk to our car.

"Make sure you print what I told you," she calls out into the night. "Make sure you let everyone know that his mother is glad he's dead."

And she closes the door with a gentle click.

In the car, I pull out my phone and see the message that arrived.

Text from Justin: *Have a nice visit?*

26

Annie and I say nothing to each other the entire ride back to my apartment. The green yards of Canfield transition to the industrial brown fields of Youngstown as we head down Route II, and by the time we've managed to walk ourselves from the car and through the door of my apartment, I can't take it any longer.

"I'm so, so *stupid*." My knees wobble and I slump onto the floor of my kitchen which, as I settle onto it, I note is in desperate need of a sweep. I don't know whether to laugh or sob, the momentum of life shattering my metaphorical spine, toast crumbs and all.

And Annie's right there. "You were just in love." She shifts my shoulders so I'm facing her, only a hint of somberness peeking through. "Love, schmove." Roll of the eyes.

Then, a wicked upturn to her mouth. "You're no dummy, Dr. Morgan Kalson."

I stutter out a half cry-half laugh. For an entire week after I defended my dissertation, and subsequently became a Ph.D., Annie had insisted on calling me Dr. Morgan Kalson. No abbreviations. *Dr. Morgan Kalson, would you like to order pizza tonight?*

Dr. Morgan Kalson, what's taking so long in the bathroom? Dr. Morgan Kalson, did you borrow my sweater and stretch out the neck hole? At the center of it, Annie was proud of me.

"Except when I am," I mutter into her armpit. She has me wrapped in a bear hug by now.

Justin's face, looking at me just before he pushed down on the gas. My hand on his. Mom calling. That scratch at the back of my mind. The empty socket of memory after the crash.

Annie lets out a deep breath through her mouth and rubs her hand over her face. I shift away, the air between us heavy and cold after being so close together. "Justin was a liar." She won't look me in the eye as she talks. "He was probably trying to hurt you—and I don't know why he would want to do that."

"Maybe I deserved it. Him. All of this." I wave my arm in an impotent arc, and accidentally knock my knuckles against the leg of one of my kitchen chairs. Annie's knees are digging into some stray poppy seeds left on the floor from the new bagel recipe I tried last week.

Fuck.

Annie looks at me from the corner of her eye. "What do you mean by that?"

What do *I mean?*

Her voice is suddenly all tension. "Morgan, seriously. . ." but is interrupted by my phone pinging, letting me know another text has arrived. I want to throw it across the room.

"What about these messages?" I thrust the phone up in the space between us, careful to keep my eyes away from the message that's appeared on the screen. I don't want to know what it says.

I don't want any of this.

I look at Annie, and her words—*our* words—come hurtling straight at me.

Survive and thrive.

Survive.

Love is my failure. The chink in my armor. But after meeting with Jean McBride, I'm certain that what Justin and I had—this thing—wasn't love. It was something else. Something that I can manage, just like I've managed everything else in my life.

"I think we should call Dana," Annie says into the silence. She reaches out and gently takes the phone from me and sets it on the kitchen counter, screen down. I let her.

"I don't know about that." I cradle the last syllable, my mind whirring into action in stutters and stops at first, until it spins at 100 rpms. "If we tell her about the text messages, she might think exactly what the police would think—that I've got Justin's phone and am sending them to myself."

"But—" Annie tries to break in, and I won't let her. This idea is picking up speed, hitting its stride. My mind hums, not with static from the past. With the future.

"I'm serious. We've already promised Dana we wouldn't do our own investigating, and so what are we going to say when she sees the texts asking about visiting Justin's parents and searching around his supposed advisor's office? She'd drop my case, and then I'd be stuck with a lawyer that I don't know and don't trust."

Annie's not trying to talk anymore. Instead, she's grabbed a seat at my kitchen table and is watching me intently, her shoulders twisted away as though she's looking for something to distract me. She's pulled a bag of gummy bears from somewhere —I vaguely remember a stash of Haribo listlessly flapped open on the counter by the toaster—and snatches a few colorful sugar bombs, shoving them into her mouth.

She tips the package towards me. I ignore her and keep going.

"So we can't tell Dana about the texts, or Jean, or even the fact that Dr. Koftura was Justin's doctor as well, because all of that information would lead her to break her contract with us."

I pause for a moment to catch my breath, stand up only to sit down across from Annie at my IKEA-born table, all sleek ash wood and plastic caps over screw holes. Annie turns herself to face me. She asks, "But why can't we just say that you knew Justin was a patient of Dr. Koftura's? We don't have to tell Dana we learned that from Jean."

"Because we need to break into Dr. Koftura's office, and I don't want Dana looking over our shoulders."

Annie leans forward in her chair, her lanky arms draped over the table. "What do you have in mind?"

The gummy bears lie forgotten on the table.

27

I'm trying to focus my thoughts on sociometric data collection for my Wednesday morning seminar, but nothing wants to settle in my brain. My phone keeps drawing my eyes over to its smooth surfaces, gleaming up from my desk in DeBartolo Hall. Emotional porn, Annie'd called it.

Total mind fuck, I'd said.

She and I decided not to reply to any more messages. Not yet, at least.

Yesterday, after Annie and I had put together a plan for getting into Dr. Koftura's office, we'd read that last text together —the one neither of us could stand to look at when it first glided into my phone as we sat in my kitchen. It was more specific than the earlier one that came just as we were leaving Jean McBride's house.

Text from Justin: *Why did you visit my parents today?*

I feel harassed, invaded. The quiet simmer of the heater in my office is infuriating. I turn on some blaring station on Spotify through my computer—Beast Mode it's called, with some ripped alpha male pumping iron on the playlist cover—but the dubstep and bass drops that shriek out do nothing for my state of mind.

Having that last message simmering in my phone feels like someone is molding my life into their own special sadist sugar cage. So I slap my folder of lecture notes shut, whip my flash drive from my computer, and shove them both into my teaching satchel. Then I pick up my phone, go to my texts, and type a reply.

I click send before I can talk myself out of it.

Justin is dead.

I glance at my watch and it tells me I'm already late for class.

I'm about to head out the door when I hear a text ping in. And then another one. I scramble to get my phone out. On the screen is a message from Annie, asking if I'm okay and how work is going. The second message is from Justin's phone.

Let me help you.

I shove my phone into my bag and rush out, hoping to somehow get to my class in negative time.

When I finally arrive at my podium, which is still covered in the same mess of the semester with a few additional pencils and blank scantron sheets added to the mix, I'm flushed from the rush of running across campus. Annie did my makeup for me again today, muttering the entire time about how ridiculous it is that I'm going back to work already, and I feel the foundation smearing around on my face with my perspiration. I can only imagine what I look like to my students, who are all staring back at me with looks that are a mixture of concern and annoyance.

I look at my watch. Ten minutes late.

I shuffle my papers and try to get started, but realize after I start speaking that I haven't clipped on my microphone.

I take a drink of water. And set my phone on the podium in front of me.

What Annie doesn't know is that I'm happy to be back in the

classroom. I need to get out of my apartment, and out of my head, for at least a few hours.

That's shot to hell now, though.

I should have listened to Annie.

"Good after. . . afternoon." I clear my throat. "Today we'll delve into popularity hierarchies in children's peer networks. To begin with, let's examine how we actually collect data on social networks. In the peer group, we call this sociometry."

And I'm off. I've given this lecture so many times before that I barely need to look at my notes. For the next twenty minutes, I'm in a different zone, a safe place, where I'm trading ideas with my students and answering their questions with enthusiasm, if not admirable precision.

I have to tell a student I'll get back to her on the equation for social impact.

Dammit.

But still, a little distraction goes a long way towards reinstating some sanity in my life.

At least until I pause to take a sip of water from my podium. Foolishly I've put my phone there, face up, out of habit I'd like to think, but can't be certain. There are two new text messages lighting up the screen.

From Justin's number: *Morgan, let me help you.*

And again from Annie: *Are you okay?*

I set my water bottle back down, but I must miss the table or set it on top of some of the stray pencils, because it topples over and a few sparks flash up from the computer tower seated underneath the lectern. My projector screen goes blank, and the room of 150 students sits in an eerie silence.

"Umm. . ." I scan around for what to do next, as if the faux wood paneling will have an answer beyond a sign reading *Turn Projector OFF. Turning to Blank Screen Does NOT Save the Bulb.* I consider just lecturing from my notes and the chalkboard, which is hidden behind the projector screen. I think about dialing the help hotline for the classroom, which never, ever helps, except to put me in touch with someone eating a sandwich and lording over microphone batteries like a dragon. Part of me just wants to cancel class and run back home to Annie.

I must have stood there, lost in my thoughts for far too long, because I hear the distinctive shuffle of book bags on the floor and the creak of moveable desks being swung back into place.

My students are leaving the room.

One young woman asks if I'm okay, and I shoo her away gently with an "I think I might have the flu" excuse. I try to place her face, and wonder if she's the same girl I shared a smile with last week when Justin came to visit. It might as well have been another life, another person who had that memory.

I start to gather up my things, as though it was my decision to let class out. Even with the cluster bomb that has hit my life, this little humiliation of having my students leave before I dismissed them stings me, and I have to suppress the blush that rises as I watch the last student exit through the doors at the back. Until someone comes through the door and heads straight for me.

I assume it's a student who's forgotten something, but as I'm turning to pick up the stationary phone used to call the tech hotline—because sandwich-eating or not, my podium computer did spark and seemingly catch fire for a few seconds—out of the corner of my eye this newly arrived figure lurches towards me.

Something roars inside my head.

Instinctively, I throw my arm back just as the intruder comes up alongside me, and my elbow connects with their shoulder, knocking them off balance. I keep my eyes on the exit, feeling the rush of energy flowing into my arms and legs as my body reacts to the threat. The shadowy figure in my periphery starts to fall over, and the edge of my arm catches their face. I hear a soft, satisfying snap.

I start to run away from my attacker, who must be the person texting me from my dead boyfriend's phone, which means they were there at the accident—that they watched Justin and I bleeding, dying, and were still able to rummage around our broken bodies and retrieve that fucking phone like they were picking up a forgotten glove—when I hear a familiar voice coming from the ground.

"What the hell?!" It's my colleague, Maria. A needle pricks my blood pressure, and I am floating down. Humiliated. Then horrified. "Morgan, what's going on?" She rubs her nose which, thankfully, is not bleeding. Her voice comes out with a nasal scratch to it.

"Oh my God, I'm so sorry," I must have said this too loud, because she flinches as I rush down to help her up.

"What are you doing here?" she asks me, irritation warping her voice more than fear. Along with her nose, which she's still cupping in both hands. I stare at her because that's exactly what I would have asked her if I wasn't trying to make up for the fact that I just basically punched her.

"I'm teaching," I say, and then correct myself, my heartbeat still swimming in my ears. "I *was* teaching. But then I spilled my water and the computer shorted-out. Or something." I offer that last part with a pathetic flourish of rising inflection in my voice so that it sounds like a question.

"Well, you're not supposed to be teaching. David asked me earlier if I could stop by to remind your class that it was canceled, just in case anyone showed up. He wasn't able to find someone to fill in today, like I did for your Tuesday class. I would have come earlier, but I had a meeting I couldn't get out of."

When I e-mailed David, I'd told him I only needed help for

Tuesday. It's not typical for a Department Head to just assume someone wouldn't be covering their own classes.

Maria sees the confused look on my face and stands up, her arms going to her side. Her nose looks normal, just a bit red on one side. No palm print on her cheek or anything, thank God.

"No one expected you to come in here just a few days after being in a terrible car crash where, you know. . ." She doesn't want to say it—that Justin died. "I'm so sorry, by the way, Morgan. If there's anything I can do." Her eyes crinkle in the corners as she talks. Her mouth folds in a kind, noncommittal way, like you'd look at a dog snarling from a rescue shelter kennel.

"So, David asked you to come down here and tell my students class was canceled." I say it as a statement, not a question, but Maria answers it just the same.

"I think he's worried about you." She ruffles her hair to fluff it back into place after her fall, and then narrows her eyes slightly. "Who did you think I was?"

"I was just in my office. Why didn't anyone mention it to me then?"

"I didn't see you come in this morning," Maria says. Being two doors down, it's true that it's hard to miss each other when we come and go, but I'd kept my door closed, not willing to have any ambushes from eager students or colleagues as I was desperately trying to not lose my mind. My face must betray what I'm thinking, because the next words out of her mouth are, "Are you okay?"

It's the only question anyone can ask me lately.

"I'm sorry about—about hitting you. You just surprised me, that's all."

"Look, why don't I buy you a coffee and we can sit down for a minute, huh?" Maria starts handing me the lecture notes I've scattered across the podium, some of them blooming with damp from the spill earlier.

I'll have to call the help desk later, I think. *Report that I extinguished a computer.Along with my professional pride.*

My bag packed up, and my coat on, Maria starts to walk with me, but the last thing I want is to be grilled by yet another person about what happened this weekend.

"I don't drink coffee," I say. "But you go ahead. I'll see you back at the office." I pass through the emergency exit door, even though it protests with an alarm. I don't care.

As I'm leaving, I catch a glimpse of Maria again out of the corner of my eye, her mouth parted with something she doesn't say and her face twenty shades of concern. The tall, imposing shape she makes in her overcoat sends a shiver up my back. Until the door slams shut behind me.

28

I head back over to my office, walking as quickly as I can, just in case Maria tries to catch up with me. I don't see a single person as I climb the stairs, and the hallway to my office is equally deserted. It's a relief, and not just because I want to be alone.

I close the door behind me and try to get my pulse to stop making my earrings vibrate. When I sit down at the tiny table next to my desk, I put my head between my legs and breathe in and out deeply. *Always focusing on my fucking breath,* I think. *That's what Dr. Koftura taught me.*

I stand up suddenly, pushing all the air from my lungs.

There's something I need to do here.

Dr. Koftura stepped into my life when I was seven, when I was hit by a car while playing in the street. Hers was the first face I saw when I regained consciousness in the hospital, waiting to explain what happened to me and that my memory might have gaps in it. That I shouldn't be scared. That this was normal when someone's brain was injured. There'd been a social worker there, too, who managed to show up one more time in her blousy top and yoga pants to explain that my mother was in jail for drug dealing and that I wasn't going home.

That's when the labels began. At first they were physical. Church-community-casserole-on-your-doorstep-worthy.

Traumatic brain injury, TBI for short. Fractured tibia. Malnourishment.

But then, somewhere between my first foster home and my first handsy "uncle," other letters started showing up in the mix. PTSD. ODD. ADHD. You name it, some well-intentioned but poorly qualified county employee tried to assign them to me. And Dr. Koftura dismissed each of them in turn with a flick of her elegant wrist and a wry eyebrow raised in my direction.

Except for one.

I pull a thick manual off my bookshelf. The *Diagnostic and Statistical Manual of Mental Disorders*, 5th edition, our diagnostic bible, and flip through to the one diagnosis Dr. Koftura let ride.

Because I want her to be wrong.

Instability in goals, career, or values. Definitely not me.

Consistent feelings of hopelessness or misery. Again, not me.

Impoverished self-image. No.

Intense and unstable close relationships. Fears of rejection or separation from significant others. Stress-related paranoia. Acting on the spur of the moment without thoughts of later consequences, especially when under emotional distress. Well, then.

BPD. Borderline personality disorder.

I know these symptoms. None of this is new to me. And yet, as I keep reading, an icy stab of fear grows in my chest.

The last time I visited them, my boyfriend wasn't dead.

Dr. Holdren had said my condition wasn't one linked with violence. Which means she's either a terrible doctor or Dr. Koftura hid my diagnosis from her.

Because being borderline means you hurt. Yourself and others.

My hand on Justin's, turning the wheel.
My phone pings twice.
Text from Justin: *I can help you.*
Text from Justin: *We need to talk.*

29

I sneak out of my office when I'm sure no one is in the hallway, and rush past Maria's door just in case she's waiting to hear my door close before whipping hers open in the hope of a post-mortem. Before I leave, I manage to grab my lecture notes for the final class of the semester and my flash drive, shoving both into my bag, along with my phone.

My stomach growls because I've forgotten to eat again, and I tell myself I need to stop and get something to eat for fear of low blood sugar adding to my erratic twitchiness of today. I don't want to go to the Starbucks in Kilcawley, and opt instead to get something at the Taco Bell on the corner of the campus where it meets Fifth Avenue. I grab a bean burrito and a Coke, a silent homage to Annie, and rush out to the road to start my walk home. I'd texted Annie to let her know I was on my way, and she'd replied to confirm that she was able to schedule my appointment with Dr. Koftura for 4pm today. She'd offered to pick me up, but I'd said I'd prefer to walk. Healing ribs or not, I wanted to think outside in the freezing air, away from the industrial white walls and central heating closing in.

I hoover down my lunch as I walk, suddenly ravenous as the

salty, greasy food shoots dopamine through my synapses. The soft tortilla and mix of beans and rice hits my stomach like a lead weight, but the shaky sensation in my limbs abates as soon as I bite in. Fifth Avenue is deserted, as most of downtown Youngstown is these days. A few cars are driving on the street, and with the sidewalk riding up right next to the road, I move as far to the side as I can to avoid slush and debris splashing up onto me. The wind is bitter, which is good for clearing my head, but I still have to move my scarf to cover my face as soon as I'm done eating.

Up ahead, there's a car swerving between the lanes of scattered vehicles.

It catches my attention, because no one ever seems to be in a hurry in Youngstown proper. Except to get back to the suburbs.

The tires of the car squeal, its body a vomit-like mottled shade of grey and brown. The rust and dried salt lines on its sides and under the wheel wells blend perfectly with the faded paint. A distinctive peeling patch of paint on the roof and hood, picture-the-Virgin-Mary-in-the-damage style, tells me it's a Chevy from the GM plant.

I also notice, too late, that it's heading towards me.

The car swerves onto the sidewalk, and its front wheel pops up onto the top of a fragment of the uneven cement where the freeze and thaw of Ohio winters has split it into shards. It misses me by a fraction of an inch, and only because I tripped on the same crack in the sidewalk as I tried to run away from the street, propelling my body forward with the force of my fall.

I hit the pavement in a graceless slump, with the same pigweed and thistle I'd admired only a week or so ago shoving their hard stalks against my cheeks. A burst of air leaves my lungs. I turn in time to see the car right itself on the road and continue at breakneck speed. I can't make out the license plate except for a few beginning letters and numbers—maybe an L, followed by a 3 or an 8—and there's no time for me to glimpse the driver behind the salt-coated windows.

You're getting old, some dank hole in the back of my brain blathers out. *Time for glasses.*

As I stand up and brush myself off, I actually think that someone might pull over and ask if I'm okay. But then I remember this is Youngstown, and that nobody helps each other here.

Well, not completely nobody. I text Annie, my mind frantically trying to make sense of what has just happened, with my hands jittering with shock. I ask her to pick me up. *Yes, I'm okay. I'll explain when you get here.*

She's with me in what feels like less than a heartbeat—"Find Your Friends" she calls out and tries to crack a smile, but immediately throws it over when she sees my face.

"Somebody almost ran me over," I shout above the roar of a diesel truck rambling by and the wind ripping across the vacant field next to the Taco Bell. A drip makes its way down my cheek, and when I reach up to wipe away what I assume is a tear—can a person really cry without knowing?—my finger is stained red. Cut by pigweed.

Annie is a tight whorl of anguish and annoyance. "What happened?" she asks, her voice just a shade below shrill. I'm waving my arms frantically and pacing up and down the same two blocks in the sidewalk, trying to process what happened.

I'm fairly sure I look like a mad woman, which means I'll blend in with the normal Fifth Avenue Taco Bell crowd.

I explain how the car ran up onto the curb. As I tell her what the car looked like, and that I think I may have caught a few pieces of its filthy license plate, my heart bumps along like an asphalt truck.

"Are you okay?" Annie asks as soon as I'm finished, an echo of her text. Of her last twenty texts, for that matter. She tries to put her hands over my arms and force me to stand still for a moment, but I shrug her off.

"Somebody wanted to run me over, Annie!"

"*What?*"

"They're trying to hurt me," I tell her, fairly convinced after all my pacing.

"*Who* is? I don't understand." Annie moves her hand to my hair, trying to brush away my bangs to look at my forehead and manifesting a tissue out of the pocket of her coat like a soccer mom, but I turn away from her fretting and blotting.

"I'm fine—just a few scratches," I say dismissively, and swat her hand away. "But you need to listen. This was deliberate. This car *tried* to run me over."

"Why? I don't understand," she repeats.

"Because of Justin," I say.

At the mention of Justin, Annie sets her mouth in a firm line. "No, it's not possible." She reaches out again to touch my arm, and this time I let her. "Nobody knew you'd be here. This isn't the way you walk home." I try to nod along as I listen to her rational thinking. "And Justin is dead," she adds, quietly.

"I got another message from his phone," I tell her, and reach into my pocket to pull out my phone and show her.

Annie scrolls through the green bubbles on my screen for a few moments, reading the messages. "Help, my ass," she mumbles.

Her breath comes out in steamy clouds as she talks. I'm freezing. It's gotten even colder outside since I started walking home.

"What's this message from you?" Annie bends down to try and catch my gaze, which I've directed at a patch of crabgrass breaking through the cracks in the sidewalk. "Why did you reply to them?"

She doesn't sound pissed at me. It's worse.

She sounds hurt.

I pull a floppy fish routine, trying to force sense out of my actions so that it'll come out my mouth, but my mouth just gapes open instead.

"Never mind," she stands up and starts to walk to her car, which is pulled into a patch of driveway in the empty lot next to the Taco Bell. Her bright orange hat bounces up and down like a homing beacon as she strides across the rubble.

I follow her, chin tucked against the wind, and come up on her just as she's unlocking the driver-side door. Old habits.

"My gut tells me this wasn't some coincidence," I argue.

My stomach gurgles audibly, right at that moment. Damn bean burrito.

"Is that what it's saying?" Annie arches an eyebrow, so far up it disappears into the nubbly rim of her hat. Then her face turns softer. "Look, I'm so sorry this happened and it must have been scary as hell, but you and I both know Youngstown drivers are awful, along with Youngstown roads being awful." She jabs her hand in the general direction of the potholes riddling Fifth Avenue like a pockmarked teenager. "Isn't it possible this has nothing to do with Justin, or Dr. Koftura, or the messages? That it was just an accident?"

No, it's not. I'm not letting this go.

"We thought Justin's crash was an accident, but it wasn't, was it?" The tenderness in my ribs aches, and I picture the blotches of blue turned to yellow bruises across my chest where the seat belt held me in.

Something flashes across Annie's eyes.

"Why did you reply to those texts? Morgan, why do you keep doing things that we agreed you wouldn't do?" She reaches out with her hands and shoves me backwards. "You need to hold it together. You can't start seeing things that aren't there. You need to *listen* to me!"

The adrenaline leeches out of me like a bloodletting. I look up at my best friend, and resignation wraps around me. I don't want to tell her about Maria. I don't want to tell her about the checklist of dangers I read to myself only an hour ago.

And, really, I don't have to.

We stand there, among the mutant lawn weeds and shards of broken asphalt mixed with used condoms and cigarette butts. A plastic Walmart bag flaps in the breeze, its smiley face putrid in the winter light as it leers at me.

And then I let Annie pull me into her rangy but strong arms and search over my face and body like a mother does after her child returns from being lost. She opens the car door for me and buckles me into my seat, like you would a toddler, and as we head back to my apartment, Annie says, "I'm going to keep you safe, Morgan. We'll figure this out together."

At the time, I completely believed her.

30

Our plan is for Annie to drive and potentially run interference, while I head into Dr. Koftura's office as a patient. Annie didn't have any trouble making an appointment for me today, especially after she explained who I was to the intake nurse on the phone, and why she was making the appointment.

It seems I'm developing quite a reputation at Dr. Koftura's office.

With my appointment set for 4pm, when the backlog of the day's appointments is bound to be catching up, I know there will be a significant wait between when a nurse would take me back to an exam room and when Dr. Koftura shows up to examine me. I hope I'll be long gone by that point.

When Annie and I arrive together at the office next to St. Elizabeth's hospital, the same emo-cute receptionist is there to check me in. Same disinterested attitude—which is perfect.

In the waiting area, Annie and I sit down and mime reading well-worn *People* magazines until we hear my name called. It's a nurse I've never seen before, and this time I'm grateful for the apparent turnaround Dr. Koftura has with her staff.

The nurse who takes me to the exam room is short, with a round, pudgy face and a microscopic ponytail encased in a pink scrunchie. The scrunchie matches her scrubs, which have pink daisies dancing across both top and bottom. Her shoes look well-worn and comfortable. Her name tag, which has blue and pink star stickers dancing at the corners, says she's Molly.

She's no Nurse Debbie, but she'll do.

I know the layout of Dr. Koftura's office almost intuitively at this point, after years of shuttling between the waiting room and the warren of exam rooms, which made it easy to draw a map on my new marker board Annie'd brought home earlier. Walking with Nurse Molly, I feel a small burst of satisfaction mixed with hope, because it's clear I got the schematics right. We turn a corner and pass by Dr. Koftura's office and the patient bathroom.

The office door is closed, and my little bubble of positivity evaporates. If they've fixed the lock on Dr. Koftura's door, I won't be able to get in. Annie and I had talked about whether I'd have the option of picking the lock, but we had to dismiss the idea almost outright. There's far too much traffic down the hallway, and even though I'm like any other malingering foster kid in that I can pick a lock the way other children say "I love you," there's no way I could do that without getting noticed. So we are banking on my being able to just walk into the office, take quick pictures of Justin's file, and then head out the exit as if I'd never been there.

Dr. Koftura can charge me for being a no-show at our appointment.

As the nurse and I pass the bathroom door, it's now or never.

"Can I use the bathroom quickly before my appointment?" I ask. I make an apologetic face, and Nurse Molly smiles in return.

"I'll wait out here," she says, and gestures to the bathroom directly behind me.

I rush into the single bathroom, lock the door, and whip out my phone. There's no time to lose. I text Annie one word—*Molly* —and wait.

When we'd discussed this portion of the plan, Annie was quick to remind me that she'd been the understudy for Ursula in our high school's production of the *Little Mermaid*. "I've got skills," she'd said. *Well*, I think, *here's hoping.*

I put my ear to the door and listen to try and decipher what's happening outside. There are faint murmurs, and the sound of footsteps. And then I hear it: frantic voices, and a group of people running. I open the door, and manage to just glimpse Molly's tiny ponytail bobbing its way around the corner and into the lobby. Annie's voice vibrates through the thin walls. "I need Nurse Molly! Please help me. I need Nurse Molly!"

I rush over to Dr. Koftura's office next door and grip the doorknob, offering a silent prayer to any and all deities that it will open. The knob turns with my hand, but I can't push the door open. I can't tell if it's locked, or just jammed, so I press my shoulder against it and give a hard push. It doesn't budge. I try again. The door shimmies slightly and begins to swing inside.

Annie's voice is more subdued now, with other voices intermingling as they say things like, "Take a deep breath," and "Can you tell me what day it is?" I catch footsteps coming down the hallway, and give one final shove on the door, turning the knob as hard as I can. It bursts into Dr. Koftura's office, and I almost fall in, quickly regain my balance, and shut the door before the person coming down the hallway can notice. Looking at the edge of the door, its sticky situation is obvious. The maintenance solution to Dr. Koftura's lock trouble was to half-heartedly replace the entire door jamb, and I thank my lucky stars that the door wasn't locked when I tried to get in.

The office is deserted—I'd briefly considered that perhaps Dr. Koftura was inside and had locked the door behind her— but just as I stand up and begin to scan the room for where Dr.

Koftura likely keeps her patient notes and files, I hear the door knob turn.

Those footsteps must have been Dr. Koftura's.

The door sticks again as she tries to open it, and I use the time to move into the only hiding place in the office—underneath her desk. I want to yelp as I squeeze my still broken body into the small space, and try to hold my breath when I hear Dr. Koftura enter, muttering a few curses under her breath about the incompetent maintenance workers. My mind follows the sounds she makes and tries to track her location inside the office. I hear her walk over to the window and pause, like she's looking out of the window, and then come around to her desk. She must be standing where the two chairs are situated for patients and family members. Telekinesis would be a handy psychologist's trick right about now. *Go away, go away, go away.*

The floor creaks, and I imagine her leaning over the desk, scanning the room, because she knows something is wrong. If she catches me here, cowering in her footwell, then my days passing as a normal, sane individual will be shot to hell. Regret tinges my mouth like a cheap mouthwash.

But then I hear her snatch something from the top of her desk. The scrape that vibrates over the wooden surface of the desk makes it sound like a coffee mug, which is odd because I've never seen Dr. Koftura drink anything over all the years I've known her. Her footsteps travel briskly out of her office, followed by the thud and clunk as she works the door closed behind her.

I'm okay, I tell myself, and let out a huge breath after holding it for so long. It's hard to wriggle out of the small space, and I wince as my elbow catches on the prong of her chair and my torso jerks backwards unexpectedly. Finally, I'm standing up and my hands fly over drawers and cupboards, searching for a piece of Justin's history.

There are bookshelves upon bookshelves filled with medical texts and journals, aligned with a row of horizontal filing cabinets. Pulling open the middle drawer, thinking that M is in the middle of the alphabet, I'm greeted with years and years' worth of files. I flip through the M's from top to bottom, but fail to find a single scrap of evidence that Justin was ever a patient of Dr. Koftura's. I move a little back into the Ks and a little ahead into the Ns, just in case something was misfiled, but still nothing.

Time is ticking away with sickening speed. I'm begging for some sort of brilliant insight of where the damn file might be, when I move around the back of her desk and my eyes land on a middle drawer I'd missed the first time because of how it blends in with the top wood panel. It's not quite a hidden drawer, but close enough.

I open up the drawer, and the gasp of disappointment that leaves my mouth is audible. It's clear with only a quick survey of the contents that there are no hidden files in here. Just a few rolls of mints, some pens, and Dr. Koftura's prescription pad.

Wait, I tell myself. I reach out and shift the pad over with a pen I've grabbed from her drawer. I'd watched way too many *Law and Order* reruns in grad school. Moving the top pad over, another one appears beneath it.

There are two prescription pads.

One endorsed for Dr. Jana Koftura.

And the other endorsed to Dr. Jawinder Koftura.

I don't have time to consider why Dr. Koftura still has a prescription pad for her dead husband. I only have time to pull out my phone, take a picture of both, and close the drawer.

My mind and body are humming. This has to mean something.

The entire wait and search must have taken only two to three minutes, but I feel like I've been in this office for hours. I know it's time to leave.

I put my ear to the door and listen. I don't hear anything at first, but then I pick up voices coming down the hallway, followed by a polite knocking on what must be the bathroom door.

"Morgan, are you alright," Nurse Molly's muffled voice says.

Shit, I think, and wonder if my estimate of time was more accurate than I'd thought. I consider just sauntering out of the office with purpose, as if I was meant to be in there, but dismiss that idea on the grounds of it being balls-to-the-wall nuts. My eyes fall on the one window of Dr. Koftura's office, and, as I make my way over there, I find myself praying for the umpteenth time today that the odds be in my favor.

The hospital building and its adjoining offices are older construction, meaning that they were built pre-central air con, and that most of the windows can still open. There's a lock on the window, and I hope the frame hasn't been painted shut by the same ham-fisted maintenance workers who "fixed" Dr. Koftura's door. I reach over, unlock the window, and push up.

The window moves freely, and a burst of cold air rushes into the room through the opening. There's no screen on the window, and since Dr. Koftura's office is on the first floor I can easily boost myself out the window and into some ancient yew bushes outside the building. A few scrapes from the untended branches of the bushes—again, I blame the maintenance crew —and I'm able to reach up, close the window, and make my way out to the parking lot.

I text Annie to tell her that I'm out, and wait to meet her at her car.

It's later, after Annie's given me the dramatic play-by-play and we've devoured a bucket of KFC, that I consider what leaving Dr. Koftura's office window unlocked will mean.

For both of us.

31

"A re you hungry," Annie asks when we are back at my apartment, chucking the greasy bucket of chicken bones in the garbage. It's as though she's added to that old adage "Starve a fever, feed a cold," and force fed me into submission chronic trauma. I tell her as much, and she gives a voluptuous cackle.

"Maybe we can write an essay on chicken soup for the psychopath's soul," she calls out from the kitchen. I'm sitting in my bedroom at the foot of my bed, staring at the wall. Annie's account of her performance in the waiting room almost made up for the fact that I hadn't found anything about Justin in Dr. Koftura's office. According to Annie, after getting my text confirming my nurse's name, she'd bolted up in the waiting room, shouting, "I need Nurse Molly! I need Nurse Molly!" as loudly as she possibly could. She'd recounted all the details as we'd driven back.

"I don't know what symptoms of which disorder I was spazzing out with," she'd said, tapping her hands on the steering wheel as we waited for our extra crispy thighs in the drive-through. "But I do know that I properly freaked everybody out."

The drive-through cashier, hair net billowing in the December wind, gave Annie a steely side-eye as she passed back our change.

Apparently a nurse who'd just entered the room to call a patient went running for Nurse Molly and a few other staff to help out, giving me the clearance to get into Dr. Koftura's office. The kindness of the nurses stretches only so far, though, and after too many minutes of indistinct chattering on Annie's part she overheard one of them mumble the word "ambulance," followed quickly by "psychiatric unit."

"It was time to shut it down," Annie said, reaching for a thigh as she winged her car into a parking spot outside my apartment building. We sat there in the fading light of the day, eating greasy chicken, proud of ourselves beyond belief.

"So I looked straight into Nurse Molly's eyes and, serious as you please, said, 'I knew you would help me. I feel so much better now.' And she just melted, I swear. Come to think of it, she is probably a pretty wonderful nurse. I don't know how anyone else could have dealt with five full minutes of my screaming her name and flailing around."

"But how did you get out?" The high of our pseudo-heist was waning, and the chicken tasted too salty and pungent on my lips.

In our planning, we'd assumed that Annie would have to at least go in for an assessment with a doctor after her episode, and I was supposed to wait for her at the car in the hospital parking deck.

"Once I'd calmed down, they really wanted me to go meet with a doctor, but I told them it was just a panic attack—was that the right thing to say?" She doesn't wait for me to answer and plows on with her story, reaching to finish my picked-apart piece of white meat. "It must have been, because that, plus my announcement that I didn't have health insurance, seemed to do the trick."

"God bless America," I'd said.

I hear Annie pressing the buttons on the microwave to make me a cup of tea—the woman won't use the kettle to save her life, as she insists it's a fire hazard—and I brace myself for the next step. I pick up my phone, half-expecting to see another text from Justin's phone, but finding none move back into the kitchen area.

Annie seems to have already read my mind, because she has two steaming cups of tea, the marker board, and a pack of whiteboard markers.

"Alright, Dr. Kalson. Let's figure this out," she says as she proffers a marker to me, and grabs one herself.

"I'm going to write down everything that you tell me, starting with the day of the accident, and you can add anything that you want to add to, or expand on. Okay?"

I nod, and for the next thirty minutes I sift through all the details of what's happened to me over the past four days. Afterwards, Annie and I both sit back and survey what we've accomplished.

At the top of the board is his name: "Justin." Underneath are his parents' names, "Ron" and "Jean," with "Estranged" and "History of violence" added in the surrounding areas. Annie wrote in Professor Farak's name, and then I asked her to create a hatched line that she labeled "Faked Being a Student." I also had Annie add "Max," with an X through the name. We both gave that one a long look before moving on. It's funny how knowing someone hurt other people is more tolerable than knowing someone hurt an animal. I should care more about Justin holding that baseball bat above his mother's head, but I don't. Most people wouldn't. Which is why animal shelters have volunteers and foster parents have to be paid.

I can't stop picturing Justin, all dark hair and deep eyes, walking his dog outside, and the poor dog following because he trusted him.

Just like I did.

"ACCIDENT" is written in capitals, and underneath there are the words "Police," followed by "Ormoran," "Miller," and "Hospital," which has the tags "Holdren" and "Koftura." Below the detectives' names, Annie and I listed their evidence against me. Dr. Koftura's "testimony" (Annie fake-gagged herself with the marker before writing that) and my "history of violence" (Annie wrote #fakenews for that one).

Annie's treading that fine line between humor and despair, and even as I'm so grateful for her being here with me, I can't help feeling like something is off. Her outrage is just a little too loud, a little too big.

I haven't told her about what happened with Maria in my classroom. And I don't think I'm going to.

Underneath "Holdren," we've written only "Believes me" and "Dislikes Koftura." For my neurologist of almost two decades, I've added "Thinks I did it," "Treated Justin," and "Has two prescription pads."

We circled the last two entries and put big stars next to them. Stars mean follow-up.

"I do the same thing in my e-mails," Annie says, sinking onto the couch. She doesn't look at me as she says it, though.

One more category: "After the accident."

Below the title, I ask Annie to write: "Visitor to the car. Who took the phone?" And then "*Who* the fuck is texting from Justin's number?" I don't have to tell her to underline the word *Who*. The "fuck" she adds herself.

I don't bring up the car on Fifth Avenue, outside the Taco Bell.

Neither does Annie.

"What do you make of the extra prescription pad?" Annie asks as she settles further into my couch. I follow, the marker board propped up against my coffee table, facing us.

I take a sip of tea, and the lemon Annie must have slipped into it makes my mouth pucker. "I don't know." Since psychologists don't write prescriptions, the procedures for use and disuse of them is kind of beyond me. I take another sip and my apartment falls silent while Annie and I mull the question over, until a thought comes to me. "I remember reading something about prescription fraud related to opioid addiction in the *Plain Dealer*. There was a doctor up in Cleveland who had hung on to his office partner's prescription pad after the partner died and was using it to write fake prescriptions for Percocet and other pain killers for paying 'patients.'" I make the air quotes as I say the word, and Annie slaps me with a couch pillow.

"You don't need to do that—I'm not an idiot," she half laughs, half snarls. I start to say sorry, and blame it on teaching undergrads with earbuds constantly stuck in, but Annie ignores me. "So do you think that's what Koftura's doing? Writing fake prescriptions to get extra cash on the side? They can't be traced back to her because they aren't under her name."

"It's definitely a possibility, but it also just might be that she's hanging onto her husband's pad as a memento of him, right?" I offer.

Annie nods her head and pulls her legs up onto the couch so she can fold her feet underneath her.

"Let me see the picture you took," she says, and after I hand her my phone she starts zooming in on the photo of the little white pad of paper with Jawinder's name at the top.

"What are you doing?"

"Looking to see if there are any indentations that might tell us what the last thing written on the pad was. Maybe a date too."

Annie's bent over my phone, with the image zoomed in as far as it will go.

I lean over her shoulder and see that the picture is just too low in resolution. We can't see much of anything beyond the stark black letters of Jawinder's name and the subsections for writing a prescription.

Annie shakes her head and hands my phone back to me. "I don't know. Do you think Justin was dealing drugs?"

I give a short bleat of laughter at the question, the way a person laughs when they think nothing could be less funny.

"You ask that as though I knew anything about him."

32

On Thursday morning, there's a new addition to my office door. Taped with one piece of Scotch tape— because apparently my dismissal isn't worth the several pieces it'd take to affix it properly to my door—is a printed sign that reads, "Dr. Kalson is on personal leave effective immediately. Any questions can be directed to Professor David Sothern, Head of Department of Psychology," and then below the memo Sheila's name is listed. Because why would David want to be bothered with 200 undergraduate students and their anxieties over end-of-semester exams?

Humiliation comes swift as a rash after being administered bargain-store Ibuprofen. No one even bothered to call me.

I check my e-mails, thinking perhaps there's an apologetic missive waiting in my inbox, full of explanations.

Nope. Nothing.

Immediately I'm down the hallway and headed straight for David's office, running through Maria's classroom visit earlier this week. Or at least parts of it.

For once, Sheila is not manning her desk, and so I am able to rush right down the middle and into one of the uncomfortable chairs I sat in just before my life turned upside down.

David—*no Professor Sothern for him, not today*—is sitting at his desk, desperately trying to eat a glazed donut without crumbs slipping down his glossy red tie.

"What the hell is this?" I ask. I snatched the poster from my door before marching down to my boss's office, which I'm now waving in his face. The poster is clutched in my hand such that David can't read it fully, but I'm sure he knows what it is. "I'm on 'personal leave?' When were you going to tell me about this?"

David takes a gulp of his coffee and does a quick reconnaissance, rubbing a hand over his mouth to make sure no derelict crumbs remain. A moment later he answers my question with a question.

"How are you doing, Kalson?"

"I'm fine, *David*. Absolutely fine." My voice squeaks on the "loo" of absolutely. And even now there's a brief moment when David shifts back in his chair, props his feet up on the desk, and I think I've persuaded him that he'll just give my classes back to me.

With his hands behind his head, David is in the exact posture I associate with almost all male academics. It's like the star pose that women are supposed to use to embolden their competitive sides, but without all the stigma. The word "manspreading" flits to mind, and I remind myself that snark has never looked good on a woman at the mercy of men.

"I think you're wrong about that."

I want to snatch his donut and eat it right in front of him.

"How so?" I ask, pitching my voice as low as possible. I consider whether a star pose in the corner of his office might not hurt.

"The police have been here to interview myself and other colleagues of yours," he begins, his forehead furrowed in concern. Despite my huff over the stupid sign and his mannerisms, I know he's trying to be kind to me.

It doesn't stop me from cutting him off, demanding to know who.

"Maria, Sheila, Doug in Cognitive Psych, and a few of your past grad teaching assistants," he lists them off, counting each on his sugar-coated fingers.

"What did they want to know?" I ask, and I try to swallow despite choking on the phantom donut.

David leans forward, his elbows perched on the table as he clasps his hands together. "This seems very serious, Kalson. You're coping with a lot right now, and I just don't see how adding the extra stress of finals week is going to help you." He looks me in the eye. "I thought you'd welcome a leave of absence, given all you've been through."

Kind eyes or not, he hasn't answered my question, but I decide not to press it. Now that I know the lay of the land—that Ormoran and Miller are sniffing around my work, interviewing my colleagues—my main goal is to get out of this meeting.

"When should I come back? And do you want me to write the exams?" I offer, recalling that just a week ago I was sitting here, being groomed for promotion. "I can do that from home, so all you'd need would be a proctor for the exam period."

David removes his feet from the desk and stares down at the glistening crescent left of his donut.

"That's awfully generous, Kalson, but I think we have it covered. Go home, get some rest, and come back to us at the beginning of the Spring semester, fresh and renewed." He tilts his head to one side. "Pending the Dean's review of your case, of course."

"Of course," I say, and offer him a curt nod.

He stands as I leave, and I watch him run his tongue over his teeth, searching for chunks of pastry lodged indelicately in his incisors, before smiling at me. "We'll miss you."

I worry he might actually wave goodbye to me—oh, and my promotion and my career, too—but he doesn't. He just closes the door.

There are two figures standing outside my office: One tall and willowy and the other short and squat. There's a bright pink purse slung over the shorter shoulder.

Indignation lights up my chest and propels me towards the two detectives before I think to restrain myself.

"What the hell are you doing here at my place of work?" I demand in a harsh whisper, hoping not to attract the attention of the other faculty. I scan my eyes down the hallway and see only one or two doors open towards the end of the hall.

"Hello, Ms. Kalson," Ormoran offers, and then gives a side-long glance to my nameplate next to my door. "I mean, *Dr.* Kalson." No hint of irony in her voice. Miller says nothing.

"Why are you here?" I ask again.

"We have a few more questions, and were hoping to talk to you. We stopped by your apartment, but your friend—Annie, is it?—said you weren't home, so we thought we'd try your office. And here you are." Ormoran smiles at me.

"I have nothing to say," I tell them, and move to put the key in my office lock.

"That's just the thing," Miller chimes in. "We're not here as a courtesy. We can either talk with you here, or we can take you down to the station and chat there. It's your choice." Miller has a pad of paper and a pen out already. I wonder what the hell she might be writing down.

I look at the sign I'm still holding in my hand after my meeting with David.

"Let's go to the station. And I want my lawyer."

33

The Youngstown City Police Department is housed just a few blocks from YSU's campus, in a building of sprawling grey stone and Victorian era carvings of gargoyles and sprites. The building served as the original courthouse for Mahoning County, before the court outgrew its original fixtures and needed to be relocated to a shiny new structure of glass and chrome just a block away. Ormoran and Miller have me ride in the back of their unmarked car, and then escort me to a small phlegm-colored room with one fluorescent light in the ceiling, a slightly off-balanced metal table, and four matching chairs. Bleak beyond words. The air smells inexplicably of cinnamon.

Dana's hair is in another elegant bun today, but her clothes are formal court attire: black pant suit and a silky blouse, sensible court shoes. When I called, I was told by her assistant she was at the courthouse for another client's arraignment. Ormoran, Miller, and I waited in awkward spurts of silence intermixed with them leaving me alone—to go to have lunch, based on the newborn smudge of washed-out ketchup on Miller's otherwise pristine shirt.

Once she got here, Dana asked to speak with me privately, and even when the room was empty except for the two of us she still leaned in to whisper in my ear that I shouldn't say anything. Just let her do the talking.

And, really, that's what I'm trying to do.

"We've been reviewing the information we downloaded from your phone—Now, Ms. Vasquez," Ormoran holds up a hand to quiet Dana's protest. "You know in Ohio we can search a phone without a warrant if there is concern for evidence being destroyed." Ormoran gives me an apologetic look. "Which we had."

She continues, "We have some very talented people in the technical side of our department, don't we, Miller?"

Miller says nothing, but does condescend to offer a slight nod.

"There's a lot of ground to cover, no doubt," Ormoran smiles as me. "You're pretty active on that thing."

Miller opens up her notebook. No huge pink purse for her in the interrogation room, apparently.

"Texts, e-mails, tweets, likes, retweets, Facebook messages, notes, to-do lists, voice memos, voice mails," Miller reads.

"Is there a question you'd like to ask my client?" Dana interjects.

Ormoran goes on. "Dr. Kalson, it's clear from the messages we read that you and Justin McBride were very close."

A wave of nausea hits and my vision blurs as I choke it back down.

Ormoran is all concern.

"Allergies," I offer, before being silenced by Dana's laser eyes.

"Sure, you'd had a fight recently. That one exchange where you were tracking him down wasn't the most pleasant thing to read." Ormoran shrugs, while Miller stares down at her notepad. "But then everybody fights."

"When did Justin break up with you?" Miller cuts in.

I take a quick sip of breath. My lawyer kicks me under the table.

"My client has nothing to say on this matter," Dana says with perfect lawyer precision.

Ormoran ignores her and keeps at me, in her calm and tender way. "You see, it turns out we didn't need his phone all that much—although we'd still like to have it, Dr. Kalson— because his laptop had most of his accounts synced up for social media, e-mail, and everything else. It was the GChats that really helped us out."

I blink. Justin and I never e-mailed. I only really use e-mail for work. And I don't know anything about GChat.

"You seem surprised." It's a statement from Miller, not a question.

"We didn't find *any* messages on that laptop from you, Dr. Kalson. Or *to* you either. It seems like Justin kept his laptop private from you. Why do you think that is?" Ormoran leans her long torso across the table, and her braids, which are loose today, fall from behind her shoulders. One strand grazes the top of the desk, and I think—just for a moment, I swear—about grabbing it and giving a hard yank.

I flash back to my memories of Justin's apartment, searching desperately for a glimpse of his laptop or computer. I don't recall seeing either. *Dammit, why didn't that strike me as odd?*

I answer myself. *Because your mind was on other things, you slut.*

Thoughts are creeping out of those dark corners.

"Don't answer that," Dana says to me. "Look, my client is here of her own free will to help your investigation, but if this is going to become a fishing expedition looking to force her to incriminate herself, I'm ending this meeting."

"You're right, Ms. Vasquez. We do appreciate your and your

client's time. We just have a few more questions, if you can stay just a little longer." Ormoran's smooth as silk, and a dangerous part of me wants to just shut down from this shit show and sink into the soft tones of her voice.

Miller shuffles up into her seat, flips back in her notebook, and starts reading from the page in front of her.

"Two days before the accident, Justin GChats a friend. Quote: 'I want to break up with Morgan so we can be together, but I'm not sure how to do it.' The *friend* writes back a few minutes later, quote: 'Just tell her and be honest. Morgan will appreciate that. She'll have to understand.'"

I know the sardonic emphasis on "friend" isn't accidental.

Every time Miller says "quote" she makes air quotation marks. Now I know why Annie wanted to slug me when I did it.

Dana shifts in her seat, and I look over to see a frown briefly cross her face before she sets her mouth back into legal counsel neutral.

For my own part, the revelation that Justin was talking about breaking up with me has no effect. It's like taking a leg that's gone asleep and stomping it on the floor to bring it back to life. It just feels numb. The pricks of pain will come later.

Miller continues, "Justin replies back almost immediately. Quote: 'You know how she is. She's so intense.' Friend—she writes back, quote: 'Intense?' And see here—this is. . ."

I interrupt Miller's recitation. "You don't need to say 'quote' every time. It's apparent from the context when something you say is a quote." I almost feel leather patches growing on my elbows. All I need is a pipe and a widow's peak.

Dana murmurs something under her breath.

Miller ignores everything and keeps reading. "Justin replies to the friend's question by, quote: (*just to annoy me now*) 'She scares me sometimes. I think she could hurt herself if I don't do it right.' He means break up with you." *As if I couldn't follow the logic.* It takes all my self-control not to punch Miller in the face when she says that.

"And that's just one example, Dr. Kalson," Ormoran says. "His laptop is littered with all sorts of similar conversations over this last week. E-mails, GChats. All with this same *friend.*"

I think back to the girl who answered the door when I was searching for Justin's office—I can't recall her name from the list of students on the makeshift nameplate outside the door.

"The friend he's chatting with this whole time is named Annie—that's your best friend's name, correct?" Miller's eyes are on mine for the first time since the interview started.

"What did you say?" I think I'm speaking in a normal voice, but when Dana puts her hand on my arm I realize I must have shouted.

"Okay, we're leaving," Dana says, and stands up in her chair, her hand still gripping my arm.

"*It was Annie?*" I ask. I feel like my brain is on fire.

"Her picture in the GChat avatar is of a white-blond woman with short hair and kind of a punky vibe. She looks very similar to the woman we met at the hospital—the friend who took you home," Ormoran offers.

"Morgan, we're leaving. . ." Dana starts to usher me to the door.

"Just wait a minute," I tell her.

"So, here's how we see it." Ormoran's talking fast now, trying to lay down her Ace before my lawyer escorts me from the room. "We think Justin had planned to break up with you on your drive this past Friday night. That's why there were no reservations at the Lodge. He was going to talk to you about it while you were both in the car, driving. Talk it over when he doesn't have to sit across from you, to avoid face-to-face. So Justin starts telling you that he cares for you, 'it's not you it's me', and you just aren't having it. You are livid—and we can totally understand that. The man had you thinking one thing, and then he goes and breaks up with you. And maybe he even tells you the truth—that he's leaving you for your best friend."

"Mmm. . ." Miller surprisingly joins in.

"Morgan," Dana says through gritted teeth, but I shake her hand off my arm. "They aren't charging you, and we need to go. They are *playing* you."

"Just go, Dana. You don't need to stay."

I think I see a silent smile pass between Ormoran and Miller.

"I'm not leaving," Dana says. "Not without you."

Ormoran goes on, "We understand why this type of behavior could just not be tolerated. So you start to let Justin know that this is not okay—you cannot just love someone, plan a romantic getaway, and then decide that is actually the perfect time to break it off and run off with your friend. You do the only thing you *could* do—you let out all your hurt onto the man who hurt you. Just like you did with Richard."

I know I should walk away from this; the detectives are baiting me, but I can't go.

Ormoran's voice is getting quieter as she's talking, now that she knows she's got my full attention.

"You're pissed—rightfully so, mind you—and letting Justin have it. And at some point, Justin gets scared and tries to call for help on his phone, and you take it and throw it out the window. And when that doesn't stop him from insisting that the two of you don't belong together, you are beside yourself." Ormoran shakes her head from side to side. And I could swear, somewhere beyond the blood pounding inside my head, that I hear her cluck her tongue in commiseration. "So your instincts kick in, and you want to hurt him, just like he hurt you. You see your opportunity as you're climbing through those windy roads. You don't want to kill him—course not, you love the man—you just want to teach him a lesson. So you see your chance with that huge tree looming up at the top of the hill. You play it safe, pretending to have calmed down a little until. . . "

The room goes quiet, Ormoran clearly hoping to conjure up twisted metal and shattered glass with her pause. But all I can think about is Annie.

"That's enough," Dana grabs me and forces me out the door.

"Thanks for talking with us, Dr. Kalson. And don't worry, Dr. Koftura isn't going to press any charges after she found you sneaking around in her office." It's the first time I've heard Ormoran's voice skew sarcastic like her partner's.

I don't have time to do much more than poorly mime nonchalance at being caught out, because Dana casts a nasty glance my way, gives my arm another forceful pull, and the two of us are outside in the hallway of the police station, alone.

"What the fuck was that all about," Dana almost spits into my face, she's so angry. We're standing outside the police station, huddled together against the cold, but still avoiding any real closeness with each other.

"I told you I'd represent you if you followed my rules. *My* rules," Dana runs a hand over her face. "What did you do?"

I pause, lots of lies tumbling over my lips but none of them sticking their landing. So I start to tell her everything. Finding Justin's parents, going into Dr. Koftura's office, and even the messages I've been receiving from Justin's phone. I lay it all out for Dana, and as I do a nuclear winter of emotions crosses her face: anger, resignation, and even, for a brief moment, pride. But as I finish recounting everything, Dana's face settles into one final reckoning.

Disappointment.

"I'm sorry, Morgan, but I can't help you," she says. "I can't work with someone who won't follow my counsel. I'm already booked beyond my capacity as it is." She nods her head towards me, her eyes not cold, but distant all the same. "Good luck to you."

I watch as Dana walks off, her court shoes clicking as she makes her way down the deserted Youngstown street and back to her office. But I don't stay too long.

I need to find Annie.

34

My lungs are about to burst as I run from the police station to my apartment. My ribs are still tender, but I push through the pain. As I run, my mind hurls backwards, looking for signs that Annie and Justin were somehow connected.

I tally up the evidence as I pull myself up Wick Avenue's hill. My legs burn viciously from not having worked them in a real run since the accident.

Annie was friends with Justin on Facebook even before I was.

Annie knew Justin was from Canfield. She said I told her all about where Justin grew up, but I don't remember telling her any of that.

And then the dumpster fire Miller set raging: *Annie and Justin were seeing each other. Messaging each other.*

Behind my back.

What if it was Annie who was at the accident? Is she the one who's been terrorizing me with Justin's phone?

There is a freight train charging through my head.

I can't run any more. I do the whole eighth grade gym class

routine—hands on knees, bent over and panting. And with my body no longer moving, my thoughts stop their kamikaze routine and find some reasonable footing again. It couldn't be Annie. She was right next to me, picking at a ham sandwich at Jean McBride's house when one of the texts came in. She couldn't have sent them, I remind myself.

Or could she?

Maybe. All dark brain static and symptom checklists aside, I have to be realistic here. Annie could be sending those messages.

If she had help.

I try to take a few steps forward, but my feet trip over each other. There are scraggly holly bushes clinging to life along the crumbling sidewalk, and I promptly vomit the farmer's breakfast Annie made for me this morning into their skeletal branches.

My best friend was fucking around with my boyfriend. And I had no clue. Not a single speck of suspicion.

If she was with Justin, and I didn't know, who else could she be with? Who else would want to hurt me?

I try to conjure up a list of Annie's friends in art school, of her ex-boyfriends and ex-girlfriends from over the years. What about the kids we shared the group home with? Could any of them dislike me enough to go along with what Annie is doing to me? The thought seems absurd, like a cruel exercise of the imagination. But so does all of this.

I run through the messages I've received since the accident. Almost all of them arrived when I was away from Annie—the only two that didn't were when we were visiting Justin's mother and afterwards in my kitchen. I'd been alone when all the others had hurled themselves onto my homescreen. And then there's the rusty Chevy running me off the road after my burrito-run. Annie was so adamant that it was just a coincidence. How did the cops know it was me who left Dr. Koftura's window unlocked? How did Dr. Koftura know, with such certainty that she'd mention it to the police? Did Annie tell her? Or did Annie tell the cops, and they went and informed Dr. Koftura themselves?

One good thing about downtown Youngstown is that nobody is ever walking around, so at least the sidewalks are totally deserted when I decide to curl up in a ball on the concrete. The ground is so cold it sends a sliver of pain up the side of my thigh and into my chest.

Why? I ask myself. *Why would Annie do this to me?*

With all the questions ricocheting around in my head, it's this one that rises to the surface with the sharp bite of recognition.

And the answer is too awful to bear.

She blames me for Justin's death.

The reality of what this means slams down onto me with such force that everything around me goes silent. All I can hear is that violent buzzing in my ears.

Because losing Justin is nothing compared to losing Annie.

A gust of wind whips itself over the freeway overpass bridge and almost buffets me into the street. I'm thinking, of all things, about Patty and Dave, the couple who wanted to adopt me. Until they didn't. Until they decided, when it got too hard, that I wasn't worth keeping.

There's a metal bar that runs along where the sidewalk and the bridge join, and with the snow that fell last night I should know to avoid stepping on it.

There's a lot of things I should know to avoid at this point in my life.

That's the thought running through my head as my foot

makes contact with the metal threshold, and for the second time on this godforsaken walk back to my apartment, I am making contact with the slush-ridden concrete. I've landed flat on my back, my bag cast askew to my side. I feel a shadow cross over my face from the winter-bright sun that's still streaming through a gray layer of cloud, much like it did in my bedroom this morning before Annie threw open the curtains.

"Are you okay?" someone says, and a shiver of fear runs down my spine because, for a moment, I actually think it is Annie. That she's followed me. But I focus my eyes on the upside-down face peering at me from beneath a woolen cap with a strange Fair Isle pattern in sunset hues. It is probably the ugliest accessory I've ever seen.

The woman's hat is drawn down against the cold, obscuring most of her forehead. There are worry lines in her face that are made more prominent by the stark winter light. Her eyes, which are set a little further apart than would allow for her to be pretty, are a startling color of green with a ring of gold around her pupil. As she leans over me, her inverted face, mouth coming at me first, and then nose and eyes, makes her look like a monster. It reminds me of an experiment I read about in graduate school, where babies preferred to look at images that depicted the array of a normal human face and avoided looking at the inverse of that, with the two eyes at the bottom, and nose and mouth at the top. My professor had explained that this showed how human beings are hardwired to force the world into patterns that are familiar to us, even if the fit isn't quite right.

The woman reaches out a mitten-clad hand towards me.

"Here, let me help. You took quite a fall, didn't you?" Her voice sounds hoarse, as though she's recovering from a nasty cold, or has spent the last twenty years smoking non-stop. I ignore her hand and pull myself up.

"I'm fine." I try to offer her a smile that is relatively normal. "Thank you for the help," I manage.

I reach down to grab my bag, but the woman has already rescued it from the puddle of slush and salt that it fell into on the overpass. She gives it a quick brush off with her hand. "No trouble at all. Be careful, now. People drive way too fast on this overpass as it is, let alone when someone is sliding off into the road."

I take my bag from her and nod in agreement. I can't manage anything else.

She might call something out to me again, across the buzzing traffic of the freeway below us, but I don't turn.

I'm already gone.

35

W hen I arrive at my apartment, Annie is in the bathroom and her phone is on the kitchen counter. I set down my purse, put my own phone into the back pocket of my jeans, and snatch hers up like a greedy toddler with a jar of Nutella. Annie and I know each other's passcodes, not just because we see each other enter them in all the time, but because we share the same one. It's 10508. October 5, 2008. The day she and I met in the attic room of our group home.

After I enter the code, Annie's home screen glows back at me accusingly. The backdrop photo is a picture of us a few years ago, our arms wrapped around each other's necks and our faces tan from a trip we'd just taken to the Jersey shore. My heart gives a lurch.

The underarms of my shirt are drenched.

I open up her e-mail first, and do a quick scan of her sent folder, looking for any iterations with identifying markers of Justin in the address: JMcBride, McBride, Justin, JMB. Nothing comes up. I click over to her trash folder, thinking that perhaps she's deleted all their correspondence but forgotten to empty the folder. The folder is empty.

The bathroom door creaks open and before I can put the phone down, Annie sees me.

"I didn't hear you come back," she says cautiously.

"I just did." I take a few steps away from her phone, which I've put back on the counter. As if physically distancing myself from it somehow erases her seeing it in my hands a few seconds ago. *Magic.*

"What were you doing with my phone?" Annie tries on a smile, but her eyes don't match her mouth.

"Nothing." I might as well smear metaphorical Nutella all over my face. I am petulant.

"What's going on?" Annie's face takes on a look of concern, and she moves towards me, her hands outstretched as though she wants to pull me towards her. "Did something happen at work?"

Liar Liar Liar. That freight train is back, charging ahead.

"How long had you been messaging Justin?"

"*What?*" There's a slight panic to Annie's voice. "What *are* you talking about?" Her face is deathly pale.

"The police have messages between you and Justin. Talking about how he was frightened of me. How he wanted to break up with me so he could be with you."

As I'm talking, the tension in Annie's body seems to slacken just a little. She looks almost relieved. But then she starts talking again.

"That is *fucking* ridiculous! How could you even think that?"

I'm staring her down, reading her tells. She might be cursing, but Annie doesn't look angry. Clammy skin and jittery hands tell me one thing. She's scared.

Good.

"But what about the messages?"

"*What* messages? When did you talk to the police?"

I don't answer, and Annie fills the void.

"Oh my God, they are *playing* you! The police are goddamn liars. I would never hurt you. You know that." There are beads of sweat breaking out at the hairline on her forehead. She looks awful. "I didn't even like him."

I used to think all of that was true.

"But you and Justin were friends on Facebook," I try, feeling more and more pathetic with each word coming out of my mouth.

Annie smiles, and this time it makes its way to her eyes as well. "Because of you, Morgan. He sent me a friend request, and I must have seen it before you saw his request."

I *so* want to believe her, and the pulsing of blood in my ears is becoming softer the more that Annie assures me all of this is just a hoax. A ploy by the cops to try and distance us from each other in order to make us weaker.

Survive and thrive.

"I'm sorry," I say, shame coming on strong and pungent like a cheap perfume. "I don't know what's happening." I push some stray hairs behind my ear. I still have my coat and scarf on, but a shiver skims up my spine all the same.

Annie moves a little closer to me, but hesitates before she tries to touch me. "I think it might be time to get you some help." Her voice is so, so quiet, and the tension in her vocal cords sings across the still air around us.

"What kind of help?" I don't want to know. I've had enough of doctors for one lifetime.

"Maybe you need to talk to someone, you know? Maybe there's some medicine that can help you."

Annie is still holding her arms out, waiting for me to let her come closer, like I'm a cornered animal who might bite her.

"So you've never met him?" I ask, not sure exactly why I need this confirmation given everything else we'd just covered, but wanting it nonetheless.

"No, never. You know that."

But, as she's talking, I see Annie's eyes involuntarily glance at her phone.

There's something she's not telling me.

I'm still closer to her phone than she is, and before she can grab it, I've taken it and run around my kitchen table, through my small living room, and into my bedroom. I don't stop to close the door, I'm so desperate to see what Annie wants to hide from me.

I frantically put in the passcode and click onto the photos app.

Because, just like Ormoran and Miller said, our generation needs to document everything.

But before the pictures can come up, Annie is in my face, her mouth twisted into a contortion of anguish and something else.

Maybe resentment, I think, just as she makes a grab for the phone from my hand.

"Give it to me—let me explain!"

I shove her away, more convinced now than ever that my life is over.

A growing fury presses on my chest. My arms feel hollow, like they have no bones, but I manage to hold Annie back with my one hand as I scroll through her photos. Most of them are of her pieces of artwork—huge, sprawling canvases with bright slashes of color that dance across the white background—but there are others interspersed throughout with people, flowers, and food. I'm looking for one face in particular.

Annie scrambles against me, growing more desperate with each passing second. She's screaming my name, begging me to give her the phone back. She's shouting every four-letter word in the English language.

She starts to scratch at my hand and leaves a deep gash in my left arm that echoes the scratches that are still healing from the accident. I turn to look at what she's done as the pain rips up my arm, and Annie takes the opportunity to wrap her arms around me in a bear hug and squeeze as hard as she can to try and get me to drop her phone.

I can't let her get it, and so I try to twist my body around to push her up against the door or my dresser to knock her off me.

But we are too far from either of them. The only piece of furniture close enough for me to brace against is the mirror standing in the corner of my bedroom. The one I'd looked into Monday afternoon, less than a week ago, as Annie ran a bath for me, to survey the damage Justin had done.

I see us in the mirror. My best friend, my companion through the hellhole of navigating life as a child without anyone who wanted you or loved you, is straddled across my back, her arms slung around me and her face bright red as she struggles to topple me over. I barely recognize my own face.

We look like two people who have hated each other for a long time.

When I slam our two bodies into the mirror, the sound is catastrophic. The glass of the mirror shatters, and the frame's cheap wood cracks under the pressure. It snaps like twigs under a Girl Scout's feet, short and crisp. Annie's arms go limp around me, and I struggle to first sit, then stand up.

Her phone is still in my hands. I scan through the pictures as quickly as I can, and find it all too easily now that I don't have Annie trying to fight her phone away from me.

Dated almost two weeks ago, there is a picture of Annie and Justin together. Their arms are around each other, and both smile into the camera. There are a few familiar neon signs in the background that tell me the photo was taken up in Cleveland at the Flats, the strip of bars, shops, and restaurants that Annie and I love to go to when I visit her.

There's no static inside my head. Only silence.

Annie's sprawled on the floor next to my broken mirror. There's a cut on her forehead that's begun to bleed, and a few scratches up and down her arms.

"Morgan," she says, her voice a mixture of an accusation and a request.

I don't answer her. I don't grab a towel to staunch the blood coming from her forehead. I don't try to pick her up and move her away from the debris of our fight.

Instead, I throw her phone down on the ground, the photo of her and Justin glaring from the screen, and I run.

From Annie. From my apartment. From my life.

And I hate myself for it.

36

I take off at a sprint, the adrenaline ripping through my body in large enough quantities that it shames the pain of my still healing ribs into silence. I don't pay attention to where I'm heading. I just keep running until finally my lungs and legs give in, wobbling like wet noodles.

I stop and try to catch my breath in embarrassingly large and noisy gasps of air, but all I can see is Annie, bloody and broken on my bedroom floor. Nothing is getting into my lungs. They are the Fort Knox of pulmonary guilt.

I try to focus my gaze on the horizon, but it's blocked by large trees still barren from the winter drought and a playground of primary-colored slides and swings. Little sips of breath find their way in as I recognize where I am: Wick Park.

The park is old, and not really used anymore. Most families have escaped to the suburbs, becoming Route 680 commuters who work in Youngstown, only to scurry back to their little three bedrooms in Boardman or Poland. Or Canfield.

There's an elderly man walking a massive German Shepherd, whose muzzle is the salt and pepper of his owner's gray beard. A woman with a long, rumpled coat slumps over on a bench, the red and orange of her hat the only thing keeping her from smudging into the drab surroundings. Otherwise, the park is deserted.

I watch the man bend down to give a loving scratch behind the dog's ears, and something cracks inside me at the gentleness of it all. People love dogs.

My phone vibrates inside my back pocket and I freeze, wanting to fling it across the park. Wanting someone to just scratch me behind my ears and take care of me.

But neither is an option.

I walk further into the park, trying to steel myself, and when I finally do pull my phone out and look down, the notification must have disappeared from my screen when my thumb touched the home button, because I'm back on my home screen again. I stifle a scream that's been rising in my throat since I woke up in the hospital a week ago.

I am on fire. Everything is burning and burning, and nothing makes sense.

I fumble with the notification menu, but my phone seems stuck.

A quick glance at the reception bars tells me that I am in a dead zone, so I walk a little further down the sidewalk, away from the older man and towards the playground. My phone captures another bar, and the notification appears.

"Find Your Friends has been updated."

I dismiss the notification with an angry flick of my thumb, and start to pace the sidewalk. The man with the dog has disappeared, but the woman on the bench is still there, all shades of tweaker post bump: shoulders hunched, hands buried deep in her pockets, face hidden underneath her garish hat. All I can see peeking out is a droopy smile.

Annie. Justin. Ormoran and Miller.

There's something tugging at the back of my mind, pleading

me to pay attention to it, but I can't get my thoughts to shimmer out of the smoke.

My phone vibrates in my hand.

Text from Justin: *You can't run away from me.*

I take off in another directionless sprint, bound and determined to prove her wrong. To prove Annie wrong, because she's the one who sent that message.

I'm certain now.

My feet pound down the sidewalk, taking me from the center of the park to the small parking lot at the edge, surrounded by a grouping of ancient elm trees. The lot itself only holds three parking spaces, and the blacktop is a roiling mess of potholes and crumbling gravel. A single car is parked there, dilapidated grey mixed with cauliflower patches of brown paint and rust. The Chevy insignia catches the low winter sun. The license plate reads L38 4G82.

Static roars inside my head. Flames gobble up my insides.

I know this car.

It's the same car that almost ran me over on Fifth Avenue.

I stop, pivot, and hurl myself away from the parking lot.

But someone grabs my shoulder, keeping me from twisting around, followed by a bright slice of pain to the back of my neck. The cool metal slams into the pressure point at the base of my skull. My boots scrabble in the gravel like I'm the star of my own after-school special.

Until they stop.

37

W hen I come to, my hands are tied behind me with the rope looped through the back of an old wicker chair. A wave of nausea washes over me as my concussed head mingles with the terror pricking at the back of my skull.

The seat of the chair has been punched through, and my legs and hips sag into the depression left by the faulty weaving. I know this type of chair. One of my foster homes had chairs like this.

One night I watched the mother of the house sit down forcefully for dinner, after having just yelled at me and the other kids there to "shut the fuck up," only to hear the satisfying "plop" of her backside as it fell through the wicker weave of the seat.

Looking around the room I'm in, I work to suppress the supernova-sized ball of fear I feel, and instead get my bearings.

Survive and thrive.

A small hint of light seeps through the curtains, which comprise a brown burlap hung from an old drapery strip on one window and a sheet with a pattern that suggests India by way of Chinese mass production stapled to the top of a window frame.

The air smells of rotting newspaper, mildew, and cigar smoke. I can make out a stack of rusted cans, with markings that look like they were used decades ago to varnish the floors. A quick survey of the floor shows that whatever was done didn't last or wasn't completed. Underneath the coating of dust, the floor was composed of jagged boards in desperate need of a sanding.

This house has good bones. The thought involuntarily crosses my mind, some TLC-watching version of myself invading my grim reality. Until the word *bones* sends another bolt of fear up my spine.

I try to move my legs, but they are also tied individually to the legs of my derelict chair. I look down to see if my phone is in my pocket, but my lap appears empty. Even if it was there, I don't know how I'd actually get hold of it. When I struggle to try and shift my arms into a more comfortable position, a voice from behind me calls out.

"You might as well make yourself comfortable."

The figure comes from around me. It's the woman who bumped into me on the freeway overpass, and then later waited for me in the park. And she's still wearing that fucking orange and red hat.

That's what the bonfire in my head was trying to point out, back in the park.

I am so, so stupid.

Even in the dim light, the green of her eyes is vivid. Her hair runs in dark ringlets over her shoulders. When she pauses to pull the hat off and unceremoniously tosses it onto a stack of old newspapers, frizzy strands escape around her scalp in a corona of frayed ends. She's wearing a large grey sweatshirt with what looks like oil stains strewn across the front, and her jeans fit loosely over her stringy frame. She offers me a smile as we come face-to-face, and her teeth have the yellowed tinge that comes from years of smoking.

Silently, she holds up my phone, the white and black of its zebra case facing me.

She leans closer to me, and whispers in my ear, "What is it, then?"

She's asking for my passcode, of course. This woman wants to get into my phone. To do what, I'm not exactly sure yet.

Her breath tickles my ear, sickly sweet.

This is Annie's partner, I realize, and for a moment I consider whether it was my quinoa salads that turned Annie against me. Maybe if I'd eaten more Little Debbie snacks. . .

"It's a pattern, not a set of numbers," I lie. "I can't describe it —I'll need my hands to do it." I wriggle my arms behind me, making my point like some kinky mime. "I don't think I can do it from behind and upside-down, though."

"Pity," the woman says. She makes for my hands, and a hot flash of adrenaline rips through me. *That was easy.*

"Oh, hang on." She's back in front of me, dangling the phone in front of my face again. It's unlocked, the little orbs of my different apps glowing from the home screen. "I'm already in." A Cheshire cat smile spreads across her sallow face. "I just wanted to see what you'd do." She turns around and walks towards what looks, in the dim light, like the kitchen. "Liar," she murmurs before disappearing through the opening into the other room.

Of course she knew my passcode. *Annie had told her.*

I pull at my ropes again, and feel a promising crackle come from the chair. Before I can do anything, though, she's returned, holding a glass of water in one hand and my phone in the other.

"Find Your Friends," she says, her eyes level on mine. A metal fist twists in my stomach. "Isn't that such a sweet name?" She cocks an eyebrow at me. "Once Justin connected you to his phone, it was so easy to keep track of you."

My mind races to make sense of what she is saying.

Justin. Annie. Justin and Annie.

"Although. . ." She leans in close again, and I grit my teeth in order to resist the urge to slam my forehead against hers. "We aren't friends, are we?"

She goes on. "I just needed to make sure you weren't connected with anyone else. Especially since Justin's here with me."

My heart lurches.

But then she reaches down and pulls his phone—red cover and "I Voted" sticker intact—out of the kangaroo pouch in the front of her sweatshirt. She strokes her fingers over the cover, tracing the edges of the sticker gently with her fingertips.

She was there, at the crash.

"What did you do?" I shout, the unexpected loss of the possibility she dangled bringing a strange new rush of grief.

Her head jolts up, her pupils wild dark pools of bitterness. "You were the one who was supposed to die. He should be here. *With me.*"

The woman juts her chin out, the expression on her face shifting from bright contempt into something with softer edges and a deeper, blacker center. Her lips move into the anguished bow of disgust.

And then I see it. The traces of him in the set of her jaw, the cut of her cheekbones. Something snaps into place in my mind.

"You're Justin's mother."

She starts, as if from a stupor, and gives me that feline smile again.

"Legally that's Jean McBride," she says, her voice tepid. She takes a sip of her water. My mouth is parched and my head's begun to throb at the base where she knocked me unconscious. "But I'm Justin's *real* mother." That flash of hot white anger in her voice again. And just as quickly, she settles back into her chair, rubbing her shoulder bones against the wooden slats as she relaxes her body.

Even though I know in every neuron in my body that I need to hold my shit together, I can't stop the terror from rising up my throat and out of my mouth. "Were you there? Were you there at the accident?"

She absorbs my questions without a single movement or twitch. *She's not worried at all*, the truth pings around my skull. I think of Justin, and Jean, and Justin's dead dog, and my mind works itself over to what I know about the genetics of psychopathy personality disorder. This woman, Justin's mother, looks as though she could be waiting for her favorite television show to come on, or standing in line at the grocery store.

I can't find any sign that she is nervous about what she is about to do.

Because I'm certain now.

Justin's mother is going to kill me.

For the first time in my entire life, I am thrilled to realize that I'm about to throw up. It lands on the front of my sweater, the tops of my thighs, and a few beads settle into the frizzy halo of the woman's head.

I may have aimed in her direction.

My captor reaches up to touch her hair, a grimace working at her mouth, and then abruptly slaps me across the face with the back of her right hand. A diamond or some other gem cuts into my face, and the warm pulse of blood oozing from my skin confirms that she's cut me with her ring. I try to straighten my face again, to see the jewel on her finger and what it might tell me about her—whether it might confirm that this house, her car, the outfit she's wearing, is some sort of persona she's playing at—but the sleeves of her nasty sweatshirt are longer than her arms and the cuffs naturally lie as cover over the tops of her hands.

"You always were a little cunt," her voice remains soothing. "Such a grasping, demanding cunt. Always wanting more."

It's the word "always" that catches at the corners of my skull. *She knows me*, I realize. *She's known me for some time.*

She's busying herself with something in her kangaroo pocket, and so I have a few moments to think through the parade of foster parents I had over the years. Bible-thumping charity seekers, barren couples testing the waters of adoption, those just in it for the "easy" money. The ones I can remember, at least, because the first few placements I had are trapped in the supposed trauma-induced amnesia of my placement into care in the first place (or so sayeth Dr. Koftura).

None of them draw a tendon to the woman holding me captive. To Justin's mother.

But of course, I want to throttle myself, *why would she be a foster parent? She had her child* taken *from her. Think, Morgan. Think!*

"I can't believe I've got you here, finally," her voice cuts in, the sound like sandpaper over stone.

"Who are you?" I ask again, because a name would expedite things in my mind.

"Call me Marlene," she says, smiling sweetly into my face. "Does that suit you?"

I hold my tongue from saying that nothing about this situation really suits me. Maybe Marlene is right—maybe I am a cunt.

"You said you wanted to help me. In your texts." I picture the messages from Justin's phone, the phone that Marlene now has tucked away into her vast sweatshirt. "Marlene, I need your help." I'm trying to rub the remnants of my expectorant from my cheeks and onto the shoulders of my sweater, but it's no use. And then, as if to prove that she was some kind of mother, once, she pulls a tissue from inside the sleeve of her sweatshirt and wipes at my face. I jerk away at her touch at first, but she clucks her tongue and tells me to be still.

The tissue is not fresh, and smells of something sour.

"Why should I help you?" Marlene says when she's finished cleaning my face.

I stare at her for a moment. She turns the broken wicker chair she's sitting in around, the back facing towards me and her legs spread like a baseball manager across the seat. She leans the billowing arms of her shirt against the top of the frame. As she does so another distinctive crackle emanates, this time from her chair.

I glance around the room and notice a few things I hadn't noticed before. Sure, there's her diamond ring, which I can see poking out from the folds of her hands. It sparkles, even in the dim light. Her hair is frizzy, but the color beneath the frizz is a rich auburn that doesn't occur in the natural world. I think back to her water glass, which wasn't really a glass at all. It was the bottom of a Nalgene water bottle. Her shoes, beneath the stained sweatshirt and ill-fitting jeans, are new, puffy Reebok sneakers. They are entirely white and without a stain of salt or a scratch from misuse on them.

It's as though she's wearing a costume. As though Marlene is playing at being poor.

But why?

"It might be about time for us to move along to the next stage," Marlene says.

A trickle of ice runs through my chest.

My phone rings.

38

Marlene pulls my phone from her pocket—the never-ending kangaroo pouch—and reads the incoming call. It's a normal ring, not the strains of Tori Amos, so I know it isn't Annie.

Annie. My mind stutters at her name. *Does Marlene know what I did to Annie?*

"Speak of the devil, and he will appear," Marlene chirps as she looks at my phone, a laugh suddenly playing at the tip of her voice. "Or, in this case, *she*. It's your Detective Ormoran." She holds the phone up to me, and I see a plain number flashing up. "Or maybe Detective Miller."

I freeze, my jaw slack, and Marlene must think I'm surprised that she knows who's calling just from the number, because she explains, "I memorized the Youngstown Police numbers a long time ago."

But that isn't what's throwing me. It's that phrase that's set my mind on fire, déjà vu seeping into every cell.

Her voice has changed over the years, morphing into a caricature of what it once was. Of the voice I've been hearing in my head for my entire life. But the words. The words are the same.

Marlene pulls her chair closer, scooting the legs of it across the dusty floor towards me. My phone keeps ringing and the screen flashes its connection to the outside world. Even though it is so close that I can almost touch it with my bound fingertips, I don't care. Right now, all I want to do is look at her.

Her eyes level on me, the look on her face appraising.

She is still only a few inches from me, and I am near enough that I can see once again the gold circle flanked by green in the iris of her eye. Looking at her, hearing her voice—memories long-dead burble to the surface.

I know those eyes. I remember how they looked at me with a mixture of hatred and ambivalence. Just like they are doing now.

What's your play, Morgan?

I know fear. I knew it when I heard tires squealing and felt my small, seven-year-old body slap up against the windshield of the oncoming car. I held it in my mouth when Patty and Dave said they wouldn't keep me, and it swallowed me whole as Justin veered the car into that massive tree. But I've never felt anything like this before. Primal, smelling of iron and licked batteries. Bloody and electric.

Survive and thrive.

The words burst into my mind, pummeling the panic threatening to take me over.

I have to do this.

"I'm sorry for whatever I did," I tell her.

She glances up from where her eyes had drifted, to a distant corner of the room.

"No, but you will be," she tells me calmly. I swear I hear a hint of resignation tugging at her voice.

I keep going.

"Mom, I'm so sorry."

She flinches at the endearment. But her face holds something more than just darkness and pain. Or the rough friction of malice. There's a hint of pride at the corners of those eyes I knew so well. Once.

"So you've figured it out," is all she says.

Almost, I think, but I don't say.

The silence sits between us for a few breaths. Almost companionable. Until I can't wait any longer. Because a deep, dark worry has hatched and is creeping out of its shell. I have to know.

"Was Justin my. . ." I begin. His name tastes like ash in my mouth.

I try again. "You're my mother," I say, over-enunciating the words to keep my voice calm. "And I didn't have any siblings. . ."

I watch her carefully, and when I see pity flit across my mother's face, I know. But I need her to say it, anyway.

She leans forward in her chair, her elbows pressed into her thighs in a way that reminds me of Detective Ormoran. "Justin was my *son*. And you were—excuse me, *are*—my *daughter*. The two of you were half-siblings. I'm not quite sure who your fathers are." She says this matter-of-factly, and as she gestures with her hands the diamond in her ring manages to glint in the dim light. "Although I'm certain you both don't have the same father. Loving men like that is too much work, and I had plenty to keep me busy already."

We sit in silence for a moment. I feel like I have no skin.

Or, rather, I *wish* I had no skin.

Because every part of me is marked. My arms, my legs, my neck and breasts—every part of me bears the stain of Justin's touch.

My brother's touch.

I manage a "Why?" between my clenched teeth. A surge of energy rushes up inside of me, and I rail against my restraints, flailing my arms and banging my wrists on the ugly, decrepit chair I'm tied to. Like I'm trying to shake myself out of my body.

Inside that syllable lives so many questions. *Why did Justin pretend to fall in love in with me? Why don't I remember having a brother? Why did no one tell me?*

Does Annie know?

Marlene stares at me as I have my little fit, her expression placid. When I've finished, hands and legs still tied to the chair, she reaches out to smooth a strand of hair behind my ear.

I valiantly resist the urge to bite her.

"Why?" She repeats my question, her face an emotionless mask.

The blow comes swiftly from the side, smashing into my right temple. She uses something harder than muscle and bone. The metal makes a dull thud as it connects with my skull. Blood trickles down through my hair, its warmth spreading across my scalp and underneath the collar of my sweater. I can't see clearly through my right eye, but my left eye spies Marlene place something back into the pocket of her sweatshirt.

It's a gun.

"You didn't deserve him," she says quietly, and despite the lack of volume to her voice the fury embedded in it electrifies the air. "He shouldn't have died—*you* should be dead, not him."

I wait, still stunned by the violence of the last few moments.

I listen.

Talking hasn't done much for me so far.

Just like I did a few minutes ago, full on shudders start to wrack Marlene's body. Her shoulders flop up and down like a gutted fish as she heaves, and words spill rapidly from her mouth. I have to turn my left ear towards her in order to catch all of what she is saying, because my right ear is plugged with the blood draining from the gash my mother has made in my skull.

"It was because of that stupid article you wrote. None of this would have happened if you hadn't shown up with that awful smirk on your face, acting as though you knew better than everyone else. Acting as though you didn't have a mother who taught you *everything*!"

Spittle flies from her mouth on the last word.

It dawns on me, like turning on a light after stumbling around in blackened rooms for hours. She's talking about my op-ed personal comments in the *Plain Dealer* this past summer. I scan back in my mind to what I'd written, and the photo that they featured with it. It was just the same faculty headshot that my department uses on their website. I was smiling in it. Just a normal smile.

The opinion piece mentioned lots of things. Foster care. Group homes. Shuttling myself back and forth between "placements" and sometimes not knowing where I was going to sleep from one night to the next. Never having anything that was my own. I spoke about how I ended up going to college, graduate school, and my work as a professor at Youngstown State helping students from backgrounds similar to mine.

I'm trying to make sense of why *that* article—this piece of pseudo-journalism that I wrote in one Sunday afternoon after a long, reminiscent talk with Annie—would bring my mother back into my life.

It didn't mention anything about my mother, because I didn't remember anything worth mentioning.

Oh my God.

A siren blares across my thoughts.

She wanted credit for what I've become.

She *wants* credit.

As if reading my thoughts, Marlene jerks her head up from where it had sunk, in an arc towards her chest, and she takes a long look at me.

I wait, wondering if I should say something. Maybe if I apologize for leaving her out, for forgetting her, she'll let me go. And this will all be over.

But there's no way I am going to apologize to this woman. I'd rather die.

You might just get your wish, I remind myself.

She wipes at her face and takes a long swig from her water bottle. I watch her as she shakes her shoulders and her head, as if she's clearing her mind.

"Now, you know that little article isn't the entire story, don't you?"

She takes another sip from her bottle.

"Revenge is an excellent motivator, isn't it, sweetheart?" The word oozes out of her mouth.

When I don't respond, she says it again, softer still. "Isn't it?"

I nod in response, and stutter out, "Yes. Yes, it is."

Marlene nods and then stands to start pacing the floor as she talks. "You see, when your brother pushed you into the street because you were being a little *cunt*—just like you always were —and that car hit you, one of our neighbors called the ambulance, and then when the emergency medical technicians came they called the cops. While you were recovering like a queen in that hospital bed, my entire life was collapsing. The drugs, the dealers, the clients—I owed a lot of money. And they took it out on me in prison." She pauses in front of my chair and puts both hands on either side of me. I brace for her to hit me again, but I also scan for a weak spot; somewhere I can grab my mother with my teeth and make her stop. But she sees me looking, and instinctively backs away from me.

"I lived like that for years," she goes on, now several feet away from me. "All because you wouldn't listen to your brother."

I can't reach her now.

My mind whirs inside my skull, working at putting the

puzzle pieces into place. So far, I only have the edges framing in the full picture, with the middle image fuzzy and undetermined.

Marlene is my mother and a drug dealer. Justin is my half-brother.

My chest spasms involuntarily again. I force myself to keep thinking.

When I was seven years old, I was struck by a car because Justin pushed me into the road, and then I was taken into child protective services.

Almost twenty years later, Marlene and Justin plan to have me fall in love with him and then die in what appears to be a car accident.

Afterwards, when Justin died instead of me and the police are closing in on their case against me, I find myself kidnapped by my mother and tied to a chair in this desolate building.

And Annie, I think suddenly, picturing her bleeding on my bedroom floor because of what I did to her. *Where does Annie come in?*

I look at my mother, and wonder how much of who I am is because of her.

A door slams from the direction of the kitchen. With it, a gust of cold air billows into the room, rousing the makeshift curtains and the hairs on my head not stuck to the side of my temple with my drying blood.

"Marlene?" a voice calls, and the tenor of it provokes a reflex in my body. One of feeling safe. But I can't place it, the wind from the door and the strange acoustics of the room distorting the sound, until I see a figure emerge from the shadows into the fading light of my captive room.

The figure—a woman, I can tell, by her build and gait—is staring at me intently. I can't see her face yet, because she is almost entirely backlit. She takes another step forward when she speaks, her voice more familiar now that she is talking in the same room I'm in. "What did you do? You were supposed to wait for me!"

"You were gone a long time," Marlene says, the calm of her voice replaced with an irritated urgency. She jerks her head over her shoulder to cast a sideways glance at the figure in the doorway.

"I had things I needed to take care of," the woman says, and as she moves further from the window and into the light, her face and voice connect.

It's Dr. Koftura.

39

"**M**organ, how are you?" Dr. Koftura makes as if she's going to approach me, her hands reaching to scan the bloody matting on the side of my head, but I jerk away from her.

"Okay, okay," she moves back, arms raised in a signal of surrender and an unfamiliar bite to her voice. "I know you must be scared. I was just trying to help."

My mouth is too dry to spit on her and her false concern. Because, even though I don't understand everything that is happening, seeing her with my mother sends a depth charge to the deepest places of my brain—the ones even Dr. Koftura couldn't touch—and the echo that comes back has confirmed one thing: that she is here to kill me. That Dr. Koftura has wanted to do that for a long time.

I just need to figure out why.

"Have you heard from the cops?" Marlene asks Dr. Koftura.

"That's what took me so long." When Dr. Koftura talks to Marlene, everything about her—her voice, her posture, her polished presence—shifts into something hard and sharp. "I needed to go into the station for some more questioning—it seems Morgan had to be manhandled out of her last interview by her lawyer. I made it clear in my follow-up meeting that erratic behavior is expected with her condition. They don't know where she is, and they don't know anything about *you*." She nods towards Marlene.

"Good," Marlene takes in a sharp breath. "So, is it time?" A quiver escapes my mother's throat, which she tries to cover with a cough.

Because she's not in charge here, I realize.

Dr. Koftura is.

"Stop talking for one moment," Dr. Koftura's tone is vicious, and I watch as Marlene cowers slightly in response. "Just let me think for a moment." My doctor scans me in the way she's done so many times before in her office, but this time her eyes catch on the visible wounds left by my mother. "You weren't supposed to leave any marks on her."

Marlene looks at the ground, and mumbles. "I'm sorry. She just . . . you know, got to me."

"I can't say I'm surprised," Dr. Koftura cuts in. Her face is devoid of kindness. Her shoulders are squared back, and she seems to move her body in fits and starts. There's no fluidity to her.

"Did you take care of everything else, at least?" Dr. Koftura asks, annoyance gripping at the edges of her voice.

My mother pulls her hands from her pocket and waves my phone, the screen black and dull. "All set."

Dr. Koftura gives a quick nod. She reaches for Marlene's shoulder and shifts her to the side so that she can sit down on the chair instead. Marlene's hands go back into her pocket, as does my phone.

"I bet you have a lot of questions," Dr. Koftura says to me.

I nod my head. I do. But I'm also playing for time.

I twist my hands behind my back, and the creak that

emerges sounds as though the bones of my wrists are made of cornflakes. I add a shout of pain to accompany it.

"Shall I start from the beginning?" Dr. Koftura ignores me and adjusts the hem of her tailored button-down shirt. She's wearing large gold hoop earrings. She must have left her coat in the kitchen, because she doesn't have it in her hands or hanging on the back of the chair. "I'm sure your mother told you that my husband was an addict?"

At my blank stare, she clucks her tongue like a displeased aunt and turns her gaze on Marlene, who stands to the side. A bead of sweat traces the side of her cheek.

"My husband had an illness, which many people chose to exploit." Dr. Koftura shakes her head with the practiced grace of an enabler. I saw this plenty of times in some of the foster homes where I lived, one parent caring for the other, making excuses for the bottles and pills and slamming doors. Missed appearances at work and disappearing grocery money.

"After he overdosed, I discovered that he'd put our family into terrible debt. And your mother, who was his dealer—right, Marlene?" Dr. Koftura's teeth bite into the consonants of my mother's name. My mother stares at me and gives a subtle nod. "She wanted to help me. She suggested I went into the business myself. Opioids were all the rage—up and coming designer drugs back then—and I had access to them by the cartload in my practice. But before Marlene and I could set up shop, you got hit by a car and your entire family imploded." Dr. Koftura rubs her hand over her lips, makes a small smacking noise, and continues. "And did I mention that before you got hit, Marlene had threatened to expose my husband and tarnish his reputation if I didn't help her?" She glances over to Marlene. "No, I didn't think you would," she says to my mother.

Marlene gives a slight shake of her head, but her expression is fuzzy and her eyes are trained on the empty space between Dr. Koftura and me.

"So how lucky I was to be attending in the emergency room the very night you got hit by a car and brought in for treatment. What a happy coincidence!" Dr. Koftura glances over at my mother, whose face has gone pale. For a moment, my mother's gaze narrows to a knife's edge on Dr. Koftura's face. But then I see her catch herself.

So does Dr. Koftura.

"Oh, Marlene. Don't look so *betrayed*. They never caught the driver of the car, did they, so we just need to look at it as an act of fate. Especially since that driver may have been aiming for *both* your children, until Justin made it that much easier by pushing Morgan into the road."

Dr. Koftura takes in a deep breath, and grimaces. "The air in here is disgusting," she says, pursing her mouth at the decay surrounding us.

She turns her gaze to Marlene. "Do something about it."

I watch as something passes over my mother's face.

When she fails to move, Dr. Koftura repeats her demand.

"Now!" she adds impatiently.

After a moment, my mother wordlessly shifts from her spot, her hands cradled in the pocket of her sweatshirt. Dr. Koftura winks at me as Marlene heads into the kitchen, past the cluster of paint and varnish cans. I hear the faucet running for a long time.

"And so our long-standing doctor-patient relationship began, and it was a good run, wasn't it, Morgan?" She actually smiles at me here. A small sliver of me still wants to smile back, but I keep my mouth flat, my eyes on hers.

"Now, did your mother mention that your brother was also a patient of mine?" She takes in my expression, which must not be as expressionless as I think it is.

A shadow passes over the entrance to the kitchen, but Dr. Koftura doesn't notice. The faucet is still running in the background.

"Oh, you already knew that, didn't you? Did little Jean McBride tell you?" Dr. Koftura reaches out and pats my knee. Her touch burns through the cloth of my jeans and into my skin. "You should know he wasn't my patient at first, like you were. That all came later, after the social workers decided, given the violence of your relationship—which, let's face it, was really all Justin—that you should be separated from each other. After your mother went to prison for her drug conviction—no second chances for drug dealers—and parental rights were terminated, Justin finally got adopted by the lovely McBride family. But I'm guessing you already know that too."

"Honestly, I couldn't believe that he'd get adopted before you. I mean, the boy had issues." She shrugs her shoulders, like she just learned that the store was out of her favorite brand of yogurt. "It just goes to show you how scared people are of 'morally corrupt' girls being churned out of foster care and what they might do to their perfect little families."

Marlene is back with a glass of water.

"This should help," she says to Dr. Koftura.

Her ring clinks against the Nalgene bottle as she holds it out for Dr. Koftura. She's shaking, but trying desperately to hide it.

Dr. Koftura takes the water as if being handed a piece of garbage. She holds it by the edges of her fingertips. It's the first time I notice she's wearing gloves. Slim black leather gloves. "Thank you," she says absently. She doesn't drink from it, but continues.

"We were just talking about Justin and his adopted family." She directs this at Marlene.

"Those McBrides brought him to me after trying to get him settled happily in their home. I played hard to get. Pretending that I didn't have space in my schedule, making them wait for months until they could make an appointment. I wanted it to be as bad as it possibly could be for them. That way, after I started planting those nasty little seeds of doubt and anger in his mind during our sessions, it wouldn't be surprising that he'd, oh, I don't know. Kill his dog. Try and bash in his mother's head. Drown a friend at the pool—excuse me, almost drown— because he cut in front of him on the diving board."

Dr. Koftura looks at me expectantly. "Do you think I'm a monster?"

The phrase floats to the surface, my mother's daughter after all. *Speak of the devil, and she will appear.*

"That's enough. I think it's time," Marlene speaks up, still standing a few steps back from both of us. Her hands are linked inside her sweatshirt. "Don't you want your drink?"

Dr. Koftura glances at her watch, ignoring Marlene's question. "I suppose you're right," she answers. "Let's finish this up." She sets down the water bottle and stretches out her hand. "Give it to me." I wait as Marlene pulls the small black pistol from the front pocket of her sweatshirt and takes a step back. There's still a wet patch on the barrel, smeared with the blood from my temple.

But instead of passing the weapon over, my mother points the gun at Dr. Koftura. Her hand wobbles as she loops her finger into the trigger. Instinctively I know that she hasn't planned this and that she's going to lose.

"This was never supposed to happen, Jana. Justin was never supposed to die!"

Dr. Koftura—Jana—stands up, her arms outstretched towards Marlene, her face shoved into a look of compassion. Steady and strong, a chill radiates off her bones. "You're right. He wasn't. I don't know why he chose to turn off at that curve in the road, rather than the one we had planned. Or why he unbuckled his seat belt. I don't know why he didn't stick to the plan."

She takes a step closer to my mother.

"If he'd stuck to the plan we made, he'd still be alive." Dr. Koftura's voice is soft and raspy, like she's trying to gentle an injured bird. And for a moment it seems to be working. My mother starts to lower the gun.

With a burst of recklessness, I shout out the only piece of information that I think might keep that gun lowered, and stop Marlene from shooting Dr. Koftura, and then me.

"You called him, Marlene. Don't you remember? You called him right before he drove off the road. He saw your name, *Mom*, flash up, and then he drove us into the tree."

Marlene turns her gaze at me. I take in the full stature of her body, which appears to be growing weaker and weaker by the moment. Her hand trembles as it tries to hold the gun. She manages to say, from her cracked lips dripping with sweat, "I never called him. I was on the road, coming down the mountain, trying to nudge him off in the safe spot we'd agreed to." I wait for her to tell me about coming to the scene of the accident, seeing her children dead and injured inside the smashed-up car. And why she decided to pick up Justin's phone from the wreckage. But she doesn't.

Instead, her eyes lock on mine. "A car coming at you is great motivation to try and keep yourself safe."

I picture her derelict car hurtling at me outside of campus, running up onto the curb but missing me all the same. *She thought that was a way to protect me? To warn me that someone wanted me dead?*

Then why am I here?

And then, louder, Marlene wails, her mouth a gaping wound, "I never called him!"

She turns towards Dr. Koftura.

"That's because I did," Dr. Koftura replies smoothly, and in one swift movement reaches out, snatches the gun, and points it at Marlene. "I told him to wait for your call. That you'd track him and let him know when he'd reached the perfect place to crash—a place that was just safe enough."

I watch my mother stand like a statue, registering what just happened. And then a split second later her body collapses into itself, even as she remains standing. In that instant, where she realizes that she is now going to die, too, pity washes over me like a forgotten spring.

"I'm glad you dressed down," Dr. Koftura says coolly, giving Marlene a once over. "I'm sure that helped to keep you less noticeable when you brought Morgan in. But, come on now, I think you need to remove that diamond ring. It's just too flashy." She gives Marlene a smile. "Here, I'll put it in my pocket for safekeeping—your pockets are just too baggy. You don't want it to fall out or anything."

Fear pinches at the edges of my mother's face, begging to come out.

Dr. Koftura stretches out her hand and waits as my mother, now openly weeping, twists the ring off her finger and sets it timidly in her accomplice's outstretched palm. "It was a gift from Justin," is all she says as way of explanation.

"I know, I know. It's very special." Dr. Koftura tucks it into the front pocket of her slim black pants. "Did I ever tell you why I went into the work that I do—neurology, I mean?"

Marlene and I stare blankly at her, not sure where the conversation is going. My mind is fixed on the gun, which Dr. Koftura has cradled in her hand like a small animal.

"They say, you know, research is 'me-search.' You've heard that before, haven't you, Morgan?" I don't respond and Dr. Koftura doesn't care. She continues talking. "I wanted to study the brain, and psychopaths in particular, because before I was even out of middle school I knew. Sometimes you just *know*." She slams the handle of the gun into her palm, and it makes a metallic slap against her skin. I look up at Marlene, and watch her face transform into something jagged and fierce as she makes her decision. Even with everything she's done to me, my instinct is to reach out and pull her to safety.

But my hands are tied.

Marlene looks at me, mouths the words, "I'm sorry," and lunges for Dr. Koftura.

But she is too late. Dr. Koftura has already fired. The shot echoes through the empty room, the empty house, and a sick sound of crumpling flesh follows. I turn my head to the side and see Marlene, my mother, slack in a spreading pool of blood on the floor, her right hand reaching out towards me.

"Takes one to know one." Dr. Koftura crosses her arms, gun balanced on her left forearm. "There's still a lot to do, Morgan."

40

Dr. Koftura moves across the room and rolls my mother onto her side so her face is looking away from both of us. But there's nothing to be done with the pool of blood, which is seeping through the floorboards. I hear soft drips where my mother's life must be finding a resting place on the cold dirt of the basement below us.

"I'm sorry to say, but your mother was an idiot." Dr. Koftura sniffs at the water in the glass my mother brought out to her just moments before. "Smells like almonds. What kind of doctor does she think I am? I mean, you're a psychologist, and I bet you know what the scent of almonds means, right?"

But her voice wavers on that last word, and it occurs to me that she's losing a bit of her control. For all her bravado, I don't think Dr. Koftura has ever killed someone else before.

Then I think of Justin.

Not with her own hands at least, I amend.

"I don't know," I say, not because it's true but because, with one dead body in the room, my mind is working frantically at how to escape. And even though Dr. Koftura might think my training is bogus, I do know with absolute certainty that there are few degrees of separation between psychopaths and narcissists.

There might still be a way for me to get out of this alive.

"What do they teach you in your little classes? How to identify emotions from cue cards?" She blinks twice. "Cyanide. Your mother was trying to poison me with cyanide that she'd dug out of some bottle of rat poison. Like I'm a two-dollar whore living down the street from her. She probably got it off one of her street junkies she still fucks once in a while—you can find pretty much anything if you know the right people. That's how she got this gun for us."

Part of me wonders if Marlene brought the poison to use on me, in case her nerve failed her, but another part of me says she brought it to protect me. That perhaps she'd always planned to turn on Dr. Koftura. Eventually.

My head throbs where my mother had slammed the barrel of the gun that killed her into my skull, less than half an hour earlier.

"She didn't know who she was dealing with," I tell Dr. Koftura, trying to keep my voice level.

Dr. Koftura looks up at me sharply. She's still standing, the gun in her hand, the weight of it causing her shoulder to dip down against her side. "Don't you pander to me," she hisses.

I also know a display of dominance when I see one.

I let out a whimper. My shoulders hunch.

"Why are you doing this to me?" I ask, letting my voice twist high into a pleading gasp.

It's a gamble I'm taking, because the question might strike her as below her stature. Or a waste of time. But I'm banking on my gut feeling being right: Dr. Koftura is dying to have someone listen to her brilliance.

"Wouldn't you love to know?" she says.

Bingo.

"Let's see if you can keep up, shall we? I know you tried to do your own investigation, but of course you didn't find anything. Such a shame I had to tell the police about your little visit to my office." She looks me up and down as she waves the gun around in the air, like a toy. "I can wait another few moments before I wrap all of this up."

She drags the chair opposite me a few feet back, and pours her long body into it like wine into a glass. Dr. Koftura leans forward, her elbows on her knees, the gun balanced carefully across her right leg.

I lean forward just slightly. She wants an audience.

"You want to know why I'm doing this? Simple. Your mother killed my husband. The love of my life. The only person who ever understood me." She exhales and purses her lips in a rosebud of revulsion. Her long braid sits like an animal on her shoulder. "I didn't see the signs until it was too late." She pauses for a quick breath in. "I blame love for that.

"He'd turned to heroin when his Percocet ran out after back surgery, and he was too ashamed to ask me for help. One day, apparently, your mother offered him a special deal, cheaper than usual but good stuff. When she came to me afterwards, she had all sorts of excuses. Said she needed to move the 'product.' That she needed the money because her daughter thought she couldn't afford to feed her own family."

She cocks her head to one side, and I try to hold her gaze steady.

My mind tracks back to one of my piecemeal memories salvaged by Dr. Koftura.

The free lunch form.

Is that what this all goes back to? My growling stomach embarrassing me in front of the kids whose faces I don't remember? To lumpy mashed potatoes and canned corn and chicken nuggets?

"Can't you just picture her selling it? Marlene had many faults—many—but she knew how to sell things. The mix had Fentanyl in it, of course, and he overdosed. The next day I found him in the bathroom at home with a needle in his arm." She picks up the gun from her lap and waves it in the air with a sharp jab of her arm. "Correction—I didn't find him. Our daughter, who was three years old at the time, did.

"She felt terrible—oh so terrible." Dr. Koftura whips her eyes to the lifeless body on the floor. "Your mother, that is. And she had all sorts of plans for how to make it up to me. But then she ended up in prison." Sarcasm invades Dr. Koftura's voice. "She must have really felt awful, because after she got out of prison she found me again. Marlene had this bright idea to use me as a front for fake painkiller prescriptions. Make me a ton of money, she said. But I was already using Jawinder's old prescription pad to write fake scripts to help cover the debts he left when he died. So no, I didn't want to follow Marlene's plan. I had a better one. I just didn't tell *her* that."

Dr. Koftura tilts her head back and blinks rapidly. *There's no way she's going to cry in front of me*, I think. But then she does.

"My husband was ill, and she took advantage of him. She ruined my life!" She shouts it out into the room, and the crying has made her voice deeper. She stands up quickly and rushes over to my mother's body. With her right leg, she kicks into the stomach of my dead mother.

"You ruined my life!" she shouts into the dense air of the room. Her foot makes a soft thudding sound, and I turn my head away from the wretchedness of it all.

I let out a sob; only part of it is forced.

"So I was left with no husband, no income to maintain our

lifestyle, and two young children. What would you have done?" She's not asking me. Not really.

"Your mother—your family—needed to pay. It was easy, becoming your doctor. Right place, right time. And your amnesia was so very convenient. Plus I knew all the tricks to keep it there, to hard-set it in your brain as it healed itself. By the time I was done with you, you couldn't remember your mother's face, your brother's existence, or what the car looked like when it hit you."

She comes down, her face level with mine. I flinch. "I'm a fantastic doctor."

Her breath is minty and fresh. The gun smells like rain on asphalt.

"So then came the waiting. What I wanted to do would take years. Partly because your mother was going to be in prison for a long time—all those new drug laws requiring extended sentences for dealing—and partly because I needed both you and your brother to grow up."

Dr. Koftura has the gun slung low at her side as she paces back and forth across the floorboards, careful not to step in my mother's blood.

"Finally, this past summer I got my chance. I'd known all along that I would get Justin to go along with hurting you, because he'd never forgiven you for causing him to be separated from your mother. Getting hit by that car—" She turns her gaze back on me, and our eyes lock. "My car—was the final stroke that set your family, such as it was, scattering to foster care, group homes, and prison. I encouraged Justin, through my work with him, to reach out to Marlene. She was the only woman he ever really loved. Now, I don't pretend to understand their relationship, but it was clear that he would do anything to make her happy. So that left Marlene—sure, she was angry about what had happened to your family and to her drug business, but

Marlene was still a mother. Can you believe that? She still *cared* about you?"

My mother's face flashes up in front of me, her mouth forming those two words just before she lunged at Dr. Koftura. "*I'm sorry.*"

"And then, the final piece came together for me. A gift, from you. You wrote that op-ed for the *Plain Dealer*, and you described your 'resilience'—God, such a cliché word—and about how you managed to survive foster care and the system by working hard, studying, staying off drugs, blah blah blah. You're a walking inspiration. And you could have left it at that, you know. But no, you had to include a little piece of extra information, and I'm going to paraphrase here." She clears her throat. "'And if I can do this without a mother or father caring for me, just imagine what children can do if they are given long-term caregivers through the child welfare system.'"

She points a finger at me, the one not holding the gun. "And it was *that* sentence that made Marlene realize you weren't pining for Mommy dearest. That you hadn't given any credit to her for your life. Not an ounce. She actually still thought of herself as your mother." She turns her head towards Marlene's lifeless and stiffening body. "At least, until I read that article to her."

She goes on. "And that article helped as well, because it included all your contact information. Who knew Twitter could be such a great research tool?"

My mind is thrown off. I'd been following along, but Twitter? I don't understand, and I let it show across my face.

"You look so confused? Such a millennial. Here, let me explain." Dr. Koftura puts her hands together, gun between them, as if she's talking to a small child. "We couldn't risk you not falling for Justin, so he became the perfect boyfriend. We studied all your posts and figured out exactly what you wanted. He was just playing at being your ideal man. The boy had a gift."

A tinge of wistfulness colors Dr. Koftura's voice as she says that last part. My stomach goes rigid as she adds one more betrayal to Justin's collection.

I'm having trouble focusing my eyes. The blood along my temple is hardening into a thick crust as shock sets in. My body is betraying me as it starts to shut down. I have to stifle a yawn.

Of course, Dr. Koftura notices.

"Listen to me jabbering on." She glances at her watch. "We've got no time to lose. We need to make sure the rigor between you and your mother is relatively close in timing. I'll be right back." And she actually winks again as she heads to the kitchen.

An unexpected surge of humiliation, shame, and radioactive anger all mix together inside me at once, counter to my body's attempt to heal itself, and threatens to suffocate me in the best way possible. Revived for the moment, I set to what I do best —surviving.

Keep her talking.

"Did you tell Justin to list you in his phone as 'Mom'?" I ask.

This makes Dr. Koftura pause and come back over to me.

"That was a little bit I'm rather proud of. When he and I were finalizing our plans—that afternoon where you were searching out Justin for lunch, you remember? And he wouldn't tell you where he was? I had him give his phone to me for a minute, supposedly because I wanted to make sure that the three of us—Justin, Marlene, and I—were all synced up, and while I had it I simply changed the label on the contact to my burner phone."

I think back to that afternoon, where I was frantically searching for Justin and convincing myself that he was lying about something, and my fear that I was regressing into some paranoid delusion.

She goes on, "I also added the Find Your Friends app, so I could follow you in the car the entire time from the comfort of my living room couch and let him know exactly where to pull off. Except, I called when you were both going up the mountain with plenty of drop-offs, which was not where we'd originally planned. And, as I'm sure you can guess by now, Justin always listened to his mother."

Next question.

"Was it your idea to have Justin unbuckle his seat belt? Just before the crash?"

Dr. Koftura shrugs her shoulders. "He was supposed to unbuckle yours. I don't know why he did what he did. Men are weak." And I imagine her picturing her addict husband between us, because her face softens for a moment. But then she's back. "Even psychopaths feel guilt sometimes."

"Do you?" I'm getting reckless. Twitchy. *Hold on, Morgan*, I tell myself.

She gives me a withering stare. "I'm not complaining. Having him dead makes less work for me in the end. Besides, he'd left everything behind that I needed him to. Those messages between him and Annie were the perfect link to tie everything together. All it took was a suggestion from me, a few fake accounts set up by Justin, and a pic of Annie snatched off her Facebook page."

My chest spasms like I've been punched. For a few moments, I can't breathe. I picture Annie, bleeding on my bedroom floor, and despair threatens to swallow me whole.

If those messages were fake, then Annie was on my side this entire time.

But wait, I remember, what about the photo of her and Justin together? Something catches inside my head.

"Did you tell Justin to go visit Annie?" I ask.

Koftura lets out a long sigh. She's getting bored. "Yes, I did. A little back-up ammunition, you know, to help sever your ties to anyone who might care about you."

Annie. Poor Annie.

I want to rip at Dr. Koftura with my teeth, call her a bitch and tell her to go fuck herself, but I have to stay calm.

Then a wave of nausea hits me with the force of an avalanche. My head lolls onto my chin for a second, but I fight my body's pull to oblivion.

I manage to compose another question, hoping this one might settle Dr. Koftura back into gazing at her own brilliance.

"Why have Marlene text those messages to me from Justin's phone? Why not send them yourself?"

But the question doesn't have my intended effect. The change in Dr. Koftura's face is immediate.

"What do you mean?" For the first time, her voice betrays something she hadn't anticipated me saying.

She's surprised.

A fresh surge of adrenaline pumps through my battered body.

"Marlene was texting me from Justin's phone, saying she could help me. I thought that was part of your plan."

"Where is it?" she starts to scramble around, searching the pockets of Marlene's body, her gloves getting covered in the viscous blood that has cooled over the floorboards. "Where's his phone? That fucking bitch!" she yells.

Her hands come up empty.

Which means my phone isn't on Marlene, either.

But Dr. Koftura doesn't notice. Instead, she stands up, gun still in her hand, and runs into the kitchen, shuffling through what sounds like a bag. I hear her talking to herself. "I thought it was destroyed in the crash. I didn't think to look. Stupid. Stupid."

And this is the moment I've been waiting for. I throw my shoulder blades against the brittle wicker of the chair, and a satisfying crack emanates from the backboard. My hands are free and I quickly undo the ropes around my wrists. I don't have time to untie my legs, and so I settle on snapping the wicker seat down the middle in order to pull my legs individually out of the rope ties. My heart throttles against my chest and I feel dizzy. I almost tip over, and have to remind myself, as my thoughts simultaneously race along at warp speed and slow down to the point of incoherence, that I have a fucking head wound.

I stand up, and just as I gain my balance, she is there, her face only inches from mine. Hard metal presses into my chest, the round nib of the gun's muzzle denting the flesh underneath my collarbone. Where my heart is tapping out its final message.

Checkmate.

I've lost.

I rush to move away from her, but Dr. Koftura grips my hair and jerks my head back so far that I can't keep my balance. I start to fall backwards, but she stops me just before I pitch over. Her arms are stronger than I'd think, considering her small frame.

"Lie down," she says, her voice like an icy stream running over me.

I lie down, her gloved hand still on my head. She twists the knot of hair at the base of my skull to the left, so the side of my temple that Marlene struck is exposed.

"Close your eyes," she says.

All her body weight is on me now, her legs straddling my waist. Justin's phone forgotten for the time being, one glance at her face shows how emboldened she is now that her plan, twenty years in the making, is finally coming to its conclusion.

She is jacked up and glittering with anticipation. But, in her excitement, she's made one significant mistake.

My arms are free.

I close my eyes and feel the muzzle of the gun lift from my chest for a moment, and then the pressure of its metal aperture is pressed to my temple. Even with all I've already been through, even knowing what I'm about to do, the connection of metal to my bare skin makes me tremble.

I am docile as a child, my breath coming in quick bursts. She reaches for my right hand—

just like I'm expecting her to—and puts all her weight on my shoulder joint to limit my mobility.

"This won't hurt a bit," she says into my ear, but her voice falters on the last word. Uncertainty echoes through the room. Maybe there's a tinge of regret. Her hands loosen on my mine, only for a second. But a second is all that I need.

I swing my left arm over her body and onto the back of her neck, making a swift survey of her vertebrae and jamming my fingers into the soft place between spine and skull. I know it will disorient her, because it's the same pressure point I learned to use in those self-defense classes Patty and Dave signed me up for all those years ago. But jabbing is not enough to knock her unconscious. Only enough to distract her.

She flinches from the discomfort caused by my fingers sliding into the pressure point, and her weight on my shoulder is relieved just enough for me to wrap my right arm around her neck to marry with my left arm. I grab her throat, and with every ounce of strength left in me, I throw her off me. Her small body comes crashing down next to Marlene's, her stomach flat on the ground, and the right side of her shirt is immersed in the pool of blood.

I am on top of her now. I grab her head in the proper hold, my knee braced against her shoulder, and a small portion of time passes until her body goes limp underneath me. I allow myself to take a deep breath. And then another.

Just as I am stepping away towards the kitchen, hoping to find my mother's phone or some other way to call for help, I hear another voice shout from the door.

"Police! Hands where I can see them!"

I don't know where the gun has gone.

41

I n the dim light, I stand with my arms above my head, waiting for the police officers to appear. My mind is trying to understand how they found us, why they are here, and what this whole rotting mess must look like to them.

I stay perfectly still, hands in the air.

And then from the kitchen, I see a black leather sleeve emerge with strong hands level to the ground, gun drawn. As the figure moves forward further, it's the familiar face of Detective Miller that appears. Behind her is Detective Ormoran, also with her gun drawn. I watch as they take in the scene in front of them. When our eyes finally meet, Miller's are cool and glassy, but Ormoran's—the best word I can think to describe the way she looks at me is shattered. Utterly shattered.

"Keep your hands where I can see them," Ormoran says, her body tense as she steps into the room. "What happened here, Morgan?" No "Dr. Kalson" when there are two bodies in the room.

Her gaze travels over the body of Marlene, and then rests on Dr. Koftura's. From the distance she's at, I know it's not likely she'll be able to see the doctor's chest moving up and down.

I start to explain that Dr. Koftura is just unconscious, but there is a sudden scramble from the floor and the three of us watch as Dr. Koftura stands. For the detectives, I imagine it's as though she's rising from the dead.

Even in the gauzy light trickling through the makeshift curtains, it's clear she has the gun in her hand. It must have fallen underneath her when I forced her to the ground, and a shock of shame runs through me for not having checked the most obvious place.

I am still standing with my hands held high when Ormoran takes control. "Jana, put the gun down. Let's talk about this."

Dr. Koftura's arm shakes, but her face is carved from stone. "I don't want to talk about anything." She swings the gun in the air, and then rests it behind her head with her arms pulled back, like she's trying to catch her breath after a long and intense sprint.

Ormoran and Miller follow her hands with their own guns.

Miller echoes Ormoran's demands, shouting for Dr. Koftura to put the gun down. "Or I'll have to shoot you," she adds.

"What does it matter?" Dr. Koftura says, her voice hoarse between sobs that are now wracking her body. "There's nothing you can do for me. You can't bring him back. Nothing will bring him back."

Dr. Koftura puts her hands out in front of her, as though she is about to let go of her hold on the gun. Ormoran and Miller start to ease up, the tension in their shoulders shrugging off slightly.

"I failed. I'm a failure," Dr. Koftura says quietly.

She looks at me.

"It was always you," she says, the hatred in her eyes burning my skin.

I want to scream out to her that I was just a little girl. A growing, desperate, lonely little girl. That I was starving, inside and out.

But I don't get the chance.

In a burst of movement, Dr. Koftura swings the gun back up, a grimace of pain traveling across her face as she tries to raise her arm and train the barrel on me. There is a sudden and violent crack that echoes through the room, and then a split second later a second burst of sound. A biting sting races across my shoulder, where the bullet from Dr. Koftura's gun grazes me.

Dr. Koftura's body collapses, the thud of her head hitting the floorboards surprisingly gently. Miller lowers her gun, but Ormoran's is still aimed somewhere off into the distance.

Ormoran and Miller exchange a quick glance with each other, and it's Miller who moves over to Koftura's body while Ormoran takes over the responsibility of assessing me.

The room starts to spin, my dehydration mixing with blood loss and the brew of hormones flooding my body as my brain tries to signal that the threat has passed. I start to stumble away from all of this death, but Ormoran takes hold of my shoulders and whispers, "I've got you. I've got you."

EPILOGUE

I wake up again, for the second time in so many weeks, in a hospital bed. For a moment, in my delirium of painkillers and liquid sustenance, I think that I'm back in the Conneaut Medical Center and that it is Nurse Debbie buzzing around me in her Gaelic boisterousness. When I focus my eyes, though, I see that the nurse is a slim, dark-haired woman whose name tag reads "Sylvia." She's adjusting something on my IV pole.

"Any chance I can get some of that good stuff, too, Nurse?" I hear the familiar fizz of Coke as she takes a swig and the liquid shifts around in the can.

Annie.

I turn towards her and she sets the can of Coke on the side table. She asks me how I'm feeling, and I do a quick assessment. There's a pulsing pain in my head, a cavernous feeling in my stomach, and I'm weak-kneed, even though I'm lying down.

I take in her face and the scab over her temple that's healing. Nothing else matters. Not really.

"Annie," I start to say. "I'm so sorry." My mouth is dry and my tongue feels like it's ten times its normal size, making my words slur slightly.

Annie looks at me, her eyes red with fatigue. "I'm sorry too."

She leans forward in her chair. I get the feeling she's been rehearsing what she's about to say, waiting for me to wake up so she can get everything out in the open.

"I shouldn't have lied about meeting Justin, but after the accident I couldn't bring it up. I was too ashamed. He'd texted the day after you and I had that fight—Do you remember? I'd just assumed you'd given my number to him at some point, but now I realize he must have gotten it off my public Facebook profile I set up for my exhibit. Anyway, he asked to meet, and when he drove up he was really sweet and wanting my advice on planning a romantic trip for you. It was supposed to be a surprise." Annie stares off into the distance. "And then he wanted to take a picture of us together, and I figured it was okay —that maybe he wanted to send it to you. Afterwards, honestly, I forgot about the photo until that day in your apartment."

The air sits heavy in my hospital room, our minds both trained back to our fight. Our arms wrapped around each other for the first time in malice rather than support.

"I shouldn't have tried to hide it that day but, Morgan, I can't pretend. I was scared of what you might do."

I nod, because we both know she was right.

"I shouldn't have assumed anything," I say finally, my mouth starting to feel more normal the more I talk. "Dr. Koftura tried to convince me that you were lying to me. She had Justin make up all those e-mails the cops found. . ."

"I know," Annie cuts me off. "You don't have to say anything more."

But I do. I pause and force myself to look Annie in the eye.

"Justin was my brother." My stomach gives an involuntary

heave. My skin feels like it's on fire, and I start to scratch at my arms mindlessly.

But Annie doesn't look away.

"Half-brother," is all she says. *So she already knows*, I think. I wonder what else the police have told her.

Her hand reaches out to mine, and I squeeze hers back.

Annie gives her head an almost indecipherable shake, and then turns away.

We may not be fine right now, but we will be.

I try to tell myself the rest of me will heal too. *Survive and thrive*. It's what I do.

I correct myself. It's what *we* do. Annie and me.

Nurse Sylvia, who's been here the whole time eavesdropping on our reunion without the slightest apparent interest, finally finishes her tasks, makes a few marks on my chart at the foot of my bed, and then leaves.

As soon as the door closes, I ask the question that's been burning in my mind since I saw Ormoran and Miller come through that doorway.

"How did they find me?"

Annie sits up straighter and squares her shoulders, like she's about to deliver bad news. I brace myself, but only slightly. *I mean, after you learn you've been sleeping with your half-brother, who's then tried to kill you, masterminded by your doctor, everything else is just party favors, right?*

"It was that woman, Marlene—" Annie looks as though she might gag on the words, but says them anyway. "Your mother saved you."

Annie continues on before I can correct her. Before I can tell her that my mother tried to save me, but that it was too late.

"I called the police station as soon as I came to in your apartment—" We both look away from each other as she says that. "—and couldn't find you. I told the intake officer that Detective

Ormoran and Miller were working with you and that they needed to come immediately. The two of them drove straight out and met me at your apartment, and after I explained about our fight and how I was worried about the way you were acting, they started asking me about where I thought you might have gone. That's when I told them about the texts you were getting from Justin's phone, and then Miller explained that they'd got some information in from their tech guys that afternoon after you left. They looked into the messages they showed you on Justin's laptop—the ones that were supposedly between Justin and me. The messages Justin was receiving from that account with my name on it were coming from a dummy profile he'd set up, complete with a profile pic he swiped from my actual Facebook page, so it was just him writing messages to himself. He'd wanted to create a trail on his laptop that would make it seem like he and I were together, and that he was scared of what you might do when you found out. They also finally got around to checking on his registration at YSU, and discovered he had never been enrolled. It turns out they were starting to think you weren't a suspect."

Annie's talking so fast at this point I can barely keep up, what with the drugs and the head wound and all. She pauses to take a deep breath.

"Slow down," I say. I give a pointed look at my IV line. "I'm not going anywhere."

This at least makes her smile, almost enough to reach her eyes.

"After they arrived and I told them about Justin's phone, Miller called into the station—that's what it's called, right?—and they start trying to track the phone again. I guess they'd done that before, but it was never on long enough for them to find a location. And, Morgan—" Annie's actually crying now—I've only ever seen her cry three times in our entire friendship—and

I'm ashamed to admit that it's not until then that I stop to consider what she must have been through since I disappeared.

"I'm sorry," I say again, the words too simple for what I want to tell her. For now, though, they'll have to do. I reach up to brush away a stream of black tears where her mascara has started to run down her face. "You're a mess, you know."

She laughs a little. "You should see yourself." She sets her shoulders straight, and I can tell the joking's over for now. "I forgot about the Find Your Friends app. I forgot that we'd linked each other up and that I could track you. I was so scared, and you'd just disappeared, and with everything that's happened over the last week—I can't explain it. I didn't remember until Miller said that thing about tracing Justin's phone. I'm so sorry, Morgan. I'm so, so sorry."

Anger flashes up my throat. There is no way I'm going to let Annie get hurt any more than she has been already. Any more than I've already hurt her.

No. Way.

"Annie, how long did it take the police to show up at the apartment?" I ask. She wipes her nose on her sleeve, even though the box of tissues is just across from her on my little hospital table. "And how long were they there before you remembered you could track my phone?"

"Maybe twenty minutes, and then—I don't know—just a few minutes. I'm not really sure."

"I'm *glad* you didn't remember until then. If the cops had come any earlier, they might have missed Dr. Koftura entirely, and we'd still think that Marlene was working alone."

Saying her name reminds me of what Annie said earlier. "I don't understand. Marlene turned off Find Your Friends so no one could track us."

"Your mo—Marlene left your phone on, and she also apparently left Justin's phone on too. I guess she hid them both behind some old paint cans to make sure Dr. Koftura wouldn't find them. She *wanted* the police to find you in that old squat."

I picture my mother's face just before she lunged at Dr. Koftura. I see her mouth, which my mind would never let me forget, along with the terrible things she called me when I was a child, mouthing those two small, enormous words. "I'm sorry."

My mother must have turned my phone back on when she left to get the water for Dr. Koftura. She was just bluffing when she said she was severing the Find Your Friends connection.

Some part of her wanted me to live.

Annie is so pale. Underneath all the bravado she puts on for others, the strain of this past week is written all over her. Dark circles under her eyes. She's thinner, as if that were even possible. I watch her rub her hands on each other, her anxiety still working itself out.

"Thank you," I tell her. "Thank you for being there for me."

"That's what friends are for." She pauses, and then adds, "You're my family."

There's a knock on the door. Detective Ormoran is standing at the threshold to my room, waiting for my permission to come in. I can't tell whether or not she's officially on duty, but then I catch a glimpse of her gun holster underneath her navy-blue blazer.

"The doctor said I could come in for a few minutes," she says, and it's clear she's not going to enter until I say it's okay. Strange how so much changes when you're not a suspect any more.

I motion her in, and Annie looks between the two of us.

"Can Annie stay?" I ask.

"I don't see why not." Ormoran's smile is dazzling, her teeth perfectly straight and white. It's a real smile, not one crafted for her job. She looks beautiful.

"We'll get a full statement from you later, once you're recovered a bit more, but right now I have just one question to ask you," she begins.

I nod, ready for whatever is coming.

"We've put together a lot of the puzzle, based on the phone records of the burner phone recovered from Jana—Dr. Koftura's —body and digging through her laptop. She kept immaculate files of her drug sales, which were a small operation but still very profitable. And we found detailed records of her 'treatment' of you and Justin in a safety deposit box under Jawinder Koftura's name. Everything's in there. The memory manipulation, the fabricated symptoms. In Justin's case, the priming for aggression. *Everything*." She smiles again, but this one's timid and hesitant, with a darker tinge burdening the corners of her mouth. "But there's something I still can't make sense of."

She pauses, and Annie and I sit there like two little kids during story time. Finally, Det. Ormoran goes on.

"What just doesn't make sense to me is why your mother wanted us to find you, after she went through all that trouble of kidnapping you in the first place?"

I think back to what Dr. Koftura told me in that run-down house. About the little bit I knew of Marlene—my mother. That the reason Dr. Koftura was able to get her to agree to the plan in the first place was because I'd removed her—my mother, my previous life before foster care—from my identity. I'd become a child with no mother, and the rejection cut her to the bone.

But then Justin had died.

Click.

"She was still a mother. She was still *my* mother," I say, the realization sinking in.

I think back to what she said to me in that burnt-out room.

What she did.

All of it.

"She knew Dr. Koftura would never stop, otherwise. That's

why she kidnapped me. To lure Dr. Koftura and stop her from finishing the plan. That's why she wanted you to find me. She needed me to survive."

I don't say the rest out loud. I barely let myself think it; it's so fragile and new.

If I survived, there was the chance I could love her again.

If I survived, I would learn to know that even when she hated me, my mother also loved me.

Ormoran considers me with her dark eyes, and as she does my explanation settles into the creases of my sheets, the edges of my body, and the gaps of air in my room. I hear the hisses and beeps that I now know come standard with a hospital stay. And then Ormoran shuffles her feet and stands up.

"I can see that," she says, and tips her head in a quick nod to me, and then one to Annie. "Mothers have instincts, you know. We all do."

She calls over her shoulder as she leaves, "I'll be back later for your statement."

And then she's gone.

The space left by Ormoran's exit seems to swallow me whole, and the rush of blood to my head leaves me feeling disoriented. The humming inside my head threatens to collapse on top of me, pushing out all my feelings in a burst of emotional incontinence.

I want to laugh, and cry, and punch my hand into a wall.

Minutes pass.

Just as I'm about to rip my IVs out of my arm and run away from everything—I've heard the Hebrides are never nice any time of year—there's a crinkling that fills the room.

Annie has pulled a backpack from the floor and up onto her lap, from which she's unwrapping a package of Snowballs from their noisy cellophane. Their bright white mounds of coconut and cake fill my room with the sweet smell only mass-produced pastry can make.

"Hungry?" she asks, reaching out her hand and offering me the contraband.

I look up at Annie's face, and see written on it not just everything these past weeks have brought to our doorstep; I see the years of heartache, and regret, and getting back up on the treadmill of life.

I see my best friend sitting next to me, waiting for the next chapter to start.

Morgan, I hear her call, and this time I don't try to lock my mother's voice away.

"Are you hungry?" Annie asks again.

I blink.

"Always," I say.

THE END

ACKNOWLEDGEMENTS

This book would not have been possible without a team of individuals supporting me during the writing and publication process.

Thank you to everyone at Bloodhound Books, including my incredible editing and publicity team, for making *It Was Always You* the best novel it could be. Also, thank you for the killer cover —I love it.

Thank you to Dea Poirier, Hannah Mary McKinnon, J.L. DeLozier, and Marisa Ferger for offering feedback and keen insights on earlier drafts of this novel, and big hugs to Dr. Jennifer Crissman Ishler, who is kind enough to read all of my writing in its earliest stages.

Thank you to my writing friends, both in person and online, for your kindness, support, and senses of humor. Brian Centrone, you are the best writing friend anyone could ask for.

I've been lucky to have many wonderful teachers in my life. Special thanks to Naomi Jackson and Paul Harding for their guidance and wisdom.

A huge thank you to Youngstown State University, where this novel is set. I would not be where I am today without the opportunities and education provided by your excellent faculty and generous scholarship programs.

My mother, Norma Holowach, is always my first reader. Thank you, Mom, for reading through drafts of my novels so quickly, and for being my unofficial publicist.

Thank you also to my mother and late father, Stephen, for loving me unconditionally, and for teaching me the value and satisfaction that comes from working hard. Thank you to my brothers, Jacob and Ben, and their families for all their love and support.

Much of this book was written in our living room, in the midst of family life. Thank you to my children, Ethan, Katherine, and Elisa, for always asking before turning your music on while I was writing. Extra hugs for helping me work out pesky plot points and drawing sample book covers. I love you all.

Finally, thank you to my husband, Joshua. None of this would be any fun without you.

CPSIA information can be obtained
at www.ICGtesting.com
Printed in the USA
BVHW070719160120
569456BV00002B/11/P